THE GHOST

AND FAMILY SECRETS

HAUNTING DANIELLE

THE GHOST
AND FAMILY SECRETS

USA TODAY BESTSELLING AUTHOR
BOBBI HOLMES

The Ghost and Family Secrets
(Haunting Danielle, Book 38)
A Novel
By Bobbi Holmes
USA TODAY BESTSELLING AUTHOR

Cover Design: Elizabeth Mackey

ISBN: 978-1-968738-23-5

Adam Nichols sat at the front desk of his property management and real estate office, Frederickport Vacation Properties, eating his lunch alone on the last Friday in January. Normally, when not going out to eat, he would have lunch in his private office, but his assistant, Leslie, had a dentist appointment this morning, and she hadn't returned to work yet. Adam needed to cover the front desk in case a customer came in. But considering it was the off-season, he doubted there would be any foot traffic today.

While sitting at the desk, eating a burger he had ordered from Lucy's Diner, Adam reflected on the changes in his life over the last five and a half years, ever since Danielle Marlow—then Danielle Boatman—moved to town.

During that time, he'd lost one of the most important people in his life when his grandma Marie died. Or, more accurately, when someone murdered her. But he got her back, thanks to Danielle.

He remembered when he first met Danielle; she was good-looking, with her long dark hair always pulled back into a fishtail braid. He only knew it was called a fishtail braid because he once overheard Mel and Heather talking about types of braids, and he found fishtail was a hilarious name for a braid.

His grandmother had been born in the house across the street from Marlow House—the house Danielle inherited. When he first met Danielle, his grandma took the young woman under her wing, seeing her as the granddaughter she always wanted. Adam remained Marie's favorite grandson—she only had two—but Grandma adored Danielle.

Initially he found Danielle attractive, but early on deemed her an airhead, especially after she made some comment about not wanting to offend whatever spirits lingered in Marlow House. But Danielle wasn't an airhead; she was a medium. They were all mediums: her, Walt, Chris, and Heather. Heck, even Police Chief MacDonald's youngest son, Evan, saw ghosts. Not to mention the little ones, yet according to Chris, they might stop seeing ghosts when they got older. Apparently, both his grandmother and Lily had seen ghosts when they were very young, but a few years before their adolescence, they lost the ability.

But the changes weren't only about Danielle and his grandma. Back then he would never have imagined he would be married now, and married to Melony, of all people. In two weeks, they would celebrate their first wedding anniversary.

Taking the last bite of his burger, Adam glanced around his office. When Danielle first hit town, he'd had more people working for him. But these days, it was only him and Leslie in the office. Now finished with his burger, Adam picked up a napkin and wiped his mouth and hands and then gathered up all the lunch debris and shoved it in the trash can under his desk. He was brushing his palms together, as if wiping off imaginary crumbs, when the front door to the office opened, and a young woman walked in, holding the hand of a little girl. Adam assumed it was mother and daughter because the child looked like the woman's mini-me. He estimated the conservatively dressed woman, with long, wavy chestnut brown hair and brown eyes, was in her late twenties, perhaps early thirties. If she wore any makeup, it wasn't obvious.

"Afternoon," Adam greeted, standing up briefly. "How can I help you? I'm Adam Nichols."

"My name is Mary Da…Mary Walsh. I'm looking for a place to rent," she said, her voice soft. "This is my daughter, Cassandra."

Adam smiled at the little girl. "Hello, Cassandra. That's a pretty name. How old are you?"

"Nine," the little girl chirped.

Adam motioned to the nearby chairs, silently suggesting they take a seat, while he sat back down. Mary pulled one chair closer to the front of Adam's desk and sat down, while Cassandra stood by her side.

"What exactly are you looking for?"

"I need something on a month-to-month basis. Fully furnished. It's just me and my daughter. We don't need anything large or fancy. We don't have any pets. I'm not sure how long we'll be staying; it depends if I can get work. I understand you specialize in vacation rentals, but I was hoping, since it's the off-season, prices might be lower at this time of year."

"Are you new to town?"

She nodded in reply.

"Can I ask what type of job you'll be looking for?"

She perked up slightly. "I was thinking housekeeping. I'll be honest, I've never had a job before. But I know how to keep house. Maybe you need someone to clean your rentals?"

Adam smiled at her offer. "I will definitely keep that in mind, but I have someone who already does that. You'll need to fill out a credit application."

Adam started opening one of the file drawers in his desk when Mary blurted, "I can't fill out a credit application. I don't have any credit. I've never had a credit card in my name or even my own checking account. Can't I just use money? I mean, if it's month to month, and I'm paying you up front, why do I need to fill out a credit application?"

Adam's hand paused. He pushed close the file drawer he had just opened. Folding his hands together on his desk, he studied Mary for a moment and asked in a kind voice, "Are you running from something?"

As he asked, he felt a gentle tug on his right ear. He froze for a moment. Another tug. His Grandma Marie was here. He wondered when she had arrived.

"Um, I haven't broken any laws. I'm looking for a fresh start."

The little girl leaned closer to Mary and whispered something in her ear. When the girl turned around again, Mary asked Adam, "Can she use your bathroom, please?"

"Certainly." Adam pointed toward the bathroom door on the other side of the office.

Mary looked at her daughter and motioned toward the bathroom, but Cassandra shook her head and leaned back toward her mother and whispered something else in her ear. A moment later Mary smiled at Adam, stood, and said, "We'll be right back." After Mary and Cassandra went into the bathroom and its door closed, the pen sitting on Adam's desk floated over the desktop and began writing on a pad of paper. When it stopped writing, Adam read the words *Help her.*

"Grandma, how long have you been here?" Adam whispered.

The pen wrote: *I followed her into the office.*

THAT EVENING, AS ADAM AND MELONY MADE DINNER TOGETHER, Adam told his wife about his new tenant.

"So you actually rented one of your properties without running a credit check? Sounds risky," Melony—always the lawyer—commented.

"You weren't there."

"No, your grandmother was." Melony chuckled as she finished grating the cheese for their tacos.

"Mel, you would have wanted to help her too. I know you. Anyway, I remembered Allen's garage apartment, which sits empty at this time of year. When I told her the rent amount, for a moment I thought she was going to kiss me."

Melony, who had just returned the unused cheese to the refrigerator, paused a moment and looked back at Adam. In a teasing tone she asked, "Was she attractive?"

Adam, who stood by the stove, frying ground beef, glanced over to Melony and smiled. "Yes, she was. But not as gorgeous as my wife." Which was a correct statement. Melony's stunning good looks had even once given Danielle a moment of insecurity, but Melony's physical appearance was not her most impressive attribute; her most impressive attribute was her distinguished law career.

"Did she like the apartment?"

"She did. But I have a feeling she would have taken it even if she hated it. She says she's not running from the law, but I suspect she's running from something."

"Leaving a domestic violence situation?"

Adam shrugged. "Maybe."

"She paid the first month's rent?"

"In cash. I gave her a receipt."

"And a security deposit?"

"When I brought up a security deposit, Grandma pinched me."

"Pinched you?" Melony snorted.

"Yeah. Grandma may not talk to me like she used to, but she has a way of letting me know what she wants. But that darn pinch almost left a bruise."

Melony laughed and said, "I assume you didn't ask her for a security deposit."

"And you'd assume right."

***

Walt and Danielle sat at the kitchen table in Marlow House, eating dinner while the twins, Addison and Jack, sat next to them, each sitting in a highchair, each eating a cookie. They had finished their dinner before Walt and Danielle started theirs.

The ghost of Marie Nichols sat at the kitchen table with them, telling them all about Mary and why they should hire her to replace Joanne. Marie wore a floral summer dress appropriate for a sunny warm day, yet outside, the temperatures were in the lower forties with intermittent rain.

"Joanne's working until the end of February," Danielle reminded Marie.

"We both know she's only staying that long because she doesn't want to leave you high and dry. She's waiting for you to find someone. Joanne is loyal. But she could take the next few weeks, train someone new—someone like Mary—and retire earlier if she wants," Marie insisted.

"You just met this person today," Danielle reminded her.

"I wouldn't say Marie actually met her," Walt snarked.

Marie ignored Walt and said, "True, but I spent all day with her and Cassandra. There is something both fragile—and fierce about that young woman."

Walt arched his eyebrows. "Fragile and fierce? One can be both?"

"Certainly," Marie scoffed. "Anyway, I'll stick around and keep an eye on things. And if she turns out to be a serial killer, I'll make sure she doesn't send anyone to my side."

Danielle chuckled. "Well, that's comforting."

"Come on, dear, the poor child is all alone."

"You said her daughter is nine? Is she enrolling her in the local school?" Danielle asked.

"I doubt it. Not from what I overheard when she was talking to the little girl. Sounds like she's homeschooled."

"What will she do with her daughter when she's cleaning houses?" Danielle asked.

"I was thinking she could just bring the girl with her."

Danielle set her fork down on the table and studied Marie for a moment. "What is it about this woman? You seem rather invested in her."

Marie considered the question for a few moments before answering. Finally, she said, "I saw her before she went to Adam's office. This morning I was with Eva at the museum. Eva wanted to visit her portrait." While some might wonder why Eva Thorndike, the ghost of the silent screen star and Walt's childhood friend during his previous life, would frequently visit her portrait at the museum, Walt and Danielle understood. A ghost could not see its reflection in the mirror, so if they wished to remember what they once looked like, they needed to look at a photograph or painting of themselves. "Mary brought her daughter into the museum right after it opened."

"And?" Danielle asked.

Marie shrugged. "I was curious and had already said goodbye to Eva, left her in the portrait room, when I noticed the two enter the museum. I followed her. She's one of those people who talk their thoughts aloud when they think no one is listening. There was no one else in the museum other than the docent, and after a few minutes, Mary thanked the docent and told her they just wanted to take their time and look around."

"You mean, she didn't want the docent following her around the museum and giving them a personal tour," Danielle said.

"Exactly. It wasn't Millie. One of the new ones. Anyway, Cassandra seemed fascinated with the displays and paid little attention to her mother's ramblings."

"But you did?" Walt asked.

Marie nodded. "From what I picked up, she's leaving an unhappy marriage. She has some money with her, but she still needs a job. You asked me why I wanted to help her. It's because she reminds me of me—of what could have happened had I not had my own money. I'm not saying I was unhappy in my marriage, not exactly. But it didn't turn out as I imagined when I initially said those vows. If I had wanted to leave, I could have because I had my own money. I suspect my husband would have tried to be far more controlling had I been financially vulnerable. While she obviously has a little money with her, she'll need a job before it runs out."

CHAPTER TWO

If an unsuspecting medium—one not familiar with the visitors of Marlow House—entered the upstairs nursery on the first Sunday in February, they would see what looked like two women, each sitting in a rocking chair. The younger of the two, a woman in her early twenties, who looked as if she was dressed for a 1920s theme party, sat primly in one chair, not rocking, as she studied the woman in the adjacent rocker.

Marie Nichols, the woman in the other rocker, held two sleeping babies on her lap as she rocked contentedly. The onlookers would wonder how the elderly woman could so effortlessly hold on her lap what might compare in weight to two twenty-pound bags of flour.

If the onlooker was not a medium, they wouldn't see the women at all. Instead, they would find two rocking chairs, one still while the other one rocked and two sleeping babies floated above the chair's seat.

"They grow so fast," Eva whispered, her gaze on the napping Marlow twins.

"In three months, they'll be a year." Marie looked up from the babies to Eva. "I could never hold them like this if I were alive."

Eva laughed at the observation. "No, I don't imagine you could, especially when they wake up and start wiggling. So, are Walt and Danielle hiring your charity case?"

"I wouldn't call her my charity case. But she's coming in tomorrow for an interview."

"I hope it works out. So, tell me, who's all coming tonight?"

"From what Danielle told me, it's just Adam, Melony, Chris, and Heather."

"Brian's not coming?"

Marie kissed the babies' foreheads before answering, "No. He's working tonight. And Lily and Ian won't be here. It's Sunday dinner with his family—across the street."

"Didn't Ian's parents used to host those weekly dinners at their house?"

"Ian suggested it might be easier with the two little ones if they hosted the weekly dinner at his house rather than packing up the baby and Connor. This way they don't have to rush home right after dinner and can just put the little ones down in their own room."

Eva didn't offer a response but silently studied the sleeping babies on Marie's lap. Finally, Marie asked, "What are you thinking?"

Eva gave a shrug and said, "I'm just wondering how long they'll continue to see us. Are they mediums like their mother, or will they be like Lily and you as a child and eventually be unable to see us?"

Downstairs at Marlow House, the friends sat around the dining room table. Walt had removed one of the table leaves before the guests had arrived, making it a more comfortable size for the six to sit around playing a game. Adam and Melony Nichols sat together on one side of the table. The couple across from them were Heather Donovan and Chris Johnson, aka Chris Glandon. Technically not a couple, they were platonic friends, and Chris was

Heather's boss. Heather liked to describe Chris as stupidly rich and handsome—which he was, and Chris just enjoyed teasing Heather, who was quirky in her own way, reminding Chris of a cross between Elvira, Mistress of the Dark, and *NCIS*'s Abby Sciuto. However, Chris didn't see Heather as a seductress like Elvira or sweet like Abby. It was more about her looks and quirkiness.

The last couple at the table were Walt and Danielle Marlow. Their relationship and history were far more complicated than their friends'. While everyone at the table was technically in their thirties, Walt had been born over 120 years earlier—at least in his previous life—and reborn about four years earlier when his spirit stepped into his cousin's body. His cousin, Walt's doppelgänger, had willingly given up his body, as his spirit was ready to move on in its journey. Danielle hadn't met Walt then, but several years earlier, when his ghost haunted Marlow House. Yes, theirs was a complicated story.

Heather counted out twelve dominoes for each player. Several open pizza boxes, along with napkins, a stack of paper plates, and bowls with snacks, were set on the nearby buffet, while each person at the table had a beverage and a plate with food on the table next to them. Hunny, Chris's pit bull, napped under the table by Chris's feet, while Danielle's black cat, Max, sat on her lap while she absently rubbed his white-tipped ears with one hand.

Melony moved her twelve dominoes closer to her plate of food and neatly organized them while saying, "I haven't played Mexican Train in ages. I hope I remember how to play."

Heather gave everyone a quick rules recap, and then Adam asked Danielle, "Did you get ahold of Mary?"

"Yes. She's coming over tomorrow for an interview."

"Sounds like she already has the job," Heather said. "After all, Marie is a pretty good reference."

Adam chuckled. "Mary has no idea my grandmother decided to be her guardian angel."

They talked about Marie for a few more minutes while each took their turn in the game. Finally, Heather changed the topic by asking Melony, "Are you and Adam doing anything special for your anniversary? It's only a couple of weeks away."

"We're spending the weekend at the beach," Adam announced.

Heather frowned at Adam. "You live at the beach."

Melony laughed. "I think what Adam is telling you, we don't plan to go anywhere." Melony turned her attention to Walt and Danielle. "What about you guys? Your anniversary is a couple of days before ours."

Danielle flashed Melony a smile and, instead of answering, played her turn. While their friends had watched Walt and Danielle get married on Valentine's Day almost four years earlier, in truth Walt and Danielle had eloped months before their wedding at Marlow House.

"We'll be staying at the beach too," Walt answered for Danielle while reorganizing his dominoes. "At a lovely little B&B."

Everyone laughed. They all understood that the bed-and-breakfast Walt referenced was Marlow House.

"I heard the place is temporarily closed down," Adam teased.

Walt shrugged. "I have an in with the owner."

"So basically, none of you are doing anything special for your anniversaries?" Heather asked.

Melony shrugged. "I imagine we'll go out to dinner. Adam and I talked about going somewhere for the weekend, but there wasn't anywhere we felt like going."

"That's what marriage does to you," Chris teased. "Turns you all into homebodies."

"Says the bachelor who's spending his Sunday night with his married friends, playing board games," Heather snorted.

"Technically speaking, Mexican Train isn't a board game. And you aren't married, either," Chris reminded her.

"True. And I don't plan on getting married. But I have a significant other."

Chris played his turn while saying, "I'm still trying to wrap my head around the idea of you two as a couple."

Heather rolled her eyes at Chris. "You can stop saying that, already. *Yeah, yeah, you used to think Brian was a jerk, and now you like him, and you didn't see what he sees in me because I'm me.* We got it. You've said that, like, a billion times already."

Chris shrugged. "I don't think it was a billion. And while Brian isn't such a jerk like I initially thought, you are still you. Which is why I still can't wrap my head around it."

The next minute Chris let out a yelp in pain, waking Hunny.

"What happened?" Melony asked.

"She kicked me," Chris grumbled while leaning down briefly to rub his injured shin.

"Oh, don't be such a baby. It was barely a tap," Heather scoffed.

"It woke Hunny," Chris countered as Hunny moved over to Walt's feet and lay back down.

"I thought no more hitting?" Danielle asked Heather in a scolding tone.

Heather shrugged. "I didn't hit him."

The banter continued between Chris and Heather. Melony didn't think either sounded angry. Heather and Chris's relationship had always reminded her of two siblings—siblings who deeply cared for and loved each other and enjoyed playful taunting. Heather certainly didn't treat Chris like her boss, and he didn't treat Heather like a subordinate. Despite Heather's interactions with Chris, Melony knew she was probably Chris's most loyal employee, and Chris knew it.

As they continued to play the dominoes game, and Melony listened to Chris tease Heather about something, Chris suddenly stopped talking mid-sentence. Melony glanced up from her dominoes and noticed Chris staring in her direction. But he wasn't staring at her but at the space between her chair and Adam's.

Melony glanced around the table and noticed all their friends staring in the same direction as Chris, none of them saying anything. Adam, his back to whatever had captured their friends' attention, frowned and turned in his seat, curious to see whatever they were looking at.

When Adam saw nothing out of the ordinary, he turned back around and asked, "What is it?"

Hunny started barking from under the table, and Max, still perched in Danielle's lap, perked up, his ears twitching.

DANIELLE, HER FINGERS STILL, NO LONGER RUBBING MAX'S EARS, stared at the wall behind Melony and Adam and watched as a faint ghostlike figure slowly emerged, as if seeping out from the wood paneling. The image—at first faint—became fully visible while remaining transparent.

"Olivia?" Danielle blurted without thought. Olivia Davis, the neighbor who had moved into the house next door—between Marlow House and Heather's house—a year earlier, stood behind Melony and Adam. It wasn't Olivia's physical body—just its image. Hunny stopped barking.

Hand now outreached to Danielle, Olivia cried, "I need your help."

"Olivia?" Adam repeated. "Danielle, who are you talking to?"

When Danielle didn't answer Adam's question, Adam and Melony turned in their seats, looking behind them, trying to understand what their friends were seeing. Like before, there was nothing unusual.

Danielle stood up. "What's wrong, Olivia?"

"I'm in danger! I need help!"

Melony turned back to Danielle. "What is it?"

"Where are you?" Chris asked Olivia.

Olivia shook her head. "I don't know. It's dark and cold."

"Are you talking to a ghost?" Melony asked.

"They—" The next moment, Olivia vanished.

Adam repeated his wife's question. "Are you guys talking to a ghost?"

"I hope not," Heather muttered as she and the rest of the mediums stood up.

Before they could explain to Adam and Melony what had just happened, Marie popped into the room.

"The twins are sleeping and—" Marie didn't finish her sentence when she noticed everyone at the table standing except for Adam and Melony. She glanced around and asked, "What's going on?"

"Marie, Olivia from next door was just here," Walt began.

"Grandma's here?" Adam asked.

"Oh my God," Melony gasped. "Olivia is dead?"

"I hope not. We'll explain later." Walt turned his attention back to Marie. "Olivia just appeared a moment ago, told us she needed help, said she was in danger, and then she disappeared."

"We need to go next door and check on her," Heather blurted.

"Marie, it would be quicker if you go over to her house—"

"I understand," Marie said, cutting Walt off. "Eva's upstairs; have her meet me next door." The next moment Marie vanished, and Heather bolted from the dining room, sprinting upstairs to the nursery.

"What's going on? I don't understand. You saw Olivia? But we didn't. And if she's not a ghost, what did you see?" Melony asked.

"Like Heather says, we hope she's not a ghost, and with Olivia, it's entirely possible it wasn't a ghost." Chris's explanation made little sense to Melony and Adam.

CHAPTER THREE

Darkness covered the early evening hours in Frederickport, Oregon. The sun had set by five thirty p.m., and the rain clouds filtered out any twinkling stars. Even without the clouds, the sliver of the night's moon would still be barely visible.

The moment Marie entered Olivia's dark house, she used her energy to turn on every light in every room. While ghosts can walk through walls and move from one location to another—faster than a Learjet—they cannot see in the dark.

Marie moved quickly through the house, searching for Olivia, and ended up in the kitchen. She stood there a moment, noting the sacks of groceries sitting on the kitchen table. Eva appeared, standing beside her, a faint dusting of glitter briefly raining down over her apparition. The glitter disappeared before it hit the floor.

"What's going on?" Eva asked. "Heather came running into the nursery, frantically motioning for me to come into the hallway so we wouldn't wake the twins. She said something about Olivia showing up briefly in the dining room, asking for help before disappearing. She told me I needed to meet you here. What's going on?"

"I'm not sure. Before you got here, I did a quick search through the house, and there was no sign of Olivia. But she obviously had been grocery shopping and didn't get around to putting her groceries away." Marie stepped closer to the two filled grocery bags sitting on the kitchen table. After looking into one, she spied a carton of ice cream. "I would think she'd put that ice cream away before leaving."

"From what Heather said, it sounds as if she may not have left voluntarily."

Marie didn't respond to Eva but glanced around the kitchen, taking inventory. She spied Olivia's cell phone sitting on the kitchen counter next to a purse. Marie moved closer to them, her attention focused on the purse. The next moment it opened, and a leather bifold wallet floated up from the purse's fabric-covered interior. It dropped onto the counter.

Eva and Marie watched as the wallet's zipper tab moved along its edge. The wallet opened, exposing several credit cards and IDs tucked into little slits on one side of the wallet.

A driver's license slipped out of the wallet, rose from the counter, and hovered in the air a moment while Marie read it. "It's Olivia's driver's license, so that's the purse she's obviously using." The driver's license floated back down to the open wallet and moved back into its slot.

"If her car is here, she should be somewhere close."

The next moment Eva and Marie stood in Olivia's driveway, next to Olivia's car. Without the motion-detector light turning on, they would remain standing in the darkness. Marie focused on a tree near the light, and one of its limbs began to sway. The light turned on, illuminating the driveway.

Redirecting her energy, Marie tested Olivia's car doors. They were all locked. Marie unlocked the car, looked inside, and found it empty. She closed the car door and relocked it.

"If she's not somewhere in the house, we need to search the property," Eva suggested.

"We should get Walt and the others first. We can't adequately search the yard without a flashlight, and when they're doing that, you and I should probably go through the house again. There might be some space I overlooked."

"So you're telling me Olivia Davis, the librarian who lives next door, astral projects? Like, her spirit leaves her body and can walk through her neighbor's walls?" Adam asked incredulously after Danielle explained about Olivia. They all sat at the dining room table, waiting for Marie's return, abandoning their game of Mexican Train.

"Yeah, but she said she wasn't going to do it anymore," Heather answered for Danielle. "So she must be stuck somewhere if she had to astral project to get help."

"And you said she knows about Grandma?"

"Yes, because—"

Adam cut Danielle off. "What else haven't you told us?"

The mediums exchanged glances, and Chris looked at Adam and asked, "What do you mean?"

"Ever since you told us about Grandma, about you all being mediums, how Grandma can communicate with animals, I got the feeling there was more. Like you weren't telling us everything. And now, this."

"I must agree with Adam. Since we learned about Marie, I keep wondering if there is something you haven't told us," Melony said.

They all sat in silence for a moment. Finally, Danielle said, "I think we told you the most important part. But telling you about Olivia while you're trying to process what you learned about Marie would have been overwhelming."

Before Danielle elaborated, Marie and Eva appeared in the dining room. Heather immediately announced the spirits' arrival.

"She's not there," Marie told them. "But her car is, and so are her cell phone and purse. And groceries sitting on her kitchen table that she hasn't bothered putting away. I searched through her house, but Eva and I want to go through it more thoroughly. And you need to search the yard; she may have fallen somewhere and can't get up. It was too dark for Eva and me to check. We need some flashlights, and Eva and I carrying around flashlights will attract unwanted attention from the neighbors."

"Did you notice if her house was locked?" Walt asked, knowing Marie might have simply moved through the wall and not bothered trying the doors.

"I checked all her doors. They were all locked except for her kitchen door. Her car was also locked up."

"Let's get some flashlights," Walt said.

ARMED WITH FLASHLIGHTS, WALT, CHRIS, AND ADAM HEADED TO Olivia's house with Eva and Marie. Danielle stayed behind at Marlow House with Heather and Melony while the twins slept upstairs.

After they left, Danielle started up to the nursery to check on the twins and make sure the monitor was on so she could hear them from the living room if they woke up. On the way upstairs, she told Melony and Heather that she was calling the chief.

"Eddy doesn't work today, does he?" Melony asked Heather as the two began clearing off the buffet and taking everything to the kitchen while Danielle walked upstairs. Heather understood Melony was referring to Police Chief Edward MacDonald and not the chief's oldest son, Eddy Junior. Melony was the only one of their friends who called the chief Eddy, as she had been the best friend of the chief's late wife.

"No, Brian said he wasn't working today. He tries to take weekends off because of his boys, but it doesn't always work out." In the kitchen, Heather moved the leftover pizza into a food container and put it in the refrigerator.

"This isn't exactly something we can call in to the station."

Heather gave Melony's comment a chuckle. "It makes it easier having the chief and Brian understand certain things. But sometimes it's tricky trying to explain to Joe and the other people they work with. And this is certainly something we couldn't call 911 about."

"I guess not. *Hello, 911, my neighbor's soul just stepped into my dining room, and she needs help.*"

Hunny and Max followed Walt and the others to Olivia's house while Walt silently communicated with the dog and cat, explaining their concern involving Olivia. He asked them both to check around the yard and tell him if they found anything. Meanwhile, Adam, who chatted with Chris as they walked next door, was oblivious to the ongoing conversation between Walt and the two animals.

Joshua had looked at a map before starting for Frederickport, so he understood an alley ran behind her house instead of the property backing up to another house. He had also pulled up the address on Google Earth, so he knew what the houses on the street looked like and that her driveway was off the alley and not on the street side of the property. The GPS on his phone took him right to her front door. He slowed down when passing her house, but he didn't stop. It was dark out, but her house was lit up as if she were having a party. Instead of stopping, he continued driving, made a right at the corner, and then drove up the alley, back toward her house.

When he spied her driveway, he slowed down but didn't stop. There were three men standing in her driveway next to a car. He put his foot on the accelerator and kept on driving. His cell phone rang.

"Where are you?" came the familiar voice.

"Frederickport."

"You know what I mean. Where exactly are you?"

"In my car."

"Funny."

"I just drove by her house. There were some guys standing in her driveway."

"What were they doing there?"

"I don't know. Just standing there, talking."

"So what now?"

"I'm going to check into my room. It's been a long day. I need to get some sleep. I hope the Seahorse Motel has a decent mattress."

AFTER STEPPING ONTO OLIVIA'S PROPERTY, WALT AND THE OTHERS stopped a moment at Olivia's parked car. Adam reached for the passenger door handle, and Chris stopped him.

"I think it best we avoid touching anything."

"I was just curious to see if her car was locked," Adam explained.

"Your grandmother already checked. It's locked up," Walt said. "And she doesn't leave fingerprints."

"You think this is a crime scene?" Adam asked.

"All I know, Olivia, who swore she was never going to astral project again, showed up at our house and told us she needed our help, that she was in danger, and then left," Walt explained.

"And if she left before explaining, that means someone disturbed her body, which, from what I understand, can pull someone back to their body," Chris added.

Max, who had been walking around the perimeter of the car, stopped at the rear of the vehicle. Peeking his head under the back bumper, his black tail swishing behind him, he meowed.

"What is it, Max?" Walt asked. Unbeknownst to Adam, Max silently conveyed an answer to Walt. Walt walked to the rear of the car, seeing only Max's tail and butt as the rest of the cat disappeared under the bumper. Walt pulled a handkerchief out of his pocket and knelt next to the cat.

Adam and Chris followed Walt and stood behind him, watching to see what he was getting from under the vehicle.

"What is it?" Adam asked after Walt reached under the back of the car and picked up something from the ground with the handkerchief.

Walt stood and showed Adam and Chris that it was a key fob. Careful not to leave fingerprints on the key fob, Walt pressed one of its buttons. Olivia's car horn honked. Walt pressed the button again, the handkerchief still between Walt's fingers and the key fob and its button. The honking stopped.

"This obviously belongs to Olivia," Walt announced.

"We didn't notice that earlier," Marie said.

"It looks like it got pushed under the car," Walt explained.

WALT, CHRIS, AND ADAM SPENT THE NEXT FIFTEEN MINUTES checking the yard and the area around the property while Eva and Marie searched through the house again. When the men finished, they entered the house while Max and Hunny performed a wider search of the surrounding area.

The men entered the unlocked kitchen door. Once inside, Chris glanced at the kitchen table and the two paper sacks filled with groceries. He walked to the open purse sitting on the counter and looked inside. Spying a store receipt, Chris picked it up and looked at it a moment before walking over to the kitchen table and looking in the bags.

"What are you doing?" Adam asked.

"Comparing the items on this grocery receipt to what's in the bags," Chris explained.

Adam frowned. "Why?"

"Because if it is a receipt for these groceries—which it appears to be because the items in the sacks match what's on the receipt—we know when Olivia bought these groceries. And if she came straight home, which I imagine she did, because there is a carton of ice cream in one sack, I don't know about you, but when I buy ice cream, I rarely drive around town running errands while I have a carton of ice cream melting in my car. We'll know when she bought the groceries and will have a better idea of when she disappeared. Because according to this, considerable time passed between the time she bought these groceries and she showed up at Marlow House."

CHAPTER FOUR

It was her and Joe's night to bring dessert to the weekly family dinner at Ian and Lily's house. Kelly Morelli thought banana splits would be a fun dessert, and it wouldn't require any baking or making a mess in her kitchen. She had gone to the store that afternoon and bought ice cream, a variety of toppings, and, of course—bananas. When at the store, she ran into Olivia Davis, the woman who bought the house she and Joe had once put an offer on.

Although the woman had beat her out of the house she wanted, Olivia seemed like a nice person. Someone—Kelly couldn't remember who—had compared Olivia's looks to Cruella de Vil from *A Hundred and One Dalmatians* because of her two-toned hair, mostly black with about a third white in front on one side. Olivia wore it shoulder-length in loose waves. Kelly had wondered if it was a conscious fashion choice or if Olivia was one of those people whose hair goes white in large sections and won't hold a dye, while the rest of it keeps its color. Kelly had to admit, on Olivia, the look was striking.

They had met in the freezer section while picking out ice cream. The two chatted for a few moments, Kelly telling her about the banana splits for their weekly family dinner, and Olivia mentioning her plans for Sunday.

But when Kelly and Joe headed over to Ian and Lily's house that evening, they had remembered the ice cream and the toppings, but she forgot the bananas and left them at home, sitting on the kitchen counter. Kelly realized the oversight during dinner when her dad asked what she had brought for dessert.

Lily didn't have any bananas at her house, she had used her last one that morning at breakfast, and when Joe offered to run home and pick up the ones Kelly had bought for tonight, both Lily and Ian immediately said they could just have ice-cream sundaes, no need for the bananas. Joe seemed immediately relieved that he didn't have to go home and pick them up, but Kelly really wanted banana splits; she had been thinking of them all day. So as soon as they finished dinner, she grabbed the car keys, announced she was running home to get the bananas, and left before anyone could try talking her out of it.

On the way to her and Joe's house, Kelly noticed Olivia's place lit up as if she were having a party, which Kelly knew was not the case, as Olivia had told her what she intended to do that night. But it looked like every light in the house was on, upstairs and downstairs.

"She obviously doesn't care about her electric bill," Kelly muttered to herself as she continued her drive, her thoughts shifting to banana splits and what she planned to put on hers.

On the way back to Ian and Lily's after picking up the bananas, Kelly noticed the lights were still on at Olivia's, yet right as she drove past the house, every light turned off, and the house went completely dark. Kelly's first thought—*power outage.*

Just as Kelly was about to turn into her brother's driveway, she noticed two cars parked across the street in front of Marlow House. She hadn't noticed them before. One was Chief MacDonald's car; the other was a squad car. Instead of pulling into Ian's driveway, Kelly stopped in the street, backed up a little, and then turned the wheel of her car slightly so that her headlights pointed at the rear of the squad car; that way, she could read its license plate.

———

WHEN KELLY WALKED INTO HER BROTHER'S HOUSE A FEW MINUTES later, she found the family still sitting around the dining room table. All the dinner plates had been cleared away, with a clean napkin and spoon sitting at each place setting. Her two-year-old nephew, Connor, ran around the table, toy airplane in one hand, making engine noises while his grandmother playfully pretended to snatch the toy from his hand when he ran past her.

Seemingly oblivious to the toddler's play, Lily held Emily Ann on her lap, feeding her what looked like orange mush, while Ian, Joe, and John good-naturedly argued about sports. After Kelly stepped into the dining room, the men stopped talking and looked her way while Connor stopped running, looked at his aunt, and yelled, "Ice cream!"

"Glad to see you still have lights," Kelly announced. She glanced at the breakfast bar and noticed the ice-cream bowls and toppings set out and assumed the ice cream was still in the freezer.

"Why would they be out?" Ian asked.

"I just drove by Olivia's house, which was lit up like a Christmas tree when I left to get the bananas, and just now, when I drove by, it went dark. All the lights turned off at the same time. Like a power failure."

"That's weird," Lily muttered.

Kelly looked at her husband. "Joe, didn't you say Brian got off at nine tonight?"

"Yeah, why?"

"I noticed your guys' squad car parked across the street at Marlow House. The chief's car is over there too. His personal car. If Brian is playing hooky, the chief obviously knows."

———

OFFICER BRIAN HENDERSON AND CHIEF MACDONALD SAT IN THE living room at Marlow House with Walt, Danielle, Melony, Adam, Heather, and Chris, along with the twins. Walt and Danielle each sat in a recliner, holding a baby. Max and Hunny had followed them home and now joined the others in the living room, while Eva and Marie had not returned with them, but continued searching the neighborhood for Olivia.

When they first arrived, Brian and the chief had parked their vehicles in front of Marlow House and walked over to Olivia's house. At Olivia's, Walt and Chris explained the situation, and the chief and Brian did another search of the property before returning to Marlow House. After locking up the house, Marie turned off all the lights.

"I'm not sure how to proceed with this," the chief admitted.

Brian's cell phone rang. He picked up his phone, looked at it, and then looked at the chief. "It's Joe."

"He should be across the street at Lily's. It's family dinner night," Danielle said. "I wonder if he saw your car."

"I'm not answering this right now. If he asks, I was in the bathroom when my phone rang. I'm not sure what I'm going to tell him." The phone eventually stopped ringing.

"He might walk over here," Heather said.

"Then we need to figure out what we're going to say," Chris said. "And how we can help Olivia."

"It's a missing person, but how do we explain we know she's missing?" Brian asked. They all looked at Danielle. The room remained silent for a few minutes.

"I could say I walked next door to borrow something," Danielle tentatively suggested. "And when over there, I saw Olivia's car, assumed she was home, and knocked on the kitchen door. It wasn't shut all the way, so it opened a little when I knocked. I called hello. When there was no answer, I walked inside. Saw her groceries sitting in the kitchen, her purse and phone still there. And when I couldn't find her, I had a bad feeling, came back here, and then Walt volunteered to go over and look around, and Adam and Chris joined him."

The chief nodded. "That would work."

"I have a question: Did you guys put Olivia's groceries away for her?" Heather asked.

"No. We didn't want to disturb anything. And the only thing that was perishable was the ice cream, and even if Olivia showed up now, that ice cream needs to go into the trash," Chris said. "I also have a theory about what happened to her, and it has to do with those groceries."

"What's that?" Heather asked.

"The groceries in those bags were all on that receipt I found in her purse. However, there was one thing on the receipt that was not in the sacks. A bottle of wine. I didn't see any wine in the kitchen, and according to Marie, there wasn't anything in the car."

"So what's your theory?" Danielle asked.

"Olivia brought the two bags of groceries inside, put them on the table, and then returned to her car to get the wine. She took the wine out of the car, closed the hatch, used her key fob to lock up the car, and when still standing behind it, someone grabbed her. She dropped the key fob. Maybe in the scuffle it got pushed under the car."

"So someone grabbed her and the wine?" Walt asked.

Chris shrugged. "It would explain the groceries on the table, what happened to the wine, and why the key fob was under the locked car. And why her kitchen door was unlocked, and her purse and phone were sitting on her kitchen counter."

"He's right!" a voice called out. But only the mediums could hear it. They all turned to the voice and saw Olivia standing in front of the fireplace.

"Olivia!" Heather called out. The non-mediums stopped talking and turned toward the fireplace. While they couldn't see Olivia, they understood she was there.

"I have to be quick; if someone comes down there, I'll be pulled back into my body again."

"Where are you?" Danielle asked.

Olivia shook her head. "I have no idea. It's dark, like a cellar. I focused on coming here. I haven't done this in a while, so I'm trying to remember how."

"Who has you?" Walt asked.

"I don't know. I was getting the wine out of the car. I had just closed the back hatch, locked it, when a car pulled up behind me from the alley. I didn't recognize the car; it was a dark sedan. The windows were dark, couldn't see inside. I thought they wanted to ask me a question, but then a man jumped out of the back seat, lunged toward me, grabbed me, and shoved a rag over my face. It smells sweet, and the first thing I think of is chloroform. I've never smelled it before, but from all the books I've read, it supposedly has a sweet smell. He dragged me into the car. I tried hitting him with the bottle of wine I'm holding, but I'm at a weird angle. I'm in the back seat of the car with him, awkwardly trying to hit him, and someone yanks the bottle out of my hand. I feel the car moving, and the man is on top of me, pressing that stupid rag on my face. I keep thinking I don't want to inhale whatever is on the rag, and I try holding my breath. But I can't, I need to breathe. Everything went black after that, and the next thing I remember is waking in a cold, damp, dark space. I was lying down on what felt like thin slats of metal. They put me in some sort of cage. I can't tell you where. And if that was chloroform on that rag, it doesn't work as fast as I've seen in the movies."

"What did the men look like?" Danielle asked.

"I can't tell you. I didn't get a good look at them. It might have been two men, or a man and a woman, or if there was a driver and someone sitting in the front passenger seat. The one who grabbed me was a man, but I didn't really see his face. I didn't see the driver or who took the bottle away from me. It might have been the same person. Why would anyone take me?"

"You need to explore your surroundings," Chris said. "Look at the people who took you. Find out as much as you can—where they have you—then come back and tell us."

"I'm trying—but—" Olivia vanished again.

"She's gone," Heather announced.

"What did she say?" the chief asked.

CHAPTER FIVE

After the mediums explained to the non-mediums all that Olivia had said, Brian picked up his cell phone. "I'd better call Joe back."

"What are you going to tell him?" Heather asked.

"You need to tell Joe what's going on. With Danielle's edits," the chief told Brian.

The next moment, everyone sat silently, curious as to what Brian would say to Joe about this evening's events.

When Joe answered his cell phone, Brian said, "Hey. I noticed I had a missed call from you." After exchanging a few words, Brian told Joe the version of the story they had all agreed on. When he finished, Brian listened quietly for a few moments to whatever Joe was saying on the other end of the call before saying, "Hold on, let me ask the chief." Brian looked at Edward. "Joe told me Kelly ran into Olivia at the grocery store this afternoon. This might make her one of the last people who saw her before—"

"Ask Joe if he would bring her over here so we can ask her some questions," the chief said, interrupting Brian, preventing him from finishing his sentence.

Brian nodded and relayed the message to Joe. A few moments

later, Brian ended the call and told the chief, "Joe said they are finishing eating banana splits, and as soon as they're done, they'll come over."

"Oh, banana splits? That sounds good," Heather murmured.

The chief looked at Walt and Danielle. "When Kelly comes over, can we use your parlor?"

Danielle nodded. "Certainly."

Adam cleared his throat before saying, "Can I ask a question before Joe and Kelly get here?"

"Sure, what?" Edward said.

"No offense, Chief, I doubt you could answer the question I have. This is more for the mediums." Adam's eyes looked over to Walt and Danielle and then to Chris and Heather. "It's about this astral projection thing. I'm sort of curious, why would anyone suddenly stop? I mean, seriously, that actually sounds kinda cool. Part of me still finds it hard to believe, but then I remember Grandma putting together her artificial Christmas tree, and about anything seems possible now. So, what made Olivia stop doing it?"

"I'm afraid meeting us played a role in Olivia's decision to abandon astral projection, and I've recently been questioning a few things, and I suspect we were wrong," Chris said.

"What are you talking about?" Heather asked.

"I think we gave her some bad information."

"Bad information, how?" Adam asked.

"After finding out about Olivia's astral projection, and her learning things about us that most people outside this room aren't aware of," Chris began.

"You mean how you can see ghosts?" Adam smiled.

"Yes. We told Olivia that if her spirit left her body, there was a possibility the spirit of someone who died, one who hadn't moved on, who hadn't accepted their death, might claim her body when her spirit was off astral exploring," Chris explained.

"You think that could happen?" Melony asked.

"Yes, it can happen," Heather answered and looked at Chris. "Why are you saying we might have been wrong?"

Chris's gaze met Heather's. "Because I've been doing some

research about astral projection. Many believe there's an energetic tether connecting the spirit or soul to its body. Some refer to it as the silver cord. This cord is only broken when the body dies. But it's the thing that will instantly bring the soul back into its body."

"But—" Heather glanced at Walt, then looked back to Chris and didn't finish her sentence.

"Those other times had nothing to do with astral projection in the way Olivia did it—we're talking about broken bodies already at the brink of death," Chris said. "Some even accepting death."

"What other times?" Melony asked.

The doorbell rang.

"Saved by the bell," Danielle muttered under her breath, not loud enough for Adam and Melony to hear.

"That's probably Joe," Brian said, standing up.

BRIAN AND THE CHIEF WENT INTO THE PARLOR WITH JOE AND KELLY, shutting the door behind them.

"Are you sure she isn't with a friend and forgot to lock her door? She told me she was planning to stay home tonight because she had a book she wanted to finish. But she could have changed her mind," Kelly said hopefully.

"I'd agree with you, but she left her groceries sitting on her kitchen table. While I understand someone might not be in a hurry to put away their groceries, I don't see them willingly going somewhere and not at least putting the ice cream in the freezer. And her purse and phone were also in the kitchen, and we found her car keys outside on her driveway," the chief explained.

"You said willingly going somewhere. You think someone kidnapped her?" Kelly gasped.

"I have a gut feeling this was foul play." *Plus, Olivia told us what happened*, the chief silently added.

"When I saw her at the grocery store this afternoon, it was about one thirty. I remember because Mom called me when I was at the store, and I looked at the time before I put my phone back in my purse. Right after that, I ran into Olivia in the ice-cream aisle."

"According to the store receipt, Olivia checked out at 2:05. But we aren't certain if she came straight home or had other errands," the chief said.

"She mentioned something about having spent the morning running errands and said that was her last stop, and how she was looking forward to spending the afternoon finishing her book."

"Which means if someone took her, it was probably within an hour from when she checked out of the store," Brian said.

"Now that I think about it, there were a couple of guys I noticed; they kept checking out Olivia. Before I talked to her in the ice-cream section, I saw her in the store, but she was some distance away, so I didn't say hi. But I noticed these two guys. At the time, I figured it was the hair."

"The hair?" Brian asked.

"Olivia has…well…sort of distinct hair color. It sort of attracts attention. It looked as if they were staring at her. They even came down the ice-cream aisle when we were there and walked by us. When I was checking out, I was at the cashier next to Olivia, and the two guys were right behind her, in the same line. They only had a couple of things in their cart, and I remember wondering how someone can walk down all the aisles of a grocery store and only walk away with a couple of things. Heck, when I go to the grocery store, I always end up buying more than I came for."

"I can vouch for that," Joe muttered.

"Can you describe what these men looked like? Have you ever seen them before?" the chief asked.

"I don't remember seeing them before. They were both tall, at least six feet. They looked to be maybe in their forties. Both white, at least, they looked white. I kinda figure they might be from out of town because they were both pretty bundled up, as if they weren't accustomed to our weather. I mean, it's not that cold out. But they both had on wool caps and gloves."

"Any facial hair?" Brian asked.

"No. But they both wore glasses. I think they were wearing jeans and dark jackets. After they checked out, they seemed in a hurry to get out of the store."

"When they checked out, had Olivia left the store?"

"Yes. The checker was about done ringing up my items when I glanced over, and Olivia had just walked out of the store, and the two guys, who had checked out right behind her, grabbed their few items, didn't even wait for the cashier to bag them up, and sprinted to the exit."

"We need to see if the store has any security footage during that time," the chief said.

OLIVIA FOUND HERSELF BACK IN THE CAGE. ONE MOMENT SHE WAS IN the living room at Marlow House, and the next she was back in her body as if someone had jerked her by the leash to return. But this time it was no longer dark. Overhead, a bright light turned on; it filled the space.

She thought the room looked like a basement, with concrete walls, no windows, and a primitively built wooden staircase against one wall, leading to the main level. She estimated the basement to be approximately four hundred square feet and empty except for the cage placed in the center of the room and a cardboard box against the far wall. The cage, her prison, was about two hundred square feet of floor space, with heavy wire walls and a padlock securing its door. The room's only light appeared to be the crude light fixture overhead, now shining harsh light down on her.

Olivia shivered from the cold, her arms wrapping around herself while her hands desperately tried rubbing heat into her skin. She was grateful she hadn't taken off her coat after taking the groceries into her house, or she would be standing here in only her light sweater and jeans. But it wasn't enough.

"Hello!" she finally called out.

A moment later a door opened, and a man appeared on the stairs and looked down at her. The fact that he didn't bother covering his face terrified her. She didn't recognize him; he was a tall white man wearing a wool cap and looked to be in his forties or fifties.

"Good, you woke up," he called down to her while standing on one of the top stairs, not bothering to walk down farther.

"Why am I here?" she asked.

"Because I put you there."

"Why?"

He shrugged. "If you weren't locked in a cage, you'd get away."

"What do you want with me?"

"Want with you? I'm not sure what you mean."

"What are you planning to do to me?"

"Nothing. Absolutely nothing."

"But why am I here?"

He shrugged. "This was the best place we could find."

"It's cold down here. I'm thirsty. I need to go to the bathroom."

He shrugged again. "That really is not my problem." He turned, walked back up the stairs, and she heard him close the door behind him.

Again alone and now trembling, Olivia sat on the floor, trying to ignore the uncomfortable cage floor. The cage reminded her of a dog kennel, but sturdier. She closed her eyes, took a deep cleansing breath, and focused her attention on what she needed to do.

* * *

OLIVIA FOUND A PRIMITIVE TWO-BEDROOM, ONE-BATH CABIN WITH A large great room upstairs. Mounted trophies: several large fish, game birds, and a buck's head decorated the wood-paneled walls. The rooms were sparsely furnished, yet she saw no sign of anyone staying in the cabin. There were no doors on the kitchen cabinets, and their shelves were empty save for a few dishes and no food items. There were drawers under the kitchen cabinets. Several cast-iron skillets hung on the kitchen wall, and by the cobwebs attached, it was obvious they hadn't recently been used to cook anything. A lone saucepan sat on the stove.

In the bedrooms, the mattresses were bare, with no sheets or blankets. In one bedroom, someone had tossed a purple bedspread on the mattress; it looked as if someone had pulled it from a dryer and dumped it on the bed. A paper sack filled with what looked like men's clothes sat next to it.

She found the man who had talked to her moments earlier outside on the covered front patio, sitting at a picnic table, talking on a cell phone. The only light on the patio came from a lantern sitting on the table. Olivia's gaze swept over the front of the house as she tried to figure out where she was. She spied a sign hanging over the front door. Moving closer, she silently read its words: *Welcome to Martin's Hideaway.*

Olivia wondered who Martin was and hoped that was a clue she could use. She turned from the front of the cabin and surveyed the perimeter of the building.

Pine trees surrounded Martin's Hideaway, and if there were any neighboring cabins, she couldn't see them; it was too dark outside. The driveway was empty, with no sign of the dark sedan.

Olivia moved closer to the man, standing beside him as he talked on his cell phone.

"As long as I'm outside, I can get reception. I can't get any service inside or on the other side of the property. We were smart to check the cell service before we decided on this place…yes…so how is the motel, all it's cracked up to be?" He laughed and said, "Yeah, it's cold down there. I might hurry this thing up and dump some water on her." Another laugh.

CHAPTER SIX

The man ended his call not long after making his strange comment about splashing water on her. Instead of going into the cabin, he pulled a pack of cigarettes from his coat pocket, removed a cigarette from the pack, and put it between his lips. After returning the pack to his pocket, he pulled out a lighter from the same pocket, lit the cigarette, took a deep puff, and shoved the lighter back into the pocket. Leaning back, he gazed off into the darkness while smoking. It was raining, but the patio overhang kept the rain off the porch and the man.

Olivia told herself she would not get any information sitting here watching the man smoke. Closing her eyes briefly, she moved upward through the patio overhang, over the house's rooftop, until she hovered above the treetops.

Rain moved through her, yet she felt neither wet nor cold. It was one advantage of astral projection. Here, she could not feel the numbing cold she felt when in her body, trapped in the cage.

Unfortunately, darkness surrounded her, and the only lights she saw were those coming from the cabin below. She stayed there for approximately fifteen minutes, organizing her thoughts and deciding which direction she should first go to determine her location and facilitate her rescue. She was about to venture away from above the cabin's rooftop when she felt a splash of icy cold spread over her face.

Olivia blinked her eyes in surprise. She was back in the cage, water dripping down her face. The man who had been smoking stood next to the cage, a lit cigarette hanging from his lips, while he held an empty saucepan in his right hand.

Confused, Olivia dried her face with the sleeve of her jacket and stared at him.

"That didn't exactly work," the man grumbled.

"Why did you throw water in my face?"

"In my defense, I wasn't going for your face." He shrugged. "I forgot about that big jacket you have on."

"Were you trying to wake me up?"

He chuckled at her question. "No."

"What was the point of throwing cold water in my face?"

He shrugged again. "Thought it might speed things up."

"Why am I here?"

"I think I answered that question already."

"Are you going to keep me here forever?"

"Of course not. You won't be here more than a week."

"Where do I go after a week?" Olivia was afraid she wouldn't like his answer.

"Not sure. Where do you think we should drop you? At the beach, near your house? Nah, that might be too risky. To be honest, we haven't really decided. I'm considering our options. But I am open to suggestions." He laughed at his own words.

Olivia stared at him for a moment. Part of her wondered if he was simply a crazy person who enjoyed abducting people. But then she remembered he hadn't acted alone; he had at least one partner. This felt like a kidnapping, but who would kidnap her? Who could they extort money from? Her sister didn't have the kind of money kidnappers demanded. Her parents were dead. She hadn't seen her sons in years, yet they didn't have that kind of money either. Not that they would pay a ransom even if they had it.

"I'm thirsty," she blurted.

"I just gave you some water." He laughed again.

"If I'm going to have to stay here a week, I need water, something to eat."

"That sounds like a you problem." As he said the words, he tapped the bottom of the pan on the cage, turned from her, and put his cigarette out in the pan. She watched him walk to the stairs, taking the pan with him. He never looked back.

When he was gone and the sound of the door closing told Olivia she was alone again, she immediately repositioned herself in her prison, trying to get as comfortable as possible to put herself into the correct state of mind to attempt another astral projection. Perhaps she had enough for the mediums now. All she needed to do was make it back to them, tell them she was in the mountains at a cabin called Martin's Hideaway. That might be enough information.

It took Olivia almost twenty minutes to relax and bring herself to the correct state of mind for astral projecting. Just as her soul was about to leave her body, the man reappeared, once again disrupting the meditative state necessary. He didn't throw water on her, but he still had the pan, and this time used it as a drum by pounding it with a large spoon.

"You aren't going to sleep on me, are you?" he shouted as he marched around the cage, slamming the large metal serving spoon against the bottom of the aluminum pan.

"Are you insane?" Olivia blurted without thinking.

He stopped his drummer-boy imitation and stood in front of her, the cage bars separating them. Smiling at the question, he said, "Crazy as a fox."

"If you aren't going to feed me or give me something to drink, why can't I just sleep?"

"This isn't a negotiation. And I don't want you to sleep." He turned and walked away, heading back up the stairs.

Olivia cried after him, "Why are you doing this?" But he didn't answer; he kept walking up the steps, his back to her. For the rest of the night, Olivia tried unsuccessfully to astral project, but she could never reach the necessary meditative state because every thirty minutes the man would return to make sure she was not asleep.

"Okay, what didn't you guys tell Joe and Kelly?" was the first thing Lily Bartley said when Danielle answered her phone on Sunday night.

"Well, hello to you too, Lily. I assume Ian's parents and Joe and Kelly left already?" Danielle lounged on the sofa in Marlow House's living room, her feet propped up on Walt's lap while he massaged her stockinged feet. While he wasn't privy to Lily's side of the conversation, Walt flashed his wife a smile at her response to Lily.

"Yes. Your guests still there?"

"No."

"So, what really happened?"

Danielle told Lily the unabbreviated version of tonight's events.

"Oh, my gosh! And Olivia couldn't tell you where she is?"

"She doesn't know. She didn't get a good look at them, but Kelly might have seen them."

"Yeah, when Kelly and Joe got back from your house, she told us the chief was really interested in the guys she noticed watching Olivia at the store. I guess the chief's going to see if the store has any security footage of the men." As Danielle listened to Lily, Walt gently lifted Danielle's feet off his lap, stood, set her feet back on the sofa, and then leaned over and gave her a kiss on the forehead before mouthing, *I'm checking on the babies.*

Danielle smiled at Walt as he left the room, and then turned her attention back to her conversation with Lily and said, "After Kelly left, the chief also called Elizabeth Sparks."

"To do a police sketch?"

"Yes. There's no guarantee there's footage, and he preferred Elizabeth to do the sketch while Kelly's memory is fresh. Unfortunately, Elizabeth is in Colorado and won't be back until Wednesday."

"Hopefully Olivia can figure out where she is and let you guys know before Elizabeth gets back."

THE MAN STRETCHED OUT ON THE BED, PICKED UP HIS CELL PHONE on the nightstand, and then looked at it, checking the time. Just as he was about to set it back onto the nightstand, the phone rang. He looked at the caller, then let out a sigh and answered the phone. "Hey."

"Did you get all checked in at the Seahorse Motel?"

"I did."

"You still there?"

"Yeah. I took a nap. Well, at least I tried to. Naps aren't my thing. But I got some rest. I've got to leave for the cabin in about fifteen minutes. I have the late-night shift."

"Did you guys take care of the car?"

"Yes. I don't think anyone is going to find it, not unless they're a fish. So even if someone saw us grab her, between the car being at the bottom of the ocean and those masks, no way anyone is going to connect her disappearance to us."

"How did those masks work?"

He laughed at the question and then said, "Those things are insane. I don't know where you found them, but dang, it was like wearing someone else's face. And with the glasses, no one noticed. Fortunately, it's cold as an iceberg, so us wearing gloves and hats doesn't seem strange to people."

"And there was no problem grabbing her?"

"No. We pretended to be looking at some ice cream and heard her sharing her plans for tonight, which was helpful. She thought she was coming straight home and spending a quiet evening alone reading a book. When we pulled up behind her house, our plan was to go inside and get her, but she was standing by the back of her car, and we just grabbed her. She was holding a bottle of wine that almost became a problem. Fortunately, we took care of that."

"I wonder how long before someone notices she's missing."

"I imagine when she doesn't show up for work in the morning, someone might come checking on her. But I don't see anyone looking tonight. She's a woman living alone. Her car is sitting in her driveway. Looks like she's home."

"Just like we planned."

"I just hope you're right about how long this is going to take."

"It will be worth it for all of us. I promise."

"I've been thinking, maybe the safest place to leave her when this is done is on the highway. Too risky bringing her back to Frederickport."

"I don't care where you leave her as long as she gets found—quickly."

CHAPTER SEVEN

On Monday morning, Heather sat at her desk at the Glandon Foundation headquarters, talking on her cell phone. Chris walked into her office, his attention on the stack of papers in his hand. He started to say something, but as soon as he heard her on the phone, he stopped talking and looked up. Heather gave him a motion with her right index finger, signaling she was about to get off the phone.

"Okay. Let me know what you find out." Heather ended the call. She looked up at Chris and said, "That was Brian."

Chris walked all the way into the office, closed the door behind him, tossed the papers on Heather's desk, and took a seat. "Have they heard anything?"

"No. Other than the grocery store will have the security footage ready this morning. While Brian and Joe wait for it, they're stopping at the library, which should be open when they get there."

Sitting across from Heather, Chris crossed one leg over an opposing knee, his hands casually resting on the chair's armrests. "Why are they stopping at the library?"

"More for show—but Joe doesn't know that. It's what they'd do if Olivia hadn't shown up at Marlow House last night."

Chris nodded. "Makes sense. If someone is missing, you'd naturally check where they work. It would seem strange to Joe if they didn't go to the library."

"Exactly. That's one reason Brian called. He asked me if I knew Olivia's schedule. I told him she usually works on Mondays, and I know the library opens at ten. But I remember Olivia once mentioned she usually gets there about half an hour before it opens."

"I imagine they'd also want to question Olivia's coworkers, see if anyone suspicious has recently asked about her or been hanging around," Chris said.

"True. Anyway, after that, the store should have the footage ready, and they can take it back to the station and watch it. While it's possible those men have nothing to do with the abduction, they need to start somewhere."

It was after ten thirty when Joe and Brian showed up at the library. They went immediately to the front desk and began asking questions.

"I've been calling Olivia's phone since I came in this morning," the woman at the front desk told Joe and Brian. "Olivia always opens. But she wasn't here when I got in this morning. Has something happened to her?"

"That's what we're trying to find out," Joe said.

The woman behind the counter leaned closer and said in a low voice, "We aren't the only ones looking for Olivia."

Brian frowned. "What do you mean?"

"Not long after I opened this morning, a woman showed up, and she was pretty upset that Olivia wasn't here."

"What woman?" Joe asked.

"She didn't give me her name. I've never seen her before. But she came barreling in here, demanding to see Olivia. When I told her she wasn't here, she asked if she had called in sick. I told her I couldn't really give out private information of employees but told her I would be happy to have Olivia call her if she would leave me her contact information."

"Did she leave it?" Brian asked.

"No. And she seemed rather annoyed that I wouldn't just give her the information. Really, now, you can't just barge into someone's place of employment and demand to know where they are if they aren't working."

"Can you describe this woman?" Brian asked.

"She was, I guess, middle age. Black, had long hair, wore it in cornrows that turn into long braids."

LAST NIGHT IAN PROMISED TO HELP KELLY WITH A PROJECT SHE WAS working on for her podcast, and they had agreed to meet at his house on Monday morning. Kelly drove down Beach Drive and noticed a car with California plates parked in front of Olivia's house. After Kelly drove by the car, she glanced in her rearview mirror and watched as a Black woman got out of the driver's side of the car.

After pulling into Ian's driveway, Kelly parked, got out of her car, and looked across the street. The woman now stood at Olivia's front door.

"THERE'S SOMEONE AT OLIVIA'S HOUSE," KELLY ANNOUNCED WHEN she walked into Lily and Ian's living room a few minutes later. Before Kelly had left her house that morning, Ian had texted his sister and told her to use her key to let herself in, as the baby was sleeping. Kelly found Lily on the floor with Connor, putting together some puzzles, and her brother sitting on his recliner, drinking a cup of coffee. Sadie, their golden retriever, who had been lying by Ian's feet, got up and greeted Kelly, the dog's tail wagging as her wet nose nudged Kelly's right hand.

"Somebody, who?" Lily asked.

Kelly gave Sadie an absent pat, leaned over and kissed the top of Connor's short red curls, and plopped down on the sofa. "I don't know. But she has California license plates. She was standing at Olivia's front door when I pulled into your driveway."

Curious, Lily stood up from the floor, walked to the living room window, and looked out over at Olivia's house. "A powder-blue SUV?"

"Yeah. Is it still there?" Kelly asked.

Lily turned from the window and faced Kelly, who was still on the sofa. "It is. But I don't see anyone at Olivia's front door."

WHEN ADAM NICHOLS CALLED MARY ON SATURDAY MORNING TO tell her he knew someone looking for a housekeeper, she was thrilled. But after he told her the potential customer lived at Marlow House, she couldn't believe the coincidence.

It wasn't that Mary had ever been to Frederickport before or even knew it existed until recently. But since that time, she had gone to the library to use their computer to research the community. She soon discovered, after Googling Frederickport, Oregon, pages on Marlow House came up at the top of the search results.

She had learned it was one of the oldest houses in town, built by the town's founder, who lent his first name—Frederick—to the town, and his last name, Marlow, to the house in question.

One article was about the *New York Times* bestselling author who now lived in the house, a distant relative of Frederick, who shared the name of Frederick's grandson and bore an uncanny resemblance to said grandson. Yet the author hadn't inherited the house; he had married the woman who inherited the estate through the grandson's housekeeper. Mary thought it sounded confusing, and she didn't try keeping it all straight.

Then there were the articles about how Marlow House had been the site of more than one murder—and some believed the house haunted. The current owners had been operating the house as a bed-and-breakfast, but it was temporarily closed.

None of that was as interesting as the fact that Marlow House was on Beach Drive. And not just anywhere on Beach Drive, but right next door to *her*.

Mary turned down Beach Drive. She didn't need to look at the house numbers because she had driven down the street when she arrived in town on Friday. Mary slowed down as she drove past the house and noticed a powder-blue SUV parked in front. She drove past the SUV and parked in front of Marlow House.

"Are we getting out, Mom?" Cassandra called out from the backseat.

"Yes, honey."

———

MARY SAT PRIMLY NEXT TO HER DAUGHTER ON THE SOFA IN THE room Danielle Marlow referred to as the parlor, her hands neatly folded on her lap as she glanced around the space, wondering when people stopped calling rooms parlors. She remembered one article she had read online about a murder that had taken place in Marlow House's parlor five years earlier. Mary wondered if it bothered Danielle, knowing someone had been killed not long ago in this quaint little room, a room that looked as if it had been decorated by a Victorian grandmother.

Danielle and her husband, Walt, sat in two chairs facing her. They had offered her something to drink before they sat down, which Mary declined. After sitting down, Danielle explained that the static they might hear was coming from the baby monitor, as their twins were upstairs taking a nap in their room.

"Oh my, how do you get them to sleep at the same time?" Mary asked.

"Part of it's luck." Danielle then added silently, *And Marie's help.*

"I wanted to thank you for letting me bring my daughter with me. I know it's not professional, but I'm new to town, I don't know anyone, and I still must work out childcare. But Cassandra is very well behaved and won't get in anyone's way if I bring her."

Walt's gaze shifted from Mary to Cassandra and noticed the

little girl staring at Max, who stared back at her, his black tail swishing. Walt knew Max wanted to say hello to the child, but Walt had warned the cat to stay back because he had no idea if the little girl was allergic or afraid of cats. Yet the little girl had been smiling at Max and covertly giving him little waves. Walt doubted she feared him.

"I'm curious, is your daughter allergic to cats?" Walt asked suddenly.

"Allergic? Umm, not that I'm aware of. And Cassandra loves cats. She loves all animals."

"Cassandra, this is Max. Would you like to meet Max? He's eager to meet you," Walt asked.

Cassandra's eyes widened. "Oh, yes!"

Walt looked at Max and said, "Max, you can say hello." Max then walked over to Cassandra, jumped up onto the sofa, and promptly climbed into her lap, lay down, and purred.

Mary looked at the cat in surprise. "That's certainly a well-trained cat."

Walt smiled. "He likes children. Children who are gentle with him."

Cassandra stroked Max's fur while softly whispering to him.

Walt looked back at Mary and said, "So, tell us a little about yourself."

"Um…I'm a single mother. I recently left my husband. As I mentioned, I just moved to Frederickport. Like I told Mr. Nichols, I've never had a job before." Mary paused a moment, as if rethinking what she had just said, and then added, "Except for the daycare at our church. But I didn't get paid for that. I married right after high school, and my job was taking care of my husband and our home. And then we had Cassandra. But now, I need to get a job…one that comes with a paycheck. I'm a hard worker."

"The twins are asleep," Marie announced as she appeared in the room, standing between the sofa and chairs. Marie then turned and smiled at Cassandra and Mary and asked, "How is the interview going?"

Danielle stood up. "Why don't we show you the house so you can get a better idea of what this job entails?"

Mary and Walt stood, but Cassandra remained on the sofa, the purring cat still sprawled atop her lap. Cassandra looked up at her mother. "Mom, can I just stay here with Max? Please?"

"I'll stay," Marie told Walt and Danielle, knowing Mary couldn't see her and assuming Cassandra couldn't.

Walt looked at Mary. "If Cassandra wants to wait here, I'm sure she'll be fine. In fact, there's a basket of toys by the window she's welcome to check out. Technically, they don't belong to our twins. We originally bought them for one of our friends' children who often visits. And there are some items for older children that we've since added to the basket that she might enjoy."

Cassandra looked up hopefully at her mother.

Mary glanced hesitantly from her daughter to the basket of toys across the room and back to her daughter. Finally, she said, "Okay, but don't touch anything other than the toys, and make sure to put everything back before we leave."

Several minutes later, Walt, Danielle, and Mary left the parlor, leaving Cassandra alone with Max and Marie. After her mother was out of earshot, Cassandra looked at Marie and said, "You're a ghost."

CHAPTER EIGHT

Startled by Cassandra's statement, Marie sat in the chair Walt had occupied moments earlier. She stared at the little girl. "You can see me?"

Cassandra nodded, her right hand stroking the length of Max's back. "Yes. You were at the museum. You followed us. But Mom couldn't see you. Neither could that other lady who was there."

"What makes you say I'm a ghost?"

"Because I can see you, and Mom can't. Mom can't see ghosts. She doesn't believe in them either." Cassandra slumped back on the sofa, no longer stroking the cat's fur. Max turned slightly and began grooming his paws.

"Who told you that people you can see—that your mother can't —are ghosts?" Marie was genuinely curious.

"My grandpa's wife."

"You mean your grandma?" Marie asked.

Cassandra shook her head. "No. She says she's too young to be my grandma."

Marie arched her brows. "But she married your grandpa?"

Cassandra nodded. "They got married on Christmas."

"This past Christmas?"

"No. The Christmas before."

"So, what did she tell you about ghosts?"

"I was the flower girl at the wedding. I told her GG said I looked pretty."

"Who is GG?"

"My mom's grandma."

"Oh, your great-grandma," Marie said.

Cassandra nodded. "When everyone was eating cake after the wedding, I told her GG said she liked my dress. But she said I was confused, and it was someone else, because unless GG's ghost was there, it couldn't have been her."

"Your GG had died?"

Cassandra nodded. "Until the wedding, no one told me she died. GG lived in one of those places with lots of other old people. Mom and I would visit her every Sunday after church. The last time we visited her was right after Thanksgiving, but GG was sick and stayed in bed the whole time sleeping. The next Sunday, we didn't go over there, and I thought she was probably still sick. But that night, after Mom tucked me into bed, GG visited me. I figured that's why we didn't go see her that day, because she was coming to our house. I saw her again at church the next week."

"When did you realize your GG was a ghost?"

"After the wedding, I asked Mom why Grandpa's new wife called GG a ghost. Mom got all quiet and said they didn't want me to be sad at Christmas, but GG had died. She said I must have talked to someone who looked like GG, because ghosts aren't real."

"What did you do then?"

"The next time GG came, I asked her. She told me she was a ghost, but that she had to move on. I think she was moving to heaven. But she wanted to say goodbye. And she told me ghosts are real, but not to be afraid of them."

"Interesting. So, am I the first ghost you've seen since your GG?"

Cassandra shook her head. "No. There's a lady ghost I saw at church, and she visited our house once. But I said hello to her, and I must have scared her because she left real quick and never came back. I'm glad you aren't afraid of me."

WALT AND DANIELLE WANTED TO GIVE MARY A TOUR OF THE ENTIRE house because she needed to understand the house's size before she accepted the housekeeping job—should they decide to offer it. They also explained that whomever they hired, their current housekeeper would train them, as she had been taking care of the house for years.

They started in the basement and moved through the first floor. When they got to the second floor and peeked into the nursery, the twins were just waking up. Walt told Danielle to finish showing Mary the second floor and attic office while he changed the twins and got them up. Danielle didn't argue. She understood Walt, with his telekinetic abilities, was better suited to wrangle two active little ones without a second pair of hands.

When Danielle and Mary walked into one of the guest bedrooms, Danielle's cell phone rang. She pulled the phone from her pocket and excused herself to answer the call without leaving the room. It was Lily.

"Hey, where are you?" came Lily's faint voice over the cell phone.

"Lily, why are you whispering?" Danielle glanced over to Mary, who now stood by the window, looking into the side yard.

"I don't want Kelly to hear. I'm in the bathroom. But I figured you'd want to know there's something going on over at Olivia's house."

"Something what?" Still holding her cell phone to her ear, Danielle walked over to the window, stood next to Mary, and looked out toward Olivia's house.

"When Kelly got here, a woman with California plates on her car pulled up and parked in front of Olivia's house. She went up to the front door. A few minutes later she wasn't by the front door anymore, but it's been over an hour, and the car is still there.

Kelly called Joe. Brian and Joe are on the way over to check it out."

"The woman is walking around Olivia's property? Because I'm looking out the window, and no one seems to be in her yard."

Mary, who had been gazing out the window, seemingly ignoring Danielle's conversation, quickly turned her head after Danielle said Olivia. She momentarily looked at Danielle before looking back out the window.

"No, I'm pretty sure she's inside Olivia's house. The curtain in one of the upstairs windows is open. It wasn't open this morning."

Danielle continued to stare out the window, her right hand clutching the cell phone to one ear. "Brian and Joe just pulled up at the back. Did Kelly describe the woman?"

"According to Kelly, she's Black. Has long box braids."

"Black? Box braids? I need to get over there. I gotta go, Lily." Danielle hung up as Walt walked into the bedroom, a baby in each arm. She looked at Walt and said, "I've gotta run next door; I'll explain when I get back." Danielle looked to Mary and added, "Sorry about this, but Walt can finish the tour."

As Danielle raced past a confused Walt, she gave her two babies a quick kiss and disappeared through the open doorway.

"Well, how rude," Walt said with a bemused chuckle. "Any idea what just happened?"

Mary shrugged. "Not sure. She just got a phone call from someone named Lily. I heard her say something about someone named Olivia."

"Olivia?" Walt's tone shifted from bemused to serious. Still holding the two little ones, he walked over to the window and looked next door. He spied the police car parked in the driveway off the alley, next to Olivia's car.

"Perhaps we should wrap up this tour. Joanne's working tomorrow, and if you'd like, you can come over and work with her. She can show you around. You'll get paid for your time, of course. It'll give you a better feel of what's expected. You might decide you aren't interested."

"Can I ask you one thing?"

"Certainly." Walt leaned down and set the now squirming twins on the floor. They immediately crawled over to the nearby bed and started pulling on the edge of the bedspread, trying to stand up.

"Is there a problem next door?" Mary asked.

Earlier that morning, Walt would have been reluctant to answer the question, but he had recently talked to the chief, who told him the newspaper would be running a story on Olivia in the morning, along with her picture. "I'm afraid our neighbor is missing."

"Which neighbor?" Mary's voice was barely a whisper.

Walt nodded toward Olivia's house. "Right next door. Her name is Olivia Davis; she's the head librarian at our local library."

Mary stared back out the window, the color draining from her face. "What do you mean missing?"

"They fear she may have been abducted from her home yesterday."

By the time Danielle arrived next door, Joe and Brian were already in Olivia's living room. They had left the side door open, and when Danielle stepped inside, she spied Joe and Brian each aiming a gun at a woman who stood midway up the stairs, her hands now raised, while Joe barked orders, telling her to move slowly.

"Guys, put the guns down," Danielle said calmly.

Joe glared over his shoulder at Danielle, the gun still aimed at the woman. He looked back at the intruder, keeping his hands steady, while Brian said, "Danielle, step outside; she may not be alone."

The woman, still holding her hands in the air, looked down at Danielle, her expression unreadable.

"She's Olivia's sister. I imagined she used her key to get in." Danielle glanced up the stairs at the woman.

The woman smiled at Danielle. Her hands still in the air, she said, "You must be Danielle Marlow. My sister has told me all about you."

"Sister?" Brian frowned. He reluctantly lowered his gun and gave the woman a nod to continue down the stairs.

"Can I hold onto the banister? Or do I have to keep my hands in the air?" the woman asked.

Brian mumbled something about how she could put her hands down, and stepped aside with Joe, their guns no longer raised, as they watched her slowly descend the staircase, her right hand on the banister.

When she reached the landing, Danielle said, "When Lily mentioned the woman with California plates was black, I figured it might be Olivia's sister, but when I saw you, you look just like your picture. You are Shanice, right?"

Shanice nodded.

"Olivia's sister is Black?" Joe blurted.

Shanice looked at Joe. "What, you didn't notice the family resemblance?" She didn't wait for an answer; instead, she looked at Danielle and asked, "Where is my sister?"

Danielle shook her head, and Brian asked, "Why are you here? Why now? Was Olivia expecting you?"

"Where is my sister?" Shanice demanded, this time her tone impatient. "Is she okay? Is she in the hospital or something?"

"Why do you assume something's wrong?" Joe asked.

"Because every Sunday night we FaceTime, and last night she didn't call, and when I called her, she didn't answer. She always answers. Finally, I got into my car and started driving. I pulled into Frederickport after nine this morning. Went straight to the library because I know she goes to work by nine on Mondays. But she hadn't come in. So I came here, but she's not home, yet her car is. And she has groceries sitting on her kitchen table that she hasn't bothered to put away, and there is a gallon of melted ice cream in one of those sacks, which tells me those groceries have been sitting there a while. And then I go upstairs to look for her, and when I come downstairs, I'm met by a couple of gun-happy cops, who apparently decided I have broken into my sister's house, and didn't bother asking before pulling guns on me."

CHAPTER NINE

Shanice sat with Walt and Danielle at their kitchen table in Marlow House while Addison and Jack sat in the nearby highchairs, eating their lunch. Brian and Joe had left Olivia's house fifteen minutes earlier, after they finished questioning Shanice and explaining to her what they knew about Olivia's disappearance. Danielle had invited Shanice to Marlow House for lunch, where they could further discuss Olivia's disappearance. Mary and Cassandra had already left Marlow House.

"Did you ever consider calling the local police station and asking them to make a welfare check on Olivia instead of just driving here?" Danielle asked as she set a plate with a tuna sandwich, potato chips, and pickles on the table in front of Shanice.

Shanice slid the plate closer to her while Danielle grabbed two more plates from the counter, one for her and one for Walt.

"Before I answer that question, I need to tell you Olivia told me all about you." Shanice picked up one half of her sandwich, lifted it to her lips, and paused a moment and looked up, watching as Danielle took a seat at the table with her and Walt.

Danielle's brow rose briefly at Shanice's comment. "Um…what exactly?"

Shanice, who had taken her bite while Danielle asked the question, shrugged her shoulders, chewed her food, and after swallowing her bite said, "Oh, that-sees-ghosts thing." Shanice glanced at Walt and added, "That spirit-body-swap thing." She looked back at Danielle and smiled. "I already knew about Olivia's astral projection."

"You believed it all?" Walt asked, genuinely curious.

Shanice picked up a potato chip from her plate and glanced over to Walt. "Yeah. I did. I do. And as for why I didn't call the local police and ask for a welfare check, I also could have just called you. Closer, right next door. Olivia had already told me about you, and while I didn't have your phone number, I could have probably looked up your B&B online for the number. But at first, when Olivia failed to FaceTime me, and when she didn't answer, I talked myself into believing something probably came up unexpectedly, and she had gone somewhere that didn't have cell service. So I went to bed early, fell asleep, and had a dream. A very vivid dream. It was my mom. And she told me Olivia needed me. And then I woke up. It was the middle of the night."

"That's when you left for here?" Danielle asked as Shanice ate her chip.

Shanice nodded and a moment later said, "I figured what was the point of calling anyone. If Olivia needed me, I wasn't staying home. I needed to come here and find out what was going on."

"Your mom's spirit visited you?" Danielle's statement was more a question.

"I think so. It was a vivid dream. Olivia told me you call those dream hops."

Danielle grinned. "Yes."

"I'm curious, when did Olivia show you a picture of me?"

"The photo book she made after the cruise. Olivia showed them to us. Looks like you two had a wonderful time. She told me she sent you the same book."

Shanice nodded. "It was a great Christmas. We had a lot of fun. I have another question. What haven't you told me that you couldn't say in front of those cops?"

For the next fifteen minutes, while Shanice finished her lunch, Danielle explained what had happened since Sunday night. Just as Danielle was about finished, the twins fussed in their highchairs. Walt got up from the table, wiped Addison's and Jack's faces and hands, removed them from the highchairs, and then set them both on the floor. Before returning to his seat at the table, he pulled a bin of random Tupperware from the cupboard for them to play with.

When Walt returned to the table, Danielle said, "The two cops you met today, Joe and Brian, Joe knows nothing about what I just told you. But Brian, along with Frederickport's police chief, knows everything."

Shanice nodded as she absorbed the information and picked up a napkin to wipe her hands.

"Do you have any idea who might have taken your sister?" Walt asked.

Shanice considered the question a moment as she crumpled the now-used napkin and tossed it onto her empty plate. "It sounds like a kidnapping, but there is no one in our family who could pay any sort of ransom. At least, not the type of ransom that risks decades in prison. Our parents are gone; it's just the two of us. We're both financially stable; our parents left us a little inheritance. We both own our own homes; our parents paid for our education. But we don't have any ransom-worthy savings sitting in some vault."

"How about someone who has a grudge against Olivia?" Walt suggested.

"You mean, like an enemy? Someone who is doing this to hurt her?"

Walt nodded.

"I can't imagine who that could be. Olivia doesn't have a wide circle. After she left her husband, which was maybe ten—twelve years ago—time goes so fast, kind of hard to keep track. But when Olivia left Texas and moved out to California to live with our parents, she didn't know anyone there. She had never lived in California before then. And at the time, well, she and I had a strained relationship."

"You seem so close now," Danielle noted.

Shanice smiled at Danielle. "It took a lot of rebuilding. But when we were younger, Olivia and I were very close. I don't know if Olivia told you, but we used to live in Frederickport before my family moved to Texas. I was four when Olivia was born. She was sort of my baby doll." Shanice laughed at the memory. "I loved helping Mom with her, and Olivia always followed me around. When I was a teenager, we lived in Texas. By that time, I had my own friends, and when Olivia was in high school, I was off at college, and she started dating Mark."

"Mark? Her ex-husband?" Danielle asked.

Shanice nodded. "Yeah. His father was the pastor at a megachurch in our town. They started dating during her junior year of high school. He was her first and only boyfriend. Since I was off at college, I only saw them when I came home for the holidays. We really didn't get to know each other, but what I knew, I didn't like. And I tried talking to my parents about him."

"What didn't you like?" Walt asked.

"My family wasn't big churchgoers. But where we were living in Texas, church was kind of a big thing. My parents didn't think her attending his family's church was a problem—something they later came to regret."

"How so?" Walt asked.

"At the time, my parents didn't fully appreciate how a young, naive girl, with little life experience, might be overly influenced by someone like her boyfriend—and his family. When I tried to talk to Mom about it, she dismissed it. I suspect she felt having an impressionable teenage daughter dating a boy who was so deep in the purity culture preached by his father was preferable to her running with some of the wilder kids in town who liked to party."

"But you noticed something different?"

"Yes. A controlling boyfriend, and during the few times I visited my parents when Olivia and Mark first started dating, he would make snide comments about how my going to college was a waste of money because a woman's place was in the home. Plus, there was that adopted-sister thing."

Danielle frowned. "Adopted-sister thing?"

Shanice nodded. "Yeah. Until Mark, Olivia had never called me her adopted sister. Obviously, everyone knew I was adopted. But the only parents I ever knew were Olivia's birth parents, and she was always my sister. But when I would come for a visit, and Olivia would introduce me to someone as her sister, he would always correct her. He would say *you mean adopted sister.*"

"What did she say?" Danielle asked.

"The first time he said it was at their church. I had come home to see my family for Christmas, and they were having a Christmas program at Mark's church. She asked me to go with her; she and Mark had been dating for a few months by this time. I stood out at that church."

"The only Black person?" Danielle asked.

Shanice nodded. "When Olivia introduced me to Mark's parents as her sister, Mark immediately corrected her, saying I was her adopted sister. At first, she looked like she wanted to contradict him, but she stayed quiet. It was weird. I remember when I was introduced to members of their church, they looked at me like I was some sort of good-deeds charity case—you know, like when churches raise money to feed the starving children of Africa. They gave me this sanguine, almost condescending expression, praising my parents for being so good as to take me in."

"Did you ever say anything to Olivia about it?"

"Yes. She said, well, you are adopted, and Mom always says adopted kids are no less loved. Like she was trying to justify it. But Mark never did that around my parents. Only because I don't think we were ever together when Olivia introduced me to someone. And then later, after they were married, Olivia had fallen into the habit of introducing me as her adopted sister."

Danielle cringed. "Wow. That must have hurt."

"It helped to erode our relationship. And when they got married, I wasn't asked to be in the wedding. But frankly, by that time, I would have declined. Our parents tried to talk her out of getting married so young. They wanted her to go to college. But Olivia was convinced God wanted her to be Mark's wife. Remember, she was very young and sheltered and fell deep into the culture of his father's church. She got married just days after her eighteenth birthday. So there was nothing my parents could do to stop it."

"I understand Olivia has two sons she never sees," Danielle said.

"Yes. My parents moved from Texas not long after the youngest was born. By that time, Olivia and I had no relationship. Mark thought I was sinful. That living-in-sin stuff." Shanice let out a harsh laugh and added, "I had lived with a couple of different boyfriends over the years."

"But you and Olivia rebuilt your relationship?"

Shanice nodded. "It didn't happen overnight. Olivia waited for their youngest to graduate from high school before leaving Mark. My parents sent her a plane ticket to California. She arrived with basically the clothes on her back. Olivia had been in an abusive and controlling relationship for years. My parents understood that long before Olivia did, but they were terrified of Olivia cutting them off completely or not being able to have a relationship with their grandsons, so they were careful about what they said. After moving to California, Mom would typically end their weekly phone calls by saying, *Olivia, remember we love you. And if you ever need anything, we're here for you.* Olivia finally understood what Mom had been telling her, and she took her up on that offer."

"It's so sad she doesn't have a relationship with her sons," Danielle said.

Shanice nodded in agreement. "They refused to have anything to do with her when she divorced their father. It broke her heart."

"That's so sad," Danielle said.

"After Olivia moved in with our parents, she enrolled in college. During that time, she started going through the process of deconstruction regarding her faith. Mom convinced her to get a therapist, and later she and I had therapy together, which helped heal our relationship. She had always loved books, which apparently had been a source of conflict during her marriage. Her husband wanted to censor and control the books she read. I think that first year after leaving Mark, whenever she had free time, she was reading a book. And that was pretty much Olivia's life since her divorce. Studying, reading, trying to figure out who she was, later starting a career, but not really socializing and making new friends. So I don't see how anyone from her life prior to moving here would have any reason to hurt her. If someone took her because they wanted to hurt her, it must be someone she met since moving to Frederickport. Or it's some random psycho."

CHAPTER TEN

Brian and Joe gathered around the monitor with Chief MacDonald at the police station, watching the security videos given to them by the grocery store. When requesting the footage, they had also asked for any videos of the parking lot during the time Kelly said they left the store.

The video taken at the register when the men were checking out captured both men's faces clearly. They watched it several times before Brian requested they freeze the frame a moment so he could get a closer look at something. Once they did, Brian moved closer to the monitor and stared at the image.

"What is it?" Joe asked.

Brian didn't answer immediately. Instead, he stared a moment longer and then let out what sounded like a sigh and said, "I think those are masks."

"Masks? What are you talking about?" Joe asked.

"Here, have a look. They have glasses on, but check around their eyes." Brian motioned to the monitor, then stepped out of Joe's way. He then grabbed his cell phone and began surfing for something.

Joe stared at the monitor, standing only a few inches from it, but he wasn't sure what he was supposed to be seeing. After a minute, still not knowing what Brian was talking about, he moved aside, giving the chief his turn to look. Meanwhile, Brian focused his attention on his cell phone, frantically looking for a website Heather had shown him in October when having a conversation about Halloween costumes.

"I think I see what you mean," the chief said.

"What?" Joe asked.

"Found it!" Brian blurted and then shoved his phone toward the chief and Joe. "There, what do you see?"

Joe reached out and took the phone from Brian. Frowning at what he was seeing on the screen, he looked back to the monitor, then back to the phone. "That mask looks like the guy on the right."

"It's because the guy on the right is wearing a mask," the chief said, taking the phone from Joe. "Look at that still frame again, Joe. Around his eyes. Even with the glasses on, I can see it: shadowing. It's not the same as dark circles under his eyes. It's because the mask has cutouts around the eyes."

The chief looked at the phone a moment and then handed it back to Brian, who swiped the screen several times before saying, "I just found the other guy."

"What do you mean?" Joe asked.

Brian showed Joe his phone. It was the product image of another mask; this one looked like the other man in the video.

"If that's the case, then we don't have a clue what these guys look like," Joe grumbled.

"Not entirely," the chief reminded them. "We have their approximate height. And we still have the footage of the parking lot. If we're lucky, we'll find their car and then find them."

"This also tells us something else," Brian said.

Joe looked at Brian. "What?"

"This morning these guys were simply people of interest. Someone Kelly noticed at the store. But knowing they were not just following Olivia, but doing so while wearing masks, these men must have something to do with her disappearance."

When they got to the footage of the parking lot, Brian thought they had hit the jackpot. He watched as the two men got into a dark sedan. What Joe didn't know—that he and the chief did, because Olivia had told the mediums—was that the men who took her were driving a dark sedan.

They watched as the men pulled out of the parking lot, and the security camera captured their vehicle's license plate. They immediately froze the frame, and MacDonald jotted down the license plate numbers.

"The guys are from Utah," Joe noted.

Several minutes later the chief was on his computer, running the license plate numbers, assuming they were getting closer to finding the men's identity. But a few minutes later, he let out a curse and slumped back in his chair.

"What is it?" Brian asked.

"Those license plates don't belong to that car. They go to a Buick wagon, not a sedan. And the owner of the Buick, according to what information I just found, is some eighty-two-year-old woman in Utah."

"So they took the plates off one car and put them on the car they planned to use to kidnap Olivia. So the question is now: did they take the license plate off a random car or a car of someone they know?" Brian asked.

AFTER LUNCH, BEFORE SHANICE RETURNED TO OLIVIA'S HOUSE, Danielle, knowing Shanice might feel unsafe staying at her sister's house alone, considering Olivia had been abducted in her driveway, invited her to stay in the downstairs guest bedroom at Marlow House. Shanice thanked Danielle for the offer but declined. She explained that she had brought her gun with her, and she wasn't afraid to use it. Walt insisted on walking Shanice over to Olivia's, saying he wanted to walk through the house before leaving Shanice alone. Shanice accepted the offer.

When Walt returned from next door, he found Danielle in the

living room with the twins, who were on the floor, playing together with some toys. "Did you get Shanice all settled in?"

"I brought her luggage in for her and took it upstairs. She hadn't brought it in yet. But she insisted I levitate it up the stairs and not carry it by hand."

Danielle giggled and asked, "Why?"

Walt shrugged and joined Danielle on the sofa. "She told me that while she believed everything Olivia told her, even about us, part of her wanted tangible proof."

"I can sorta understand. And how did she react?"

Walt leaned back on the sofa, crossing his right leg over the opposing knee. "The best I can describe it—pensive. Like part of her was surprised despite already saying she believed Olivia. She also seemed tired and stressed. She is obviously worried about her sister, and I suspect exhausted from the long drive here. I made sure the house was locked securely. I asked her if she wanted to call a locksmith."

Danielle frowned. "Locksmith? Why?"

"Olivia dropped her car keys when they grabbed her, and I wondered if she might have her house keys with her, maybe in a pocket. And locking up the house will not protect Shanice if the kidnappers return and have the keys."

"Did she want to?"

"No. She checked her sister's purse, the one sitting on the kitchen counter. Her house keys were there, and Shanice said her sister would have no reason to have an extra house key on her. But when I left, she was wearing her handgun in a holster."

"Like a cowgirl?"

Walt chuckled. "No. One on her body, not around her waist. Like a private eye."

"That's good…I think." Danielle's cell phone rang. She picked her phone up from the coffee table and answered it. It was the police chief.

Walt sat quietly next to Danielle on the sofa, silently listening to her side of the conversation. When she ended the call, he asked, "What was that about the car?"

"According to Kelly, the guys following Olivia drove a dark sedan, and the camera captured a shot of the car's license plate."

"That's great."

"Not so great. They were Utah plates, but for a Buick wagon, not a sedan. I say plates, plural, but it was only one license plate. Anyway, the owner of the Buick is an elderly woman who hasn't driven her car for the last couple of months because of some medical issues. Her driveway situation is similar to ours, in the rear of her house. That's where the car has been sitting, and she didn't notice the plate was missing. The chief had someone from the police department where she lives interview her. According to the woman, the only visitors she ever gets are from her church and her daughter. And none of those people ever go out to the back of her house. But according to the officer who interviewed her, it would have been easy for anyone to pull up behind her house and take the license plate with no one seeing it. They hoped one neighbor might have a security camera that captured footage of someone messing with her car, but unfortunately there were no security cameras back there. I guess it's a rural area."

"You say they got video of the car, what about the men?"

Danielle explained about the masks. When she finished filling Walt in on the conversation she'd had with the chief, the two leaned back on the sofa for a minute, silently contemplating the current situation. After a few moments, Danielle looked at Walt and said, "Oh, what about Mary? I completely forgot about her. Did you show her the rest of the house?"

"No. I suggested we call her tomorrow, tell her when Joanne will be here, and if she wants to come over, Joanne could finish the tour and then tell her what the job entails. But I wouldn't be surprised if when we call her, she says she's no longer interested."

Danielle frowned. "Why do you say that?"

"She asked me what was going on next door. The police car was parked behind Olivia's house. Since the newspaper is running a story in the morning, there was no reason to keep it a secret. I told her our neighbor was missing, and then I said we suspected someone had abducted her when she was in the driveway."

Danielle cringed. "Yeah, I can understand not wanting to take a job next door to where someone was just abducted, and knowing the kidnappers are still out there. She's a young woman who seems to be all alone, responsible for a child."

"What's going on?" Marie asked when suddenly appearing.

"Where have you been?" Danielle asked.

"After Mary came downstairs to get Cassandra, I decided to go find Eva and see if she's heard anything."

"Cemetery gossip mill?" Danielle snarked.

Marie shrugged. "Something like that."

"Has she heard anything?" Walt asked.

"Not really, but Eva feels that wherever Olivia is, she's still alive. Anything new here?"

"I agree with Eva about Olivia being alive. I'd expect her ghost to come back here before moving on." Danielle then updated Marie on all that had happened since she had gone upstairs to take Mary on a tour.

"I didn't realize you'd left the house and gone next door," Marie told Danielle. "I was in the parlor with Cassandra when her mother came down to get her, and no one said anything about you leaving."

"You didn't stick around and give me a chance," Walt reminded her.

"True. And by the way, Cassandra can see ghosts."

"What?" Walt and Danielle chorused.

Marie recounted the conversation she'd had with the little girl.

"Considering her age, I have to assume she is more a medium like Evan instead of like Connor." Walt and Marie understood what Danielle was saying. While babies and young toddlers typically could see and hear spirits, when those children grew older and the adults around them treated those ghosts like the product of the child's imagination, then the child lost the ability, as Lily had done as a child, when she grew up believing the ghost who had befriended her had been an imaginary friend. And while Lily now understood and believed in the existence of ghosts, she no longer had the ability to see them.

"Unfortunately, if Walt is correct, Mary probably won't want to come back. I worry about children like Cassandra and wonder if Mary will decide to leave Frederickport altogether, as it probably doesn't feel like the safe little quaint town that she probably assumed it was. Will she go back to where they're from? Wherever that is. We never got around to asking her," Danielle said.

"I know where she's from," Marie said.

"Cassandra told you?" Walt asked.

"Not exactly. It was her license plate. I noticed it when I followed them out of the museum the other day. And this morning, when talking to Cassandra, she confirmed that fact when I asked."

"Where are they from?" Walt asked.

"Texas. They drove all the way here from Texas. Just the two of them."

CHAPTER ELEVEN

Gina Bellemore didn't like hospital cafeteria food, and she certainly would not feed it to her mother. Before leaving her home, she lovingly prepared a box lunch for them to share, which included chicken sandwiches made with her home-made wheat bread and some of the chocolate cookies Gina had baked the day before. She also filled a thermos with her homemade tomato soup, because her mother needed something warm.

Instead of driving herself to the hospital, Gina's husband had agreed to take her and drop her off. Her mother's car was already there, so they would drive that home—after.

After. After her father died. Her father had been sick for over a year with congestive heart failure and had been going to the hospital for weekly treatments in the ICU. But after his treatment on Friday, he didn't go home the next day as he normally did. This time he stayed. He wouldn't be coming home.

Her mother had been going to the hospital since Saturday, sitting by his bedside for hours before going home at night. Gina stopped by each day to sit with him. Her father was always asleep, and when he woke up, he didn't recognize her.

An hour earlier her mother had called to tell her the nurse said his organs were shutting down, and it wouldn't be long. Her mother told her she wasn't going home tonight; she wanted to stay with him in case this was the night. She didn't want her husband to die alone.

When Gina stepped into the ICU hospital room, she found her mother, Nancy Martin, sitting exactly in the same place Gina had seen her sitting the previous day: in the chair pulled up next to her father's bedside. He looked to be asleep, his body hooked up to an assortment of monitors, the digital display flashing information Gina didn't understand.

Holding the thermal lunch bag with both hands, her purse draped over one shoulder, Gina quietly walked to the counter and set down the bag and purse. Nancy looked up and smiled at her daughter, saying nothing.

Hands now free, Gina walked to her mother and briefly took the hand Nancy offered, giving it a gentle squeeze. Dropping Nancy's hand, Gina stepped closer to her sleeping father and kissed his brow.

Gina turned from the hospital bed, walked to the other side of the room, grabbed an empty chair, and dragged it next to her mother's chair and sat down. The moment Gina sat down, the two women held hands.

"Thank you for coming," Nancy whispered.

"I'm staying until you go home. Richard dropped me off, so I don't have my car here. Are you hungry? I brought you something to eat."

Nancy shook her head. "No."

"When was the last time you ate something?"

Nancy smiled at her daughter and patted her hand and, before looking back at her husband, said, "I ate a granola bar about thirty minutes ago. And I have my bottle of water."

They sat in silence for about twenty minutes before Nancy said, "He woke about an hour before you got here. He actually knew me. He seemed like his old self."

Gina squeezed her mother's hand gently. "What did he say?"

"It was the first time he talked about dying."

That surprised Gina. Since her father's diagnosis, they had been ignoring the elephant in the room. The pending death. It was the topic they danced around while her father took his weekly treatments and had some good days, some bad, yet never addressed the reality that his time was quickly running out.

"What did he say?" Gina asked.

"He told me he wanted to be cremated. That he wanted his ashes spread at the cabin."

"Really?" Gina looked over at her father. She wasn't surprised he wanted his ashes spread up at the cabin. After all, it was one of his favorite places. But she was surprised he'd finally acknowledged he was dying.

THE HEART MONITOR'S ALARM RANG. ALLEN MARTIN, WHO HAD BEEN sleeping in the hospital bed, sat up abruptly and opened his eyes. He found himself staring into the faces of his daughter and wife, both of whom looked sad.

"I'm fine. But get the nurse in here to shut that thing off!"

Two nurses ran into the room. The way they rushed toward him freaked out Allen, and he jumped out of the hospital bed.

A moment later, Allen stood a few feet away from the hospital bed and could hear his wife and daughter crying. But it wasn't the crying that had captured his attention; it was the man in the hospital bed whom the nurses now fussed over. A man who looked like him.

Allen took several steps back from the bed, his attention still riveted on what had been his body. The nurse told his wife and daughter, "I'm sorry, but he's gone."

"Well, crap," Allen grumbled, now standing on the other side of the room, still watching the scene. "I guess I'm finally dead." His wife and daughter were now hugging each other, and when they let go, he watched as his daughter walked closer to his bed, leaned over, and gently kissed his cheek.

From across the room, his daughter whispered, "I love you, Daddy."

Allen smiled wistfully. "I love you too, Gina. You'll always be my little girl. I'm glad I got to watch you grow up into such an amazing young woman."

Gina stepped away from his body, allowing her mother to say her last goodbye. Allen watched as Nancy leaned over his bed and kissed his forehead. "I love you, Allen. I'm going to miss you." Her right hand gently brushed the side of his face.

"I'm going to miss you too." Allen glanced around the room. "Okay, where is the white light? I'm here."

Whatever Allen imagined would happen next didn't happen. His wife and daughter continued to cry and hug each other while the nurses fussed around the hospital bed.

Eventually, Allen followed his wife and daughter out of the room into the hall. The pair stood at the front desk, talking to one nurse. Finally, he called out, "Let's go home. This hospital is depressing."

***

ALLEN SAT IN THE BACK OF HIS WIFE'S CAR AS HIS DAUGHTER DROVE them home. It was late afternoon on Monday, yet Allen had lost track of what day of the week it was. Nancy sat in the passenger seat, and Allen felt like a voyeur, listening to them talk. He understood they didn't know he had come with them from the hospital.

The moment he climbed out of that hospital bed and looked back and found his body still in the bed, he understood. He was dead. It was not as if it came as a surprise to him. The last year and a half had been brutal. First, he and Nancy had traveled to Utah for that experimental treatment, which obviously didn't help.

When back home, his doctor eventually started a treatment that required him to spend one night a week in the hospital. Back then he pretended his condition wasn't dire, and he would call the weekly treatments his tune-up, as if it were a joke. But it had never been funny.

Allen had never been a religious man, and for most of his life he believed that when a person died, they simply went to sleep. Sleep without dreams. Lights out. Nothing else.

While he and his family never discussed his impending death, he knew they were thinking about it. Nancy began reading books on near-death experiences. She never showed him the books, but he found them in her nightstand once when looking for his reading glasses.

Allen understood it was Nancy's way of processing and accepting what humans can't prevent from happening. One day, when Nancy was at the store, he took one of her books from the drawer and began reading. While he had never been much of a reader, this topic captured his attention.

The books spoke of a death that was more than sleep. They chronicled near-death experiences, and the most common theme was about following the light. But after he died, there was no light to follow. He simply was. Just as he had been before, this time without a body. At least, not a body anyone around him could see. Not sure what he was supposed to do without a light to follow, Allen decided to just go home. Perhaps the light would come for him there.

Gina pulled her mother's car up along the side of their garage and parked. Allen remained sitting in the back seat while Gina opened one of the back doors. She had placed her purse and the lunch bag on the back seat. When grabbing the items off the seat, she did not realize her father's spirit was just inches away.

"If you're hungry, we have some sandwiches and soup," Gina called out to her mother as she slammed the car door shut before allowing her father to get out.

Allen soon discovered he didn't need an open door to leave the car. The next moment he stood behind his wife and daughter as they started toward the house. Allen glanced down at his legs and noticed his bare knees peeking out from under the hospital gown.

"I don't want to walk around for eternity wearing a nightgown!" Allen grumbled. The next moment the gown he wore vanished, and in its place, he wore his favorite pair of slacks and a flannel shirt. Allen smiled in surprise. "Well, that's better!"

They had only walked a few steps when Gina stopped abruptly and glanced up at the apartment over her parents' garage. She noticed a light on and the curtain open. "Mom, is there someone in the apartment?"

"I forgot to tell you. I let Adam rent it out. They moved in on Friday."

"Is that a good idea? Do you really want strangers around right now? And we could use the room for family to stay when they come in for Dad's service."

Nancy let out a sigh. "Perhaps. But when Adam called, he told me it was a young mother with a little girl. They needed somewhere to stay."

"You aren't talking vacation rental?" Gina asked.

Nancy shook her head. "No. It's month to month. She seems very nice."

"Well, might be nice having someone else here," Gina conceded.

The next moment the topic of their conversation showed up when Mary's car pulled up into the empty parking spot next to Nancy's vehicle.

"That's her now," Nancy said. "Her name is Mary Walsh."

Gina and Nancy remained standing next to the garage, watching as Mary got out of her car. A moment later, a little girl climbed out of the back seat.

Several minutes later, Nancy was introducing Mary and Cassandra to her daughter yet chose not to mention her husband had just died. Nancy wasn't emotionally prepared to accept condolences from a virtual stranger while still processing the loss of her life partner.

While Mary had been told Nancy and her husband owned the property and Adam rented out the garage apartment for them, Adam Nichols had never mentioned the husband was in the hospital when she moved in.

Cassandra stood quietly by her mother as the lady who lived in the big house introduced them to another woman who she said was her daughter, Gina. Behind them, a man stood quietly, making no attempt to introduce himself. When no one acknowledged the man, Cassandra wondered why. When he turned to look at her, Cassandra gave him a big smile. The man's eyes widened in surprise.

CHAPTER TWELVE

On Tuesday morning, Danielle walked into the kitchen at Marlow House, holding her cell phone. Walt was already sitting at the kitchen table, drinking a cup of coffee and reading the morning newspaper, while the twins sat in nearby highchairs, being fed spoonfuls of oatmeal by Marie.

"Well, that was a surprise," Danielle said as she placed her cell phone on the counter and poured herself a cup of coffee.

Walt looked up from his newspaper, while Addison and Jack briefly greeted their mother by excitedly waving their hands at her, yet pivoted their attention back to Marie.

"What was a surprise?" Walt asked.

Danielle turned to face Walt, coffee cup in hand, as she leaned back against the edge of the kitchen counter. "I just talked to Mary on the phone. She asked what time we want her to come in today."

Walt set his newspaper on the table, his eyes on Danielle. "She's still interested in the job?"

Danielle shrugged and took a sip of coffee before saying, "I guess. I told her I'd call Joanne, double-check the time, and then call her back."

Walt picked the newspaper up while Danielle walked to the table with her cup of coffee. Before sitting down, she kissed the tops of Addison's and Jack's heads and said a few words to Marie.

"The article about Olivia is in here," Walt said. "Nothing we don't already know."

"I also talked to Heather this morning, hoping she had news from Brian. But nothing new." Danielle took another sip of coffee.

"I spoke to Eva this morning," Marie added. "Nothing new from that front."

Walt handed Danielle the newspaper without her asking. She set her coffee cup on the table, took the newspaper from Walt, skimmed the article about Olivia's disappearance, and then handed the paper back to him. "I'm so worried about Olivia. I kept waking up last night."

"I know you did, so did I." Walt folded the newspaper and tossed it to the other side of the table. "Kept hoping she'd come back, tell us where she is."

"The only positive thing, we haven't been visited by her ghost," Danielle said.

CASSANDRA WALKED DOWN THE GARAGE APARTMENT STAIRS LATE Tuesday morning while her mother trailed behind her. Mary paused midway down the stairs to look in her purse, double-checking to see if she had the shopping list she had prepared that morning.

Cassandra didn't stop but continued down the stairs and walked to their car. When she reached it and turned around to face her mother, she spied the man from last night. He stood at the foot of the stairs, staring at her. He hadn't been there a moment ago.

Mary said nothing to the man when she passed him; instead, she used her key fob to unlock her car and told Cassandra to get in and buckle up.

Minutes later, after both mother and daughter were in the car, buckled up, with Mary driving the car down the street, heading to the grocery store, Cassandra asked, "Mom, who was that man?"

"What man?"

"The man standing at the bottom of the stairs."

Mary frowned and glanced in her rearview mirror at her daughter's reflection. "What are you talking about?"

"You know, the man. He was there yesterday with the lady and her daughter. The lady who owns the place we're living at."

"Cassandra, I don't know what you're talking about. Where was there a man?"

Suddenly Cassandra understood. "Never mind. I was thinking about something else." She slumped back in the seat and remained quiet for the rest of the car ride.

MARY DIDN'T HAVE THE ENERGY TO DEAL WITH CASSANDRA'S GAMES of make-believe this morning. She needed to get to the grocery store and pick up some food for herself and her daughter. Since leaving Texas, they had been eating fast food, which wasn't healthy. Plus, it was expensive, and she needed to guard her resources. If she got the housekeeping job with the Marlows, it would help, but it wouldn't solve her problems. However, according to Adam Nichols, Danielle's housekeeper was planning to retire, and she had other clients in town. If Mary did a good job with Marlow House, perhaps the retiring housekeeper would consider recommending her to some of her other clients.

It was raining outside, so Mary tried to park close to the store's entrance. She wasn't sure how she was going to deal with the wet, damp, cold weather of the Oregon coast, a big change from where she lived in Texas. But she didn't come for the weather, she reminded herself, and it wasn't as if she intended to stay in Oregon indefinitely. Considering what she'd learned yesterday from Walt Marlow, she might leave before next month's rent was due. Mary felt a little guilty about that possibility because the Marlows seemed like nice people, and if they offered her the job, it would help her out in the immediate future—yet would leave them without a housekeeper if she left suddenly.

"Can we get some ice cream?" Cassandra asked her mother as

Mary grabbed an empty shopping cart after they entered the grocery store.

"Isn't it kind of cold for ice cream?" Mary asked as she pushed the cart from the entrance into the main section of the store, Cassandra trailing behind her.

"It's never too cold for ice cream."

When the row of checkout registers came into view, Mary paused for a moment and looked around, trying to get her bearings before proceeding. "I'll tell you what, if you don't ask for anything else, stay right next to me, and be on your best behavior, I'll buy a box of ice-cream bars."

Cassandra agreed to the bribe and followed her mother to one end of the store. From there, they began walking down each aisle, not sure where they might find the items on their list.

They had been at the store for about thirty minutes and had traveled from the produce section to the other end of the store, where the bakery and deli sections were. It was there Mary spotted him; he was standing at the deli counter, ordering something. Mary froze upon seeing him. *Joshua, he's here.* She looked down at Cassandra, currently distracted by the cupcakes in the nearby bakery section.

Mary quickly steered the cart toward the pastry section, away from the deli department, and grabbed her daughter's hand, desperate to escape this part of the store before he saw her. Or before Cassandra noticed him.

ALLEN COULDN'T KEEP HIS MIND OFF THE LITTLE GIRL. SHE HAD seen him. He was certain of that fact. He wondered, could she also hear him? If true, it meant there might be other living people who could see and hear him.

"Mediums," Allen blurted when the word popped into his head. "That's what they call those folks who can see dead people."

When alive, Allen never believed in mediums. When seeing them on television, he always assumed it was nothing but a parlor trick, and here he was, dead, and a little girl could see him. But where was the light? Allen still hadn't seen the light.

Inside the house, his daughter was still with his wife. She had spent the night and even slept in the bed with Nancy last night, which Allen thought was sweet. This morning his son-in-law came over with his grandchildren, and now the three adults sat around the kitchen table, drinking coffee and talking about his memorial service up at the cabin and how Gina and her husband would go to the funeral home and arrange for his cremation later that afternoon while the grandkids stayed with Nancy.

Because of the weather, Gina had suggested having the memorial in town and waiting until it was warmer to go up to the cabin to spread the ashes, while Nancy wanted to have the memorial at the cabin too.

Allen had left his family inside the house to discuss his memorial while he wandered around his backyard, remembering when he and Nancy first moved into the house and their much younger selves planted the colorful hydrangea bushes. He was glad he had hired someone to cut them back last month so Nancy didn't have to, and she could enjoy their blooms come spring. He wondered if he would be here in the spring, or if the light would come for him. If there was a light.

His thoughts drifted back to the conversation he had overheard inside, about the cabin and spreading his ashes there. Pausing by the bare hydrangea bushes, he closed his eyes and thought about the cabin, wondering what might need to be done there to prepare for his memorial.

When Allen opened his eyes, he was startled to discover he was no longer standing in his backyard in Frederickport but was now standing at the end of his driveway at the cabin.

"Wow, that's a new level of transportation," Allen blurted before starting up the driveway toward his cabin. But he stopped abruptly when a strange man came walking out of his cabin's front door. The man took a seat on the picnic table, and a moment later took a cigarette out of his pocket and lit up.

"Who are you? And what are you doing at our cabin?" The next moment Allen was no longer standing on his driveway, but was now on his front porch, inches from the stranger sitting on his picnic table.

The man, unlike the child living in his garage apartment, could not see him. Despite that, Allen continued to shout at him, demanding an explanation. Finally, in frustration, Allen took several swings at the intruder, his fist moving through the man's head and then chest. After a few swings, Allen gave up and decided to check inside the cabin to see if there were more people with the man.

He moved through the cabin, and other than some toiletry items sitting on the bathroom counters, and a purple bedspread—that he did not recognize—thrown on the bed, along with a sack that appeared to be filled with some clothes, there did not seem to be anyone else there, nor did the cabin seem disturbed. Whoever the stranger was, at least he hadn't vandalized the place.

After checking out the main floor, Allen moved down to the basement. What he found there caused him to freeze. It was nothing like he had expected.

In the center of the basement was an enormous kennel-like cage he had never seen before, with four heavy-wire walls and a ceiling and floor made of the same material, and a door secured with a padlock. The most disturbing thing was a woman sitting in the center of the cage, curled into a fetal position.

Allen didn't need to run to the woman—just wanting to be by her side was enough to take him to her. Now in the cage, he stood over her and looked down. The woman's head was turned to one side, one tear-streaked cheek visible. Allen leaned closer; if he got any closer, his face would disappear into hers. She was still alive, barely.

CHAPTER THIRTEEN

When Cassandra and her mother returned from the grocery store, Cassandra expected to see the ghost man again, but he wasn't there. She helped her mother bring in the groceries.

"After I put these away, I'll make us some lunch. After lunch, we're going back over to Marlow House," Mary explained.

"The house you're going to clean?"

"I hope so. I still don't know if they're hiring me, or if I'll just be working today." Mary began removing the items from her grocery bags and set them on the small kitchen counter.

"What am I going to do when we're there?"

"I want you to bring a book with you, and while I'm working, you are to sit quietly and read."

"Where at?"

Mary picked up a now-empty grocery bag and folded it. She looked at her daughter. "I'm not sure. I'll ask Mrs. Marlow where she'd like you to stay when I'm working. It's nice of them to let me bring you, so you need to be on your best behavior."

Thirty minutes later, Cassandra sat at the small kitchen table, eating the ice-cream sandwich her mother gave her after finishing lunch.

"While you eat that, I'm changing my clothes into something more suitable for cleaning. When you're done, I want you to wash up."

Cassandra gave her mother a nod and watched as Mary left the room. A moment later, the bedroom door closed. Cassandra was just about finished with her ice cream when the ghost man she had seen earlier appeared, sitting at the table directly across from her.

"Please don't be afraid," the man said. "I'm not going to hurt you."

Cassandra smiled at him. "I know. Ghosts can't hurt me."

He returned the smile. "So, you can see me? Ghost? Is that what I am?" He pondered that thought a moment and said, "I guess you're right. My name is Allen, by the way. You're sure a brave little girl. I thought all kids would be afraid of ghosts."

Cassandra shrugged. "My GG told me ghosts can't hurt people. And GG never lied to me. I knew you were a ghost because my mom can't see you."

"Can I ask your name?"

"Cassandra."

"Hello, Cassandra. It's nice to meet you. You are very brave, and I am hoping you can help me."

"Help you how?" Cassandra took her last bite of the ice-cream sandwich and then licked her fingers.

"We need to call the police and help a woman."

"What woman?"

"I don't know who she is. But some bad people have her, and you can help me save her."

Mary stepped back into the room. "Who are you talking to?"

Cassandra looked from her mother back to Allen. "Um, Allen?"

"Allen?" Mary frowned.

"Um, he needs my help. He's the man I saw earlier; he…"

"Stop!" Mary shouted. "I don't have time for your make-believe. You've finished your ice cream; I want you to throw away your napkin and go wash up. And I don't want to hear about this imaginary man of yours again, or you're going to be in big trouble, young lady. I've told you how I feel about this nonsense."

Cassandra's eyes widened in fear. She looked from her mother to Allen, back to her mother.

"It's okay," Allen said gently. "I don't want you to get into trouble. I'll figure something out. If you can see ghosts, I'm sure there are others like you." The next moment, he vanished.

* * *

ALLEN FOUND HIMSELF BACK AT HIS CABIN, AGAIN STANDING AT THE end of his driveway. But this time there was a white dual-cab pickup truck in the driveway, with a Utah license plate. Instead of one man sitting on his front porch at the picnic table, there were two men. The next moment he stood on the patio with them, listening to them argue.

The man he had seen during his last visit kept calling the other man "Bud" while Bud kept referring to him as "Dude." Allen didn't think the one man was actually named Bud, or the other one was named Dude. The way they said it was like one might call another person a nickname like bro or princess.

They were arguing about the woman in the basement, and Dude thought it was ridiculous that someone always needed to stay at the cabin. After all, it wasn't like she was going anywhere. But then Dude did something that shocked Allen.

"Bud, is this really necessary?" Dude grabbed hold of his own neck and pulled his skin, making it stretch out about six inches. For a moment Allen thought that was his skin, but then he realized Dude was wearing a mask. Moving closer, he saw Bud was also wearing a mask and holding a newspaper.

"Damn sure it's necessary," Bud confirmed.

"But no one is here but you and me. And even if she sees what I really look like, who cares? She won't be around long enough to tell anyone."

"What happens if she escapes?" Bud asked.

"And exactly how is she going to escape?"

"What if someone comes up here and finds us? If we're in disguise, we can jump in our truck and take off before they ever find her, and all we need to do is ditch the masks, like we did the first pair of masks, and swap out the license plate."

"You are paranoid. For one thing, no one is coming up here. Didn't you say the guy who owns this place is in the hospital?"

Bud shrugged. "Actually, I read the guy kicked the bucket last night."

"Better yet," Dude replied.

"That's rude," Allen grumbled.

"No point in being careless. Not now. You never know who might come driving up. Maybe a ranger or a neighbor. It's going to be over soon, anyway. Tomorrow it will be three days. And it's entirely possible by tomorrow afternoon she'll be with the guy who owns this place."

"They say it can take between three and seven days to die without food and water. She might be the one to stretch it out seven days."

"Which is exactly the reason we need to be careful and keep these masks on." Bud tossed the newspaper on the table; the front page of the newspaper landed faceup. "There's an article in this morning's newspaper about her. They know she's missing. I didn't think they'd start looking for another week or so."

Dude picked up the newspaper and started reading the article after saying, "We knew someone would start asking questions when she didn't show up for work on Monday."

"Yeah, but I didn't expect them to publish an article in the paper just because the librarian failed to show up for work. I figured she'd be dead and found before there was anything in the newspaper about it. This is why we need to keep these masks on."

Allen moved behind Dude and began reading the news article.

"Okay, if we leave the masks on, can we at least get out of here for a couple of hours? It's not like she's going anywhere. And frankly, it would be better not to have a truck in the driveway, just in case someone drives by who knows no one is supposed to be up here."

"But then no one will be here to check on her every half hour to make sure she isn't sleeping. If she's sleeping, her body won't use as many resources, and then this will drag on for an entire week. We both want this to be over as soon as possible."

"True. But there is another way to keep her from sleeping."

"How's that?" Bud asked.

"I found a radio in one of the cabinets, and the thing works. It's staticky and annoying to listen to, but perfect to keep someone from falling asleep. It gets loud."

"Okay. But until this is finished, unless we're at the motel, the masks remain on."

By the time Mary and Cassandra reached Marlow House, the rain clouds had disappeared, replaced by blue skies and bright sunshine. Danielle opened the front door for them and welcomed the mother and daughter into her home.

"Joanne's in the kitchen," Danielle explained as she closed the front door. "She's expecting you." The three stood in the entrance hall for a moment as Danielle continued, "Walt and I are going out with the twins, so we'll be out of your way. When we get sunshine, we like to get out and enjoy it."

Mary smiled at Danielle. "I understand. Cassandra brought her book with her. Where would you prefer she read while she waits for me?"

Danielle flashed Cassandra a smile and then looked back at Mary. "She's welcome to sit anywhere she wants downstairs. The library, parlor, living room, kitchen. Wherever she feels comfortable."

After Walt and Danielle left with the twins twenty minutes later, Joanne and Mary went upstairs while Cassandra sat at the kitchen table, eating cookies Danielle had offered her, along with a glass of milk. Her book sat on the table next to her.

When finished with her cookies and milk, Cassandra rinsed out her glass, set it in the sink, wiped up all the crumbs from the table with her napkin, and threw it in the trash. Walking back to the table, she picked up her book.

After Danielle had given Cassandra the cookies, Cassandra asked about Max. She hadn't seen the cat again since arriving at Marlow House. Danielle told her that the last time she saw Max, he was napping in the attic office. Cassandra was disappointed by the news. She also wondered about the ghost she had seen at Marlow House before. Would she see her again?

Cassandra walked to the kitchen window and looked outside. It was sunny today. This was the first day of sunshine she had seen since coming to Oregon. Cassandra stepped outside onto the back porch, and a moment later she had the answer to one of her questions when Marie appeared on the patio.

"Well, hello again," Marie greeted.

Cassandra smiled at the grandmotherly ghost. "You're the second ghost I've seen today."

Marie arched her brows. "I am?"

Cassandra nodded. "Yes. A man named Allen. He was at the house we're staying at."

"Allen?" Marie frowned. She had been there when Adam rented Allen Martin's garage apartment to Mary and Cassandra. She had also heard Allen had passed away last night.

"Oh my, I know Allen."

"Do all ghosts know each other?"

Marie laughed. "No, dear. But Frederickport is a small town. My grandson is the man who rented your mother the garage apartment. And Allen and his wife own that apartment and live at the house there—well, he lived there. Allen has been sick for a while, and I heard he passed away last night. So I can understand why he would be over there. Close to his wife until he moves on."

"He asked for my help."

"Your help?"

Cassandra nodded. "Yes. He wanted me to call the police because some bad men have a woman somewhere. I tried to tell my mom, but she doesn't like it when I talk about people she can't see."

Allen moved from the porch to the basement, where the men held Olivia prisoner. He knew who she was now: Olivia Davis. While Allen hadn't been to the local library for years, he remembered hearing about the new head librarian last year. It had been what everyone was talking about back then. Someone had murdered the woman who was replacing the head librarian. Olivia, who had just moved to town to fill the job left vacant by the incoming head librarian, had ended up with the murdered woman's new job.

He had never met Olivia before, yet he remembered hearing she had moved into the house next door to Marlow House. The house Olivia purchased had some sort of scandal attached, but he couldn't recall what it was. Closing his eyes, he tried to remember what the house looked like, but his mind's eye could only see Marlow House. He couldn't remember what the houses next door to Marlow House looked like.

Allen opened his eyes a moment later; he was no longer in his cabin's basement; he now stood in the backyard of Marlow House.

Marie's back was to the fence surrounding Marlow House's side yard, and beyond that, Olivia's house, as she faced Cassandra, listening to the child explain how Allen had showed up at their apartment, but left when her mother got upset. Cassandra went on to explain how her mother believed demonic forces made people hear voices or see images other people couldn't, and when Cassandra had initially tried telling her mother about her GG, Mary got extremely upset. Cassandra didn't believe her GG's ghost was demonic; her mother just didn't understand.

While explaining all this to Marie, Cassandra suddenly stopped and pointed behind Marie. "There he is!"

Marie turned abruptly and saw Allen standing about six feet behind her. "Allen?"

"Marie? Marie Nichols? Well, I'll be!" Allen smiled and then looked past Marie and spied Cassandra. "Cassandra, you're here!"

"Allen, I'm sorry to hear about your death. Cassandra was just telling me she saw you over at your house, and you asked her to help you."

Allen's smile vanished, his face now serious as he moved closer to Marie and Cassandra. "Some men have Olivia Davis."

"You know where Olivia is?" Marie asked. "We've been looking for her."

"She's at my cabin, they have her locked up, and I don't think they've given her any food or water for a few days."

"Allen, don't leave; I need you to take me to your cabin. I don't know where it is."

"What can you do? You're obviously a ghost like me. After all, I remember attending your funeral. That was nasty business, by the way. Being murdered and all. But you look great now, even younger."

Marie smiled. "Thank you. But trust me, there is something I can do."

Marie turned back to Cassandra, who had been watching in fascination the exchange between the two ghosts.

"Listen carefully," Marie told Cassandra. "You have a gift. Not everyone can see spirits. Walt and Danielle Marlow also have this gift. But don't tell other people because they won't understand."

"My mom doesn't understand."

"When you see Walt or Danielle, talk to them privately. Tell them Marie went with Allen Martin's ghost up to his cabin. That's where they have Olivia. They will understand. I need to go now."

Marie and Allen vanished.

LOUD, STATICKY SOUND GREETED MARIE AND ALLEN WHEN THEY arrived in the basement of Allen's cabin. Marie found Olivia sitting in the center of a cage, her hands over her ears, trying to block out the intrusive noise.

"Where is that coming from?" Marie glanced around. She spotted the radio before Allen did. Moving toward it, she focused her energy on its on-and-off knob. The next moment the noise stopped, and the basement went quiet.

"Thank God," Olivia muttered from the cage. "It stopped."

Allen glanced toward the stairs. "If those men are still here, they'll probably come down here when they realize the radio's off."

"How many men?" Marie asked.

"I just saw two. Their truck is parked in the driveway. They mentioned something about leaving for a while, but I don't know if they've left yet. How did you turn the radio off?"

"I'll explain later. I'm going upstairs. If those men are still here, I need to take care of them before we help Olivia." Marie vanished, leaving behind a confused Allen wondering how Marie had managed to turn off the radio and how she might take care of the men.

Upstairs, Marie found the cabin empty. Outside, there was no vehicle in the driveway, no men in sight. She went back into the cabin, but before going back to the basement, she focused her energy on the drawers in the kitchen, opening each one. After opening the third drawer, she found what she was looking for: a pen and a pad of paper.

The pad of paper and the pen floated up from the drawer, landing on the counter. Using her energy, Marie wrote several words on the paper with the pen. When finished, her energy tore the top sheet of paper from the pad and returned the pen and pad to the drawer before closing it.

Just as she was about to leave, she noticed a wooden bowl sitting on the other end of the counter and, inside it, a key. Moving closer, she inspected the key.

"Could this unlock the padlock on the cage?" Marie asked aloud.

BELIEVING SHE WAS ALONE IN THE BASEMENT, OLIVIA TRIED steadying her breath. Now that the sound had stopped, maybe, just maybe, she could focus on astral projection. Yet, even if she could, would they be able to figure out where Martin's Hideaway was?

Motion from her right caught her attention. Still sitting on the floor of the cage, she looked toward the staircase, and to her surprise, she spied what looked like a sheet of paper floating toward her.

"I'm now hallucinating," she groaned. But she didn't look away from the paper as it came closer and then moved through the bars, landing on her lap. Olivia looked down and read the words written on the piece of paper: *You aren't alone. It's Marie. I've come to help you escape.*

Olivia's eyes widened. "Marie? Is it really you?" Olivia felt a gentle tug on her right earlobe. Tears slipped down Olivia's face. She looked around the room, wondering where Marie was. It was then she saw it: a key, floating outside the cage. Olivia's attention had been so focused on the floating piece of paper that she hadn't noticed the key trailing behind it. She watched as the key floated toward the padlock on the cage and then slipped into the keyhole. It turned, and then the padlock opened, jiggled slightly, and then slipped from the cage, falling onto the floor, making a sound like a glass bottle falling onto a tile floor without shattering.

The cage door squeaked open a moment later. Olivia tried to stand, yet stumbled, falling back onto the floor of the cage.

"OH MY, THE POOR DEAR HAS NO STRENGTH," MARIE MUTTERED. "Let me help you, dear." The next moment Olivia's body lifted from the floor. Olivia immediately tensed with the unexpected levitation, but then she seemed to understand what was happening and relaxed.

Allen, who stood a few feet away, watched in fascination as Olivia floated out of the cage and up the stairs, Marie following behind her. Had Olivia been able to see Marie, like Cassandra could, Marie might have presented the illusion that she was physically carrying her, in the same way the twins or Connor saw Marie when she picked them up, when in fact it was Marie's spiritual energy that was doing the lifting, not a physical body.

Allen followed Marie up the stairs, and while he wanted to ask Marie a million questions, something told him to ask the questions later; Marie needed to concentrate on what she was doing.

When they got upstairs, Marie set Olivia on the sofa. She then walked to the kitchen, took a glass out of the cabinet, and filled it with water. The glass floated across the room to Olivia.

"If she hasn't had anything to drink, you don't want her to gulp that," Allen warned.

"Yes, I understand," Marie said.

Olivia sat on the sofa; her eyes focused on the glass of water coming her way. When it was a few feet away, she grabbed for it, spilling some water on herself as she brought it to her lips. She wanted to gulp the water, but Marie's energy prevented Olivia from taking too much water at once, pulling the glass away after each sip.

"We need to get Olivia out of here before those men come back. But I can't exactly fly her to town. How would that look? I need to put her somewhere safe and warm until the police get here. And when they get here, it would probably be best to put Olivia on the road not far from this cabin. But until then, I need to find somewhere to put her temporarily. Someplace safe and warm. Maybe one of the neighboring cabins. One that's empty, of course."

Allen considered Marie's words a moment before saying, "The Morgan cabin. It's about a half-mile from here. The way the roads are at this time of year, no one can drive back there. But she should be safe there until the police arrive."

WHILE HER FIRST INCLINATION WAS TO GULP THE WATER, OLIVIA understood why Marie kept pulling the glass away. At least she assumed it was Marie. After a few minutes the glass pulled completely from her grip, and she wanted to jerk it back, but Olivia told herself she needed to trust Marie. The glass floated into the kitchen and landed on the counter.

After a few minutes she noticed a purple bedspread floating her way. She had been so focused on the water glass sitting on the counter that she didn't notice the bedspread coming out of one of the other rooms in the cabin. She felt something lift her to her feet, and while she was standing, she understood she was not holding herself erect—Marie's energy held her. Should Marie let go, Olivia worried she might fall to the floor.

Olivia stood passively, her body devoid of strength as the bedspread wound around her, making her think of a swaddled baby. Lifted by invisible arms, Olivia floated up from the floor, then out of the cabin, and then down the road, as if traveling on a magic carpet, a carpet wrapped around her body, keeping her warm.

CHAPTER FIFTEEN

The two men Allen had heard calling each other Bud and Dude returned to the cabin. Bud pulled the truck up into the driveway, turned off the engine, and said, "I'm using the bathroom before I leave."

They both got out of the car and walked into the cabin. Bud headed straight for the bathroom. When he returned several minutes later, Dude glared at him. "Hey, Mr. Obsessive Control Freak, who insists we keep these masks on and wear gloves at all times, and one of us has to stay here and the other one needs to be in town to monitor any news, I thought you said we can't use any of the glasses here because we might leave DNA on them?"

Bud frowned. "What are you talking about?"

Dude pointed to the half-full glass of water sitting on the kitchen counter. When Bud looked at the glass, his eyes widened. "Did you use that glass?"

"No, I didn't use it!" Dude snapped. "You obviously did."

Dude started to say something else when Bud's gaze darted to the far end of the counter. "The padlock key! Where is it?"

Exasperated at his partner, believing Bud had been the one to use the glass after once going on and on about why Dude wasn't to use any of the dishes in the cabin and to only use what they had brought with them, Dude glanced to the end of the counter, prepared to point to the key when he saw the bowl empty; he froze.

Neither man said another word; instead, they both raced to the stairs leading to the basement. When they reached the basement, Bud let out a curse and said, "This is why I wanted one of us here!"

Dude had no response. Instead, he stared dumbly at the padlock now on the floor, the key still in the keyhole as the cage door hung wide open. "How is this possible?" he muttered.

Bud stepped to the cage and found a piece of paper where their prisoner was supposed to be. He reached into the cage, picked up the paper, and looked at it. "Who in the hell is Marie?"

BY THE NOTE FOUND IN THE CAGE, IT WAS OBVIOUS SOMEONE HAD helped their prisoner escape. Since Bud had traveled the only road into the cabin three times that day and had passed no one, he was convinced their prisoner and Marie were somewhere close or had traveled farther down the road, to the remote cabins deeper in the forest. He knew there were no phone lines back there or cell service. Of course, it was always possible they'd used a cell phone on the front porch of the cabin—the only place they had service—and were now hiding out, waiting for the cavalry.

When planning the kidnapping, Bud had made a contingency for such an event; he called it *Abort Mode*. Looking for Marie and their prisoner was not an option because their plan fell apart if they were forced to capture—or eliminate—a second prisoner.

Still standing in the basement looking at the empty cage, Bud said, "Abort mode. I'll get the drone. You know what to do."

Without response or argument, Dude hurried to the cardboard box sitting in the basement's corner. From it he pulled a cordless drill. It was already charged. That had been another one of Bud's obsessions—*keep it charged*.

Before coming to the mountain, Dude had practiced assembling and disassembling the cage a dozen times. Bud had said it was important because they couldn't leave anything behind, and they might be forced to move quickly. Dude began disassembling the cage and stacking the pieces neatly.

Upstairs, Bud had gone outside and taken his drone from the car. Within minutes, it was in the air as he monitored the surrounding area. He watched the drone's camera from his tablet. There were no vehicles on the long, desolate road leading from the highway to the cabin, and when he moved the drone deeper into the forest along the same road, there were no vehicles—no signs of their escaped prisoner.

But then the drone captured a peculiar flying object—a purple kite or perhaps a bird? But it was too large for a bird, and the head was on the wrong end, and the head—it looked like a human head. Bud tried maneuvering the drone to get a better look, but crows came out of nowhere and began circling in the air between the unidentified flying object and the drone.

"Are the roads clear?" Dude's voice broke Bud's concentration. Bud turned and watched Dude carry a stack of panels from the cabin. Dude shoved the panels into the back of the pickup truck. Bud looked back at the monitor, and whatever the drone had captured was no longer in sight.

"It had to have been some weird bird," Bud muttered to himself before saying, "Yeah. I'm bringing the drone down now, and I'll help you get everything."

Less than ten minutes later, the basement was almost empty. Dude gathered his meager belongings while referring to his checklist to make sure he forgot nothing. The only thing he didn't have, the bedspread. Bud had insisted he bring something to use as a blanket; he couldn't use anything from the cabin. The bedspread wasn't anything special, just an ugly purple one they had picked up at a thrift shop on the way to Oregon.

Meanwhile, Bud cleaned the water glass and put it back in the cabinet. He walked back down to the basement one last time and looked around. It looked just as it did when they first arrived—except for one thing. The note he had found in the cage was in the corner. His partner had overlooked it. Bud walked to the corner, picked it up, and read it again. *Who is Marie?* he asked himself again. Shaking his head, he folded the note several times and slipped it into his shirt pocket.

Bud headed back upstairs. He walked through the cabin and checked to make sure it looked as it had when they first arrived. After he finished going through all the rooms, his partner walked in the door. "Ready?" Bud asked.

"I put all the stuff in the car, but I can't find the bedspread."

"What bedspread?"

"The one I bought on the way up here. It's not here."

"This cabin isn't that big; go look again; it has to be here."

"I already looked twice."

"It couldn't just walk away," Bud snapped. But then he cringed and said, "Or perhaps it could."

"What do you mean?"

"Our escapee may have taken it with her to keep warm."

"Oh, wonderful," Dude grumbled. "My DNA's all over it."

"Now you're worrying about DNA. Thought I was the one being obsessive."

"Oh, shut up."

"Considering where we picked that thing up, it probably has more than your DNA on it. And if she's dragging it through the forest with her, I can't imagine they could get any real evidence from it if the police ever get ahold of it."

"Whatever. Let's get out of here. Don't forget to turn off the heater and the lights."

***

THEY HAD ALMOST REACHED THE HIGHWAY, BOTH GRATEFUL THEY hadn't passed any other vehicles. Instead of continuing to the highway, Bud turned off a side road they had explored when first scoping out the area. They drove down the dirt road about a quarter mile, parked, removed all the cage paneling, and tossed them into the nearby brush.

After disposing of the cage panels, they got back into the truck, turned around, and headed to the highway and then to the ocean. They drove to the spot where they had disposed of the sedan. Pulling off the highway, they parked on the far end of the overlook where trees obscured the view of their truck from the highway, with the other side of the truck facing the ocean.

Both men pulled off their masks and turned them inside out. Bud tossed his mask to Dude, and then got out of the truck, slamming the door behind him. Dude reached into the glove compartment, pulled out an aerosol can, and then opened the passenger door. He turned around in the seat, facing the open door and the ocean. Leaning out of the truck, he used the can to spray both masks and then tossed them on the ground.

Bud had said he needed to do that to destroy whatever DNA was on the masks. Dude thought it was overkill since the masks were going into the ocean anyway, but he didn't argue. He had been taking orders from Bud since he was a little kid.

He returned the can to the glove compartment, got out of the truck, and reached into the back seat and pulled out a small, rusty metal box. Dude stuffed both masks, now smelling like chemicals, inside the container. He scooped up some rocks and sand from the ground and tossed them on top of the masks. After closing the lid of the metal container and securing it, he picked it up, stood up straight, and walked to the side of the cliff, facing the ocean.

Looking back at the truck for a moment, he watched as Bud switched out the license plates. Their truck's license plates now matched the information they had given to the Seahorse Motel when checking in. The routine had been, when away from the motel, they wore the masks; they also changed the identity of their vehicle. Turning back around to face the ocean, Dude hurled the box outwards and watched as it eventually fell into the water and disappeared in the waves below.

* * *

TEN MINUTES LATER THEY WERE BACK ON THE HIGHWAY, HEADING TO

the Seahorse Motel. Both men had taken off their gloves and tossed them onto the back seat. "Now what?" Bud asked.

"We're registered for the rest of the week, so we stay. If this Marie was successful saving her, then we need to see what story she comes up with. Leaving early might draw unwanted attention to us, and that is the last thing we want. So we're stuck here."

"She might still die. She didn't look very good this morning."

"While that's a cheerful thought, it might complicate matters."

Dude shrugged. "Maybe not. Nothing to connect us to her."

"I should have listened to my gut and let you take the truck while I stayed with her. We shouldn't have left her alone."

Dude shook his head. "Not sure about that. I think if this Marie, whoever she is, had shown up, and you had to deal with her, then this would get even more complicated. And was this Marie alone?"

"What I can't figure out, why the note?"

Dude frowned at Bud. "What do you mean?"

"What was the point of the note? It freaked me out when we got there and she was gone, and then I read the note. But after thinking about it for a while, why would this Marie bother writing a note? Was she mute or something?"

Dude shook his head and shrugged. "No clue."

Bud kept wrestling with that thought in his head as they silently continued down the road to the Seahorse Motel. Finally, Bud asked, "Hey, that blanket she took. What color was it?"

"Purple. Why?"

CHAPTER SIXTEEN

Cassandra wanted to stay outside on the back patio to read her book, but not long after Marie and Allen disappeared, her mother came downstairs and found her outside. Mary told her to come into the house and not to go outside again without her permission. Cassandra didn't understand why her mother was so upset. It was a fenced yard, and it wasn't like there was a swimming pool or something in the yard that she might fall into and drown. But she didn't argue and came inside, sitting back at the kitchen table with her book.

Cassandra found it impossible to concentrate on reading. She kept silently recounting what Allen said, about what Marie had told her, and what she had to tell Mrs. or Mr. Marlow. But to do that, she needed to talk to them alone. What would happen if she and her mom left before the Marlows got home?

It had been about an hour, maybe less, since Marie and Allen disappeared. Mrs. Marlow had said Cassandra was welcome to read anywhere downstairs. Cassandra decided to go back to the little room they called a parlor. When she got there, she was happy to see Max was in the room, napping on the windowsill.

Cassandra walked to the windowsill and gently stroked the length of Max's back. Max opened his eyes and looked up. He began to purr. Cassandra smiled while petting Max. She leaned over and lightly kissed the top of his head.

After kissing the cat, Cassandra took her book and walked over to the sofa and sat down. Max, who had watched her walk away, stood up, stretched, and jumped down to the floor before strolling to the sofa and jumping up onto the sofa cushion to join Cassandra.

Upstairs, Joanne and Mary stood in the bedroom Mary had been in when she first learned the news about Olivia from Walt. Joanne was explaining that unless the Marlows had company staying in the room, it only needed light cleaning, and it wasn't necessary to change the sheets. As Joanne talked, Mary wandered to the window overlooking the side yard, Olivia's house in clear view.

When Joanne stopped talking, Mary asked, "Do you know anything about the neighbor who's missing?"

"Olivia?" Joanne walked to the window, stood next to Mary, and looked outside. "Only that no one has seen her since Sunday."

"No one has any idea what happened?"

"I understand she had just returned from the grocery store. Her groceries were still sitting on her kitchen counter. They had been sitting there for a couple of hours before anyone realized she might be missing. Apparently, they found her car keys in her driveway, like someone took her when she was outside locking up her car after coming home from the store."

"Are you afraid?" Mary whispered.

Joanne looked at Mary. "Is that why you didn't want your daughter outside?"

Mary nodded.

Joanne looked back outside. "I understand your fear; it's reasonable. But I don't believe there is some guy out there grabbing random women from this neighborhood. I suspect Olivia went with someone, maybe a friend or an acquaintance. I say that because, well, frankly, there have been some concerning incidents over the years that have occurred on this street—and even in this house. But none of them were because of some random stranger without a connection to the targeted person. I feel Olivia's disappearance is about her. That whoever took her—if someone did, and she didn't leave of her own accord for some reason—it was about her specifically. So, no, I'm not necessarily afraid, although I'm being careful. Because I might be wrong, and I probably wouldn't want my daughter outside alone right now, either, considering what we don't know yet."

"I saw in the newspaper that she's the local librarian. Does she have family? If so, I imagine they're very worried."

"From what I understand, Olivia has been divorced for years before she moved here. She has a sister, which I only know because Olivia was invited to spend this past Christmas at Marlow House, but she declined because her sister was taking her on a Christmas cruise."

"Her sister? She has a sister?" Mary said more to herself than to Joanne.

Cassandra found it impossible to concentrate on her book. She kept wondering when the Marlows would be home. Would they get home before she had to leave? It suddenly dawned on her that when they came home, they would likely come through the kitchen door, and if so, she should wait in the kitchen instead of the parlor if she wanted to talk to them alone. She slipped Max from her lap, kissed the top of his head, gave him a soft goodbye pat, and grabbed her book and raced from the room, heading to the kitchen.

Danielle walked into the kitchen first, carrying Addison, while Walt trailed behind her, Jack in his arms and a diaper bag draped over one of his shoulders. They found Cassandra sitting at the kitchen table with her book, yet the book wasn't open.

Cassandra leapt to her feet, her expression looking as if she had been caught doing something she shouldn't be doing and was desperately searching for something to say to explain her misdeed.

Joanne's and Mary's voices drifted in from the hallway through the open doorway. Cassandra glanced frantically toward the doorway and back to Walt and Danielle before saying in a rush, her voice a whisper, "Marie told me to tell you she's getting Olivia; she's being held prisoner at Allen's cabin. Allen's a ghost."

She had barely delivered the words when Joanne and Mary walked through the doorway. Cassandra promptly sat back in her seat, opened her book, and stared down at a page.

Still trying to process the little girl's words, Danielle looked from the child to Joanne and Mary. Joanne began explaining what they had done so far, while Mary walked to her daughter and gave her shoulder a gentle pat in greeting. Cassandra sat rigid, pretending she hadn't just uttered an insane declaration.

Walt, who had heard what Cassandra had said, placed Jack in a highchair and then redirected the conversation by fabricating a concern he had with the cleaning routine in his attic office. He asked the two women if they would go to the attic now so he could show them before he forgot. The three left the kitchen, leaving Danielle and the twins alone with Cassandra.

Danielle secured Addison in a highchair next to her brother and gave both twins a cookie. She peeked out into the hallway, listening for sounds telling her Walt was on the way up the stairs with the two women, and when convinced she and Cassandra had the necessary privacy, she walked to the kitchen table and sat across from Cassandra.

Folding her hands on the tabletop before her, Danielle looked at Cassandra, who was still staring down at her book. "Marie told us about your gift."

Cassandra looked up to Danielle with wide eyes. "My gift?"

Danielle nodded. "You're a medium, as am I. When I was a little girl, I began seeing ghosts—the first one being my grandmother at her funeral."

"My first was my GG."

Danielle nodded again. "But people didn't believe me. So I learned to be careful whom I told."

"Mom says ghosts aren't real. She says when someone says they see ghosts, it is really demons trying to fool you."

"I understand why your mom feels that way. And I hate contradicting something your mother believes."

Cassandra frowned. "Contradicting?"

Danielle smiled. "Disagreeing. Saying she's wrong. Your mother loves you, and she wants to keep you safe. But sometimes, well, even the best moms don't understand certain things. Mine didn't."

Cassandra nodded. "I think Mom's wrong. Mom doesn't understand. I know what I saw. I talked to GG. It was her, not a demon."

"I just wanted to tell you I understand what you're going through. Because I'm like you. But now, I need you to tell me everything Marie told you about Olivia."

Cassandra closed her book, took a deep breath, exhaled, and recounted everything about her discussion with Marie—meeting Allen, and how he had lived at the house where she and her mother now stayed.

When Danielle arrived at Frederickport Vacation Properties, Brian Henderson was already there, sitting in his police car in one of the parking spots in front of the office. He had just arrived. Danielle pulled her car into the space next to Brian and parked. They got out of their vehicles at the same time.

Brian looked over his car at Danielle. "The chief said I needed to meet you here; it was important. But Joe walked into his office about that time, so he couldn't elaborate. He told Joe he needed him to do something at the station."

"I'll explain inside," Danielle told him.

Fifteen minutes later, Danielle and Brian sat alone with Adam in Adam's office, the door closed. Danielle had just finished updating Brian and Adam about Cassandra, Allen, and what Marie had said.

"Dang, Grandma is out there on another rescue mission," Adam said with pride. "But you obviously didn't come here to tell me about Grandma's current escapades. What do you need from me?"

"The chief says he can track down this cabin of Allen's, but thought since you handle his garage apartment rental, you might not only already have its address but can tell us something about it. Something that might be helpful before charging up there. While we now know where they took Olivia, the chief is waiting to see what Marie finds because he doesn't want to rush up and put Olivia in more danger; he wants to be prepared when they go," Danielle explained.

Adam leaned forward, placing his elbows on the desktop, and said, "While I don't have the address, I'm fairly sure it's in the mountains not far from where those crazy witches took you guys." Adam looked at Brian when he said *you guys*. He leaned back and turned to his computer. "But I can get you the address."

"Do you know anything else about the cabin?" Brian asked.

"When I put Allen's garage apartment in the rental program, we talked a little bit about it. This was before he got sick. He told me how he and his brother had bought the cabin up in the local mountains about thirty, forty minutes from here, and they used to go up there and fish. He'd take Nancy and Gina there during the summers when Gina was little. When his brother passed away—he was never married—he left his share to Allen. I assume Allen and his family haven't used it much the last couple of years, since Allen got sick."

"If someone found out about the cabin and that Allen had been sick for the last year, I can understand why our kidnappers would choose the place," Brian said.

"Plus, Allen was in the hospital the last couple of days," Adam added.

Danielle looked at Adam. "Considering what happened when she rescued you, it would probably be best if Marie got control of the situation before the police arrive."

"Yeah, I could just see the cops pulling up to the cabin in time to see kidnappers being tossed around by an invisible force." Adam snickered. "But I'm afraid I don't really know much about the cabin aside from the fact that it has two bedrooms and a decent-sized basement. But I can get that address for you." Adam turned to his computer and started searching through the county database, looking for property owned by Allen Martin. After a moment, Adam blurted, "Bingo!" and then grabbed a piece of paper from the desk, jotted down the cabin's address, and handed it to Brian.

CHAPTER SEVENTEEN

Unlike the road to Allen's cabin, the Morgan cabin was off an unpaved side road, and Marie understood why Allen felt this might be a good place to hold Olivia. While the road was unpaved and there probably wasn't a Wi-Fi connection—which was of no use to a ghost anyway—there was electricity.

Moving Olivia inside the cabin required opening the front door or a window, and to do that, Marie needed to find some place to set Olivia outside where she wouldn't get wet, while Marie used her energy to test the locks. She found that place on the wooden porch swing under the patio overhang.

Marie found all the doors and windows securely locked, and while it was entirely possible for Marie to use her energy to manipulate the lock mechanism on the door, it would be easier to use a key, as she had with the cage back at Allen's cabin. But instead of looking for a hidden key under the rocks around the cabin, Marie decided it would be even easier to move the lock lever on the front window and slide it open. The window was large enough for Olivia to move through, and there was no screen that needed to be removed.

Once inside the Morgans' cabin, Marie had no way to tell how cold it was inside; after all, she had no body; and the Morgans didn't have a thermometer hanging on any of their interior walls. But Olivia had been shivering since leaving Allen's cabin, even wrapped in the bulky bedspread.

After looking through the cabin, Marie moved Olivia into its only bedroom. Choosing the room was not so much for its bed, but for its electric heater, and that the small room had a door, which Marie reasoned, if closed, might mean the room would heat quicker.

As Marie closed the bedroom door and turned on the heater, Allen asked, "Is she asleep…or like us?" He stood over the bed, looking down at Olivia still wrapped in the bedspread.

Marie moved from the heater to Olivia and took a closer look. She gave Olivia a gentle nudge. When she got no response, Marie nudged Olivia again, this time firmer. After a third nudge, Marie muttered, "Oh dear."

"Is she dead?"

"No, but she seems to be unconscious. I suspect moving her, especially in this weather and how we got here, might have been too much." Marie looked up to Allen. "I can't leave her. If those men showed up after I left, there would be nothing you could do. I need you to get a message to one of the mediums."

"Mediums? Cassandra?"

Marie shook her head and then explained what she needed him to do.

***

ALLEN KNEW WHO WALT AND DANIELLE WERE. EVERYONE IN Frederickport did. However, he had never met them, but he had seen their pictures in the local newspaper, and once, when he and Nancy had been at Old Salts Bakery buying cinnamon rolls, Nancy had insisted they were the couple they passed when entering the bakery, but Allen hadn't gotten a good look at them.

Even if Allen couldn't remember how they looked exactly, he figured if he simply showed up at Marlow House and started asking questions, whoever answered would have to be a medium or another ghost. And if he couldn't find a medium at Marlow House, Marie told him to go to the Glandon Foundation headquarters, because Heather and Chris were both mediums who could help.

Allen didn't bother asking Marie to elaborate on the identity of Heather and Chris, whom she obviously assumed he knew, which he didn't. Allen nodded along, silently telling himself he would use the same find-a-ghost-or-medium-tactic he planned to employ at Marlow House. As it was, he already had enough to remember regarding this plan of Marie's; he wasn't asking Marie to give a physical description that he needed to remember.

CHIEF MACDONALD CALLED JOE AND BRIAN INTO HIS OFFICE. BRIAN already knew what the chief was about to say. But Joe had no idea, and Brian had to pretend he was hearing everything for the first time.

They had spent the last fifteen minutes playing a frantic and bizarre game of Ghost Telephone. Different from the childhood game of Telephone, where a child whispers a message to another child, who then messages it to another…and another; in the game of Ghost Telephone, it involves a series of ghosts, mediums, and non-mediums, where messages are passed back and forth.

"They said you needed to see us; sounded urgent. What's up?" Joe asked when he and Brian walked into the chief's office.

Edward, who sat behind his desk, looked up. "We just got an anonymous call I want you both to listen to." Edward turned to his computer and played the file, reportedly a recording of a call that just came into the police station.

Edward clicked play: *I just drove into Frederickport with my wife, and we saw something along the highway, by the Crest Bay turnoff. Looked like a rolled-up piece of carpet to me, like it flew off the back of someone's truck. But my wife insists there was a human head sticking out of one end. I told her she was imagining things, but she insisted I call. Says the hair on the head was black on one side, white on the other. It's probably nothing, but she insisted I call.*

The caller hung up before the operator could ask for his name.

Brian looked for Joe's reaction. What Joe didn't know, Danielle had written a script, which Chris delivered using a software program to alter his voice. And the phone used to make the call? Some time ago, Chris had decided they needed to purchase several untraceable cell phones with prepaid minutes for times such as this —when the mediums needed to find a way to pass information to the chief that he could more easily explain to others by claiming he had received an anonymous phone call.

"It might just be a carpet, but when that car said black and white hair…"

Right on cue, Brian interrupted the chief and said, "You think it could be Olivia Davis?"

"How would she get out there?" Joe asked.

"We can debate that later," the chief cut off. "I'm sending an EMS to the scene, and I want you to accompany them."

JOE DIDN'T REALIZE BRIAN WANTED HIM TO DRIVE BECAUSE BRIAN needed his hands free so he could pass on information to Heather. The drive out to the Crest Bay turnoff was about thirty-five minutes, but that was driving at the speed limit, and the ambulance and police car were driving at top speed with their sirens on.

The plan required Marie to move Olivia to where the fake anonymous caller claimed to have seen the rolled-up carpet. But she didn't want to do it too soon, as the kidnappers might return to Allen's cabin before the police arrived, and she didn't want the kidnappers to find Olivia on the side of the road.

Allen had been busy passing messages between her and the mediums, arranging Olivia's pickup, and during that period he had stopped by his cabin several times, and when he didn't see the kidnappers' vehicle, he assumed they hadn't returned and they didn't realize their prisoner had escaped. But Allen had remembered the truck, so he passed a general description to Danielle, who gave it to the police so they could be on the lookout for the vehicle.

Unfortunately, he hadn't paid attention to the truck's make or model, or the license plate number, only that it was a Utah plate.

"I bet we'll just find a roll of carpet," Joe said while steering the police car down the highway at high speed. "Someone else would have stopped by now, found her, and called in."

"You're probably right," Brian said, glancing from the car's odometer to the cell phone in his hand, his index finger primed to send a prewritten text message to Heather. In a couple more miles, he would press send. Once Heather received his text, she would tell Allen's ghost to go back to the Morgan cabin and tell Marie it was time to move Olivia.

Initially, when the chief and Brian had calculated how long it would take to reach Crest Bay turnoff at the speed they would drive, and factoring in how long it would take Marie to move Olivia—using Marie's estimate—they knew approximately how many miles they needed to travel down that highway before Marie moved Olivia to get her there in time, yet not too early.

Ideally, Allen could have stayed at that point, and the moment he saw the police car and ambulance, he could have instantly returned to Marie and told her it was time to move Olivia. Unfortunately, Allen had no way of calculating exactly where that point on the highway might be. While a ghost can walk through walls, they can't estimate mileage, in the same way they can't see in the dark or feel the air's temperature. Which was why Allen stayed with Heather in her office, waiting for Brian's text.

OLIVIA HADN'T REGAINED CONSCIOUSNESS, AND MARIE ANXIOUSLY waited for Allen to return. Marie had already turned off the heater and opened the front window of the cabin. After seeing Olivia safely in the ambulance, she planned to return to shut and relock the window and go to Allen's cabin. When the kidnappers returned, she planned to keep them there until Edward could send his men to arrest them. She wasn't certain how all that was going to work, but for now, her focus was on Olivia.

"It's time," Allen said as he appeared in the cabin's bedroom.

Marie said nothing; instead, she focused her energy on Olivia. Still wrapped in the bedspread, Olivia lifted from the mattress, floated from the bedroom into the living room and then out the window.

"Go ahead of me and warn me if any cars are coming," Marie told Allen.

Allen nodded and started down the road. Olivia—who looked like a horizontal, elongated purple cylinder with a peculiar tuft of black and white hair on one end, floated some ten feet above the ground and moved away from the Morgan cabin and down the dirt road, keeping below the treetops.

Marie intended to move Olivia toward the treetops when passing Allen's cabin, but when his cabin came into view, there was no vehicle in the driveway, and she assumed the kidnappers hadn't returned.

When they made it to their planned destination, Marie gently placed Olivia on the side of the highway after several cars passed, and right before the ambulance and police car came into view.

Marie and Allen watched as the ambulance and police arrived. The following minutes became chaotic, with members of the EMS scrambling to assess Olivia's condition before moving her, while Brian and Joe closed off part of the highway to divert traffic.

When the ambulance finally pulled away, the sirens blaring again as it raced to the hospital, Marie felt a flood of relief. They had saved Olivia. At least she hoped they had.

After Marie secured the Morgan cabin, and she and Allen arrived back at Martin's Hideaway, Allen asked, "What now?"

"Now we wait until the kidnappers return. See what they say when they realize their prisoner is gone. I need to find out as much information about them as I can to tell Edward." Allen had already told Marie that according to the mediums, the police would not be releasing any information regarding Olivia, not wanting to tip off the kidnappers that she had escaped.

When they entered the cabin, nothing seemed different. Marie and Allen failed to notice that the water glass was no longer sitting on the counter. The two ghosts sat together in the living room, and while waiting for the kidnappers' return, Allen took this time to ask Marie the questions he had been wanting to ask her since she freed Olivia from the cage.

"Why can you move things, and I can't?"

Marie smiled. "Danielle calls it harnessing energy."

"When that piece of paper floated into the basement, and I saw you had written that letter—"

"Oh, the letter!" Marie blurted.

"What?"

"I forgot about the letter. I left it in the cage. Thanks for mentioning it. I need to get it. We don't need the police finding it. I'll be right back."

Marie disappeared.

The next moment, Marie stood in the middle of the basement. Stunned, she looked around the now empty space.

"Oh my…"

CHAPTER EIGHTEEN

The mediums of Beach Drive, along with their support group, gathered around a large table in a private alcove at Pearl Cove late Tuesday afternoon. They chose this restaurant instead of Pier Café to avoid Carla, who would have likely waited on them at Pier Café and, in doing so, would have lingered nearby, hoping to catch snippets of their conversations while asking them if they had heard what was happening in the missing person's case involving Olivia Davis.

Had Joanne and Mary not still been cleaning at Marlow House, they might all have gone there. They didn't want to meet at the offices of the Glandon Foundation headquarters, as there were too many foundation employees underfoot. Another reason they met at Pearl Cove to discuss the current situation was that both Danielle and Heather expressed a craving for Pearl Cove's clam chowder.

The mediums at the table included Walt, Danielle, Chris, and Heather. The support group included Ian, Lily, Adam, and Melony. Also sitting by the table, each in a highchair, were the twins; Ian and Lily had left Connor and Emily Ann at home with Ian's mother babysitting.

Danielle had just finished briefing the support group on what had happened that day, right up to when Brian sent a text to Heather, and Heather passed the message on to Allen, who in turn passed it on to Marie. Before Allen left to tell Marie it was time to move Olivia, Heather told Allen she was going to Pearl Cove, and that was where he and Marie would find the mediums for the next hour or so. Right after Allen returned to Marie, Heather and Chris drove to Pearl Cove, arriving around the same time as their friends.

"I keep thinking about my mom and dad," Adam mused after Danielle finished her update.

Adam's friends all looked his way, and Melony asked, "What do you mean?"

Adam shrugged and leaned back in his seat. "Oh, how after Grandma broke her hip and had to stay at that facility for rehab, and then Mom and Dad showed up right before Thanksgiving, convinced she needed to be put in assisted living permanently and shouldn't come home. Like she wasn't mentally or physically able to care for herself anymore—despite the fact they were never around and had no idea what she might be capable of. And now she's out on rescue missions."

Heather's cell phone rang. She picked it up, looked at it, and before answering announced, "It's Brian." The table went quiet—except for Jack, who made bubbling sounds while his sister giggled. The adults anxiously listened to Heather's side of the conversation.

After a few minutes, the call ended. Heather set her phone on the tabletop and looked at her friends. "They have Olivia, and they're on the way to the hospital."

A cheer went around the table, not loud enough for the next table to hear, but a spontaneous expression of relief, knowing their friend was in safe hands.

"How is she? Has she been able to tell them anything?" Lily asked.

Heather shrugged. "Brian says she's disoriented. According to the EMT on the scene, her vitals are weak, and they're trying to get to the hospital as fast as possible. Brian had to get off the phone because he didn't want Joe to hear him talking to me, and Joe was ready to leave."

"What did the kidnappers do to her?" Adam asked.

"There's no sign she was physically abused. But it looks like she's been deprived of food and water since she was abducted on Sunday. And something that Danielle didn't tell you when she explained what happened today." Heather paused a moment and glanced at Danielle and back at Adam. "Because I doubt Danielle knows. When Allen's ghost was with me, waiting for Brian's text, he was telling me what he saw and heard over at his cabin. It sounded as if the kidnappers' intention was to kill Olivia. But they weren't doing it directly."

"What do you mean directly?" Lily asked.

"Like how that crazy nurse smothered Marie with a pillow. Or how Chris's whacked-out uncles tried to get Danielle and Chris to drink poison wine, or how Agatha Pine was pushed down the stairs at Marlow House, or—"

"Okay, we get it! Enough!" Chris blurted.

Heather gave Chris a shrug and continued, "Their plan was to withhold food and water, basically starve her to death. I suspect it would have been the lack of water that would get her before the lack of food. From what I understand, someone can die within three days without drinking anything, while people can go much longer without any food."

"Did Brian tell you what the prognosis is for her recovery?" Walt asked.

"He didn't really say. I don't think he knows. He said she was severely dehydrated, out of it, and he overheard one of the EMTs say she may not have lasted another day."

"Did Allen tell you if they tied her up? Bound her wrists, shackled her ankles?" Melony asked.

"From what I was told, Olivia was being held in a cage, no restraints, only the padlock on the cage's door," Danielle answered for Heather.

"Almost sounds like they wanted it to appear as if she died of natural causes," Melony mused. "They obviously wanted her dead, but they didn't want to leave any marks on her body that showed she had been tied up or held captive when her body was eventually found."

"I understand what you're saying," Ian said. "A woman living alone suddenly wanders off after coming home from the grocery store. There is no sign of an intruder or foul play."

"Just her spirit-self coming to Marlow House and asking for help," Heather interjected.

Ian shrugged. "True. But we're the only ones aware of that. Olivia is a woman living alone. No family here. People might wonder if she wandered off, had some sort of mental break. She comes home from the grocery store, and instead of putting her groceries away, she just wanders off. Like I said, there was no sign of foul play. No one saw anyone abduct her. Each year hundreds of older people—often those who suffer from some sort of dementia—die from dehydration or malnutrition. While Olivia has a few years before she's considered a senior citizen, and dementia and Alzheimer's in your fifties might be uncommon, it can happen."

"You're suggesting someone wanted Olivia dead and didn't want people to see her death as a murder," Walt said.

"Or they're just psycho and don't have a motive," Chris grunted.

"Hopefully we'll find out soon, random psycho or someone with a motive who wants Olivia dead. Marie went back to Allen's cabin to wait for the kidnappers. I imagine they're going to be unhappy to discover their prisoner escaped," Danielle said. "I assume they'll start searching around the cabin, and if they don't find her, they'll want to take off before the police show up—assuming they panic, realizing if Olivia manages to contact the police, she'll lead them to the cabin. When they leave, if they leave before the police get there, they won't be leaving alone, Marie will be with them, and hopefully she'll be able to figure out what this was all about."

"That's my grandma," Adam beamed. "From rescue mission to private eye."

Adam was still grinning with pride when Marie appeared at the table, standing next to him. When the twins started waving in Adam's direction, Adam's grin widened, thinking he'd somehow captured their attention. But when Heather whispered Marie's name, he realized the twins weren't looking at him.

"You're back? Is Allen with the kidnappers?" Danielle asked.

Marie shook her head. "No. They're gone. Everything is gone. There's no trace of them ever being there." Marie then explained what she and Allen had discovered when returning to Martin's Hideaway. After her explanation, Heather recounted it to the non-mediums.

"We'd better call the chief," Danielle said.

POLICE CHIEF MACDONALD STOOD IN THE HOSPITAL HALLWAY WITH Joe and Brian, near the door to Olivia's hospital room, waiting for the officer to arrive to stand guard by her door. MacDonald had ordered round-the-clock security for Olivia. He told Joe it was until Olivia could tell them what had happened, yet Brian understood the chief was more interested in Marie's report. According to Allen, the kidnappers had worn the masks at the cabin, so Olivia wouldn't be able to identify them. The times she had reached out via astral projection, the only thing she seemed to know was that someone had grabbed her in the driveway—not who or why. They needed the information Marie could provide.

When the chief's cell phone rang, he looked down to see who was calling. It was Danielle. He excused himself and stepped away from Brian and Joe so that he could talk privately. He didn't need Joe hearing him ask Danielle if she had heard from Marie.

When the chief got off the phone, Joe and Brian were now at the other end of the hallway, talking to the police officer who would be standing guard by Olivia's room for the night. A moment later, Olivia's attending doctor stepped out of her hospital room into the hallway.

"How is she doing?" the chief asked the doctor.

"She's stable. Conscious, but confused and disoriented. Ms. Davis is extremely dehydrated. We need to get fluids into her."

"Can I talk to her?"

The doctor shook his head. "Not today. Has the next of kin been notified?"

"Next of kin?" the chief repeated.

"I'm assuming she has family, someone the hospital can call."

"As I explained to admitting, for the time being, we need to keep Ms. Davis's admission to the hospital confidential. We have evidence that leads us to believe someone tried to kill her."

MacDonald and the doctor talked a few more minutes, and when the doctor said his goodbyes and left, MacDonald pulled out his cell phone and called Danielle back.

"Hey, Chief, any changes?"

"Olivia is stable but confused. She won't be up to talking to us until tomorrow. I was wondering, is Marie there?"

"Yeah, did you want me to ask her something?"

"Yes. Since she won't be hanging out with our masked kidnappers, I was wondering if she might go over and hang out with Olivia's sister."

"I was going to ask you about Shanice. You told us not to say anything to anyone outside of the medium circle about finding Olivia. But now that Olivia's at the hospital—"

"We can't tell her yet," the chief cut in.

"Why?"

"We don't know Shanice. That's why I'd like Marie to go over to Olivia's house and observe her sister. I understand she's aware of your secret, but don't tell her a ghost is hanging out at her house."

"You want Marie to spy on her?"

"I want to see how she's reacting. If she was part of this, she probably knows Olivia escaped by now, so I want to see how she behaves when she's alone."

"I get it, Chief. I don't like it, but I get it."

CHAPTER NINETEEN

When Ian and Lily returned home from Pearl Cove, they found Kelly's car parked in the street in front of their house, while Ian's mother's car was parked in their driveway.

"Your sister's here." Lily stated the obvious as Ian pulled into the driveway, parking next to June's car.

"I'm assuming Joe hasn't told Kelly that Olivia has been found." Ian turned off the ignition.

"According to Danielle, none of us are supposed to know. So if Joe can't keep a secret or slips and tells her, you know what that means."

Ian let out a sigh and unbuckled his seatbelt. "Yes, if she tells us, we pretend it's the first time we've heard about it. I'm not terrific at those types of lies."

Removing her seatbelt, Lily facetiously side-eyed Ian. "What type of lies are you good at?"

Ian chuckled and opened his door. "You know what I mean."

"Luckily for you, Joe tends to be a stickler for rule-following, so I suspect he won't tell Kelly. But we'll still need to do some acting."

"Acting how?"

"As far as Kelly knows, we're still concerned about Olivia. So we need to dial down the cheerfulness."

As Ian got out of the car, he said, "You have a point."

———

SADIE GREETED IAN AND LILY AT THE FRONT DOOR, HER TAIL wagging and no barking. They found Kelly and June in the living room, with June sitting in the rocking recliner with Emily Ann, and Kelly on the floor with Connor, assembling wooden train tracks.

"How were the kiddos?" Lily asked after saying a quick hello to her sister-in-law.

Upon hearing her mother's voice, Emily Ann began squirming. Wrestling with the now restless baby, June laughed and said, "Fine until you got here. This one wants her mama."

Lily grinned. "Let me wash my hands really quick."

While Lily rushed to the kitchen to wash her hands, Kelly looked at Ian. "Mom says you guys ate at Pearl Cove. Must be nice."

"We just had clam chowder. Nothing crazy." Ian reached down and ruffled his son's hair.

"Who was all there?"

As Ian listed off everyone who had been with them at Pearl Cove—except for Marie—Lily returned from the kitchen and took Emily Ann from her mother-in-law. She intended to take the baby to the sofa with her, but June stood up, insisting Lily sit in the rocking recliner with the baby. After Lily acquiesced, June took a seat on the empty sofa.

"I like clam chowder," Kelly said with a pout.

"I'm sorry, Kelly. I figured Joe was working, and it was pretty much couples."

"You said Heather was there. Brian's working too. Are Heather and Chris a couple now?"

"It really was spur of the moment," Lily interrupted, now cradling Emily Ann in her arms. "Heather started craving clam chowder, so Chris suggested they leave work early and go to Pearl Cove. He called Walt and Danielle to see if they wanted to join them, and Walt and Danielle had been talking to Mel and Adam about getting together, so Danielle called me and asked if we wanted to go too. I didn't really want to take the kids out, so we called your mom, and she was sweet to come over on such short notice."

"You two rarely ask me to sit for these two; it was nice spending grandma alone time with them. And not once did Connor talk to his imaginary friend since I've been here." Ian and Lily understood exactly what imaginary friend she was referring to—Marie.

Ian sat on the sofa next to his mother. Connor dropped the piece of wooden train track he had been holding and walked over to his dad and climbed up onto his lap. The four adults sat together in the living room, with Ian and Lily each holding a child while Sadie curled up under the coffee table.

"Kelly and I were talking about your missing neighbor," June told Ian. "Kelly says they're still no news on her. I understand her sister is still staying over there."

When Marie arrived at Olivia's house, she found Shanice carrying a stack of books into the kitchen. They looked like photo albums. Shanice dropped the books on the kitchen table and walked to the stove, picked up a teakettle, walked to the sink, and filled the kettle with water. She was just setting the kettle on the stove when a cell phone rang.

Shanice turned on the burner and walked over to the other end of the counter, picked up a cell phone, and answered it.

"Hi. No, nothing. No word." Shanice leaned back against the counter next to the stove while she talked on the phone. "I'm not coming back until my sister is found...I don't care how long it takes...I refuse to believe that...no...yeah, thanks, but my neighbor is watching my house...I appreciate your concern, but I need to be here. When Olivia is found—and she will be found—she's going to need her big sister. And it's not like I need to worry about rushing home for a job...Okay. I'll call you as soon as I find out something."

Shanice and the caller exchanged a few more words before she said goodbye. After that, she set her cell phone back on the counter, and the teapot began to whistle.

Five minutes later, Shanice sat at the table with a cup of hot tea, looking through one of the photo books. Marie moved closer. The book in her hands seemed different from the other photo albums Shanice had placed on the table. Unlike the family photo albums Marie had made during her lifetime, this one didn't have individual photographs affixed to removable pages in an album. This was a printed book, the type people order online after uploading image files to a photography website. The front cover, printed like a commercial book, showed a photograph of a cruise ship with the title *Christmas Cruise 2019.*

Marie watched as Shanice slowly turned the pages of the book, looking closely at each picture. The pictures on the pages showed the smiling faces of two sisters—laughing, posing, surrounded by other people on the cruise with them. There was one of Olivia and Shanice standing in the buffet line, making goofy faces. By the pictures in the book, it looked as if they'd had a wonderful time on the trip.

Shanice paused on one page and ran a fingertip over a picture of Olivia and herself. They both looked so happy. When she finished looking through the book, she closed it, set it aside, and grabbed the top photo album from the stacks sitting on the table. She placed it in front of her and opened the book to the first page.

Marie looked over Shanice's shoulder at the open photo album. She recognized the couple in the first picture, Shanice and Olivia's parents, Elmer and Helen Mallory. They had been friends once. Not close, but Marie remembered them.

The next picture showed Shanice as a little girl, holding a baby. According to the writing in the album, the baby was Olivia. Shanice stared at that picture.

Marie remembered when Elmer and Helen had adopted Shanice. She was only a year old. Esther Meek, who had been a close friend of Helen Mallory, had once told Marie about the adoption. While several people from the church they attended had assumed

Shanice had first been a foster child that the Mallorys adopted, that wasn't the case.

According to Esther, before moving to Frederickport, the Meeks had been close friends with Shanice's birth parents, Roy and Angela Lee. How the story went, Angela and Helen had been childhood best friends, and Elmer met Roy in boot camp. When Elmer came home on leave after boot camp, he brought his buddy Roy home with him. It was then that Roy met Angela, and they fell in love. Later, Roy and Elmer deployed to Vietnam. Before leaving, Roy and Angela married, while Elmer and Helen remained engaged.

Roy and Elmer were in the same unit. While in Nam, Roy received a letter from his bride; he was going to be a father. Days after receiving the news, their unit was ambushed. Elmer came home early with a permanent injury to his right leg, while Roy returned home in a box.

Devastated over the death of her husband, Angela worried about her unborn child—what would happen if something happened to her? She had been the youngest child, with a wide age gap between her and her older siblings. Her elderly parents couldn't raise a baby, and her siblings were raising teenagers. Because of this, she made a will, assigning Helen as her child's guardian should something happen to her.

Tragically, Angela died in childbirth. Helen and Elmer, who were planning to get married later that year, cancelled their wedding plans and married at the courthouse days after Angela's death.

The newlyweds brought Shanice home with them, and after dealing with the red tape, they eventually adopted their friends' daughter. While they gave her their surname, they kept Lee as Shanice's second middle name.

According to Esther, Helen and Elmer doted on little Shanice. When Olivia was born, Shanice doted on Olivia, excited to have a little sister. From what Esther told Marie, the relationship between Olivia and Shanice changed drastically after Olivia married the pastor's son.

Marie watched as Shanice looked through one photo album after another. When she got to the last album, Shanice opened its first page and stared at the picture—it was of a bride and groom. The bride was a much younger Olivia, her hair solid black—like Heather's.

Shanice stared at the picture, making no attempt to turn the page. Then Marie noticed—tears—tears slid down Shanice's face. Shanice slammed shut the album, stood, and walked out of the room.

WALT AND DANIELLE SAT SIDE BY SIDE ON THE SMALL SOFA IN THEIR bedroom, each reading a book while a fire flickered in the fireplace. The twins were asleep in the nearby nursery.

Marie suddenly appeared in the bedroom, standing between the sofa and the fireplace. It wasn't Marie's apparition that got their attention; it was what she said upon arrival, her tone both agitated and firm. "You need to call Edward right now! He needs to tell her immediately!"

Startled by the unexpected outburst, Walt and Danielle looked up.

"He needs to tell who, what?" Danielle asked, closing the book on her lap.

"Shanice. I've spent the last couple of hours spying on the poor dear, and she is an absolute wreck. When I got there, she was on the phone. Obviously not talking to anyone involved in Olivia's abduction. Then she started looking at family photo albums. Those made her cry. I followed her into the living room, and she started shouting to…I'm not sure exactly who she was shouting to…but she wants her sister back. Olivia is the only family she has left. She did a lot of stomping in frustration. Talking to herself. Some praying. A good deal of praying. You need to tell Edward to stop this nonsense. She needs to know her sister is alive."

"I agree. I wish the chief hadn't asked me to ask you…" Danielle groaned. "This is going to be awkward."

"Awkward how?" Walt asked.

Danielle looked at Walt. "She'll find out the chief didn't tell her right away. She's going to ask why. Even if I don't tell her about Marie spying on her, after Olivia tells her about the rescue, she will eventually figure it out. Awkward. And if I come out and tell her that's why we didn't immediately tell her Olivia was in the hospital, still awkward."

CHAPTER TWENTY

Marie and Walt silently listened as Danielle talked on the phone to Chief MacDonald. She began by telling him what Marie had observed and told him of Marie's insistence that Shanice be told Olivia was in the hospital. But what surprised them was when Danielle volunteered to be the one to tell her.

When Danielle ended the call, Walt asked, "After you pointed out how it would be awkward, I'm surprised you offered to tell Shanice the news."

"I figure it would be less awkward than having to face Shanice after the chief told her. While he wouldn't have told her about Marie, she's still going to have questions, and I don't want her to wonder why I didn't tell her she was being surveilled. Seemed less awkward somehow." Danielle stood up. "I'm going over there now."

"Would you like Walt to go with you?" Marie asked. "I can stay with the twins. Or I can go with you."

"No. I'd rather do this alone."

"Then I'll stay with Walt in case the twins wake up and he needs some help."

Danielle started for the bedroom door but paused as she reached for the doorknob and looked back at Marie, who stood by the loveseat where Walt remained seated. "Umm, maybe next time you might want to knock before suddenly appearing in our bedroom? Now, that could have been even more awkward than me talking to Shanice." If Marie could blush, she would have turned bright red.

SHANICE SAT ALONE IN OLIVIA'S LIVING ROOM. IT WAS DARK outside, and she hadn't bothered turning on the living room lights. Earlier she had built a fire in the fireplace, and its flames flickered, providing subtle lighting.

The doorbell rang, interrupting her mindless scrolling on her cell phone. She tossed the phone next to her on the sofa and stood up. *Maybe it's the police,* she wondered, *coming to deliver news about Olivia.* But when she looked through the door's peephole, it wasn't a police officer standing on the front porch; it was Danielle Marlow, wearing a heavy jacket over what looked like pajamas.

Shanice opened the door. The moment she did, Danielle said, "They found Olivia; she's okay and at the hospital."

SHANICE'S FIRST IMPULSE WAS TO GRAB HER PURSE AND JACKET AND head down to the hospital, but Danielle stopped her, telling her they needed to talk first. A few minutes later, the two sat on the sofa together. Before sitting down, Shanice had turned on one of the overhead lights.

"I need to explain a few things first. About the rescue and why the police didn't immediately inform you."

"What do you mean they didn't immediately inform me?"

"Your sister has been at the hospital for a couple of hours. No one knows she has been found—only those involved with her rescue and the medical staff. For the time being—for Olivia's safety—no information is being given to the public, and as far as most people know, she is still missing. But first, let me explain her rescue."

Danielle told Shanice about the rescue, beginning with Allen's participation, then help from Marie, and assistance from the mediums. She told her of the kidnappers' intent to kill Olivia and her current stay at the hospital. "Right now, Olivia isn't up to talking to anyone, not even the police, but the chief plans to speak to the doctor and see if you can see her in the morning."

Shanice leaned back on the sofa in disbelief. She shook her head. "This entire thing—ghosts on a rescue mission—there was a time I would think you were insane to even suggest such a scenario. When Olivia first started reading about astral projection, I always assumed it was just part of her spiritual journey. Not that she would try—or succeed at astral projecting."

"Olivia told us about her spiritual journey."

"When I was little, I remember our family going to church when we lived in Frederickport. But we had to move to Texas for Dad's job. After we moved, we tried a few churches, but none that Mom and Dad felt comfortable at. I grew up identifying as Christian in sort of an abstract way. We celebrated holidays like Christmas and Easter. We said our prayers at night, and Mom would tell us Bible stories. By the time Olivia was in high school, I was off at college. That's when she started dating Mark Davis.

"I think I mentioned before, his father was the pastor of this megachurch in the town. Lots of the kids in Olivia's school went there, and Olivia started going with her girlfriends. I think she wanted to fit in. My parents were okay with it. They always believed each person had the right to make their own choices regarding religion and faith. Something my parents came to regret." Shanice said that last sentence with a snort.

"Mom was devastated when Olivia chose to marry right out of high school instead of going to college. I'd seen the warning signs when she first started dating Mark in her junior year. Probably because I was off to college and only saw them when I came home for weekends or holidays, so the change was more noticeable to me. I tried to warn Mom, but she said Olivia was just going through a phase and getting involved with church wasn't a bad thing."

"Olivia has told us about her abusive marriage. How her church friends told her she needed to be a better wife, and how after the divorce she started deconstructing her faith."

"Yes. It was right after she left him and came to live with Mom and Dad that she started looking closer at her father-in-law's brand of Christianity, comparing it with other Christian denominations. She also explored other non-Christian faiths, which led her to astral projection. Like I said, at the time I didn't think much of it. And when she first told me she had done it, I…well…thought…that it was in some ways the other side of the coin from her life with Mark. Delusional, but in a new way."

"When did you start believing her?"

Shanice laughed. "She told me she would prove she could astral project. Told me to put something next to my bed that night, and she would visit me and tell me what it was the next morning. Since I was on vacation at the time, across the country from her, it wasn't like she could show up in the middle of the night and sneak in my house to see what I'd put next to my bed, so I said sure."

"I assume you put something by your bed that she got right the next day."

"She sure did. It was a souvenir I'd bought for one of my friends' kids. A stuffed raccoon. I hadn't told Olivia I'd bought any souvenirs, much less a stuffed raccoon. But when she talked to me the next day on the phone, she asked if I'd bought the raccoon for myself or a friend."

"So you believed her?"

"Yes. And I started reading more and more about astral projection and other things she was exploring. Olivia didn't tell me everything about her neighbors here until after Christmas. She told me she was afraid if she told me everything about you guys, I would think she was having a mental breakdown."

"But you believed her."

Shanice nodded. "Like I said, I had started reading more about such things…going down the rabbit hole, so to speak. Mysteries of the world, how some believe in reincarnation, timelines, ghosts."

"Speaking of ghosts. I need to explain why the chief didn't immediately tell you Olivia had been found."

Ten minutes later, after Danielle explained about Marie spying on her and why, the two women sat quietly, one processing the information and the other worried that the person sitting next to her on the sofa was going to be angry.

"Actually, I understand," Shanice said when she broke her silence. "None of you have ever met me before, and if someone wants my sister dead, who? A random person? Or someone close to her? Or someone who was once close to her?"

CASSANDRA SAT IN THE LIVING ROOM OF THE GARAGE APARTMENT, watching television while her mother was in the bathroom taking a shower, when Allen appeared, standing between Cassandra and the television.

Cassandra let out a little gasp of surprise but smiled at the ghost.

"I'm sorry. I didn't mean to scare you."

"You didn't. You just surprised me. Is Marie with you?"

"No. But I wanted to stop by and tell you thank you for everything."

"Is Olivia safe?" Cassandra still didn't know who Olivia was; she just knew she was in trouble and someone needed to help her.

"Yes, she is. So thank you, and I won't be popping in here and bothering you again. I understand this all makes your mother uncomfortable, so we should respect your mother's boundaries. But I wanted to tell you thank you and let you know everything was okay."

When Mary got out of the shower, Cassandra didn't mention seeing Allen's ghost. Instead, she took a bath, and when she returned from the bathroom, dressed in her clean pajamas, she found her mother sitting at the kitchen table, reading the newspaper.

Cassandra walked up to the table, but her mother, engrossed in whatever she was reading, didn't look up and seemed unaware of her daughter's presence.

"What's wrong, Mom?"

Mary startled and then looked up at her daughter and smiled weakly. "Nothing, honey. I was reading a news article."

"About what?"

Before Mary could answer, Cassandra leaned over her mother's shoulder and read the headline and said, "It says a lady named Olivia Davis is missing."

Mary quickly folded the newspaper and pushed it aside. "Nothing for you to worry about."

"Oh, I know. Olivia is safe now." Cassandra turned and walked back to the living room, leaving her mother staring at her in confusion. But Mary didn't ask Cassandra what she meant.

Later that night, after Cassandra climbed into bed, Mary sat alone on the sofa in the living room. The television was on, but she had turned the volume low so as not to keep Cassandra awake, who was in the bedroom they shared, its door closed. Mary had lost interest in the television program over fifteen minutes ago and had been sitting on the sofa, lost in thought. After a few more minutes, she picked up her cell phone from the end table, looked at it, and made a call. While waiting for the party to answer, she picked up the TV remote from the same end table and turned off the television.

"Hello?" came the familiar male voice.

"Hello, Joshua." Mary set the TV remote back on the end table and leaned back on the sofa, still clutching the cell phone to her ear.

"Mary? Mary, is that you?"

"Yes."

"Where are you?"

"I'm safe."

"And Cassandra?"

"She's fine. Where are you?"

"Me…umm…home. Of course."

"Olivia is missing."

"What are you talking about?"

"Olivia, they say she may have been abducted."

"Where did you hear that?"

"There is this thing called the internet." Mary wasn't about to tell him she read it in the local newspaper. And she certainly would not tell him she was in Frederickport.

"Why would anyone abduct her? For what reason?"

"You honestly hadn't heard anything about it?"

"She probably just left on her own and didn't tell anyone."

"Like before?" Mary asked.

"What is that supposed to mean?"

"Any changes, Joshua?"

"With whom, me?"

Mary let out a snort, then said, "No. You will never change. I was thinking of the patient lying in the hospital. Are they awake? Have anything to say?"

CHAPTER TWENTY-ONE

It had rained all night. Back in California, where Shanice lived, it rarely rained through the night, but when it did, the steady rhythm typically helped her fall asleep, in the same way the movement of the cruise ship had rocked her to sleep during her Christmas vacation. But Shanice had slept poorly last night, unable to take her mind off Olivia, and she found the persistent rainfall more annoying than soothing.

She woke by six but didn't get up until seven. By eight she was up, dressed, and downstairs, pouring herself a second cup of coffee. Her plan was to call the police station around eight thirty, assuming the police chief would be in his office by that time. He had promised to check with Olivia's doctor and see when she could go to the hospital to see her sister.

The doorbell rang while she drank her second cup of coffee. She wondered if it was someone from the police station stopping by the house to talk to her in person instead of calling. But when she opened her front door, it wasn't a police officer standing on the front porch, but a young white woman, with straight jet-black hair woven into two long braids falling past her shoulders, reminding her of

Wednesday from *The Addams Family*, a Wednesday with straight-cut bangs falling mid-brow.

Despite the childish hairstyle, she wore dark eye makeup and darker lipstick. Her clothing choice included a heavy jacket over a black dress. The dress fell mid-calf, revealing a pair of stylish black rain boots that Shanice guessed probably reached the woman's knees. However, because of the dress's hem length, she could only guess. Before Shanice said anything, the woman introduced herself.

"Hi, I'm Heather Donovan. I'm your sister's neighbor, on the other side." Heather pointed toward her house and grinned. "My boyfriend, Brian, he's one of the cops who had you at gunpoint when you first arrived."

"You're one of the mediums," Shanice said, recognizing the name.

Heather's grin widened. "Guilty."

Shanice flashed Heather a smile, opened the door wider, and invited her to come in. Heather gave a nod and stomped her boots on the front mat before entering the house.

"You're one of the mediums who helped rescue my sister," Shanice said as she shut the front door.

"I simply played interpreter."

Five minutes later, the two women sat together at Olivia's kitchen table, each drinking a cup of coffee.

"I didn't just come over to introduce myself or to check on you. Brian asked me to bring you a message."

Shanice arched her brows and sipped what remained of her coffee before asking, "The one who drew a gun on me?"

"In fairness, I heard both him and Joe pulled a gun on you. But don't feel bad, I'm pretty sure he once did the same thing to Danielle."

Shanice smiled and set her now-empty cup on the table. "So, what is this message?"

"The chief—Police Chief Edward MacDonald—has assigned Brian to lead this case. He can't really assign anyone else because—"

"The others don't know about the ghosts?" Shanice finished for Heather.

Heather nodded. "Exactly. Anyway, Brian is going over there this morning to interview your sister. The doctor said it was okay. He was planning to be there by eight thirty. The chief already talked to the doctor about you going over, and he said you can see Olivia."

"That must mean she's doing better."

"Sounds like it. But Brian wants to talk to her first. He doesn't expect to be there more than an hour, and after that you can see her. The security guard at her hospital door will let you go in. Brian wanted me to remind you, if you talk to anyone, keep acting like you're worried about your sister."

"I am still worried about my sister."

"I mean like she's still missing. Anyway, Brian also wanted me to tell you her room is 220. And after your sister comes home and the world knows she's been found, whatever you do, don't say anything to anyone—including cops, especially cops—that me, Danielle, and the other mediums knew anything about Olivia being in the hospital before the rest of the public."

***

THE NURSE HAD HELPED OLIVIA ADJUST THE HOSPITAL BED TO elevate her head, allowing her to sit up in a comfortable position. Olivia remained hooked up to monitors and an IV. She wore a hospital gown, and the nurse had laid a light blanket over her nightgown and combed her hair. The doctor had told the nurse on duty to expect someone from the police department after eight thirty to interview the patient, and the nurse wanted Olivia to feel comfortable, especially after the trauma she had already endured.

Before leaving her patient alone with Officer Henderson, the nurse asked Olivia one more time if she needed anything. Olivia assured her she was fine, and a few minutes later Brian was alone with Olivia. He sat in a chair by her bedside.

Olivia and Brian weren't strangers. Olivia had initially met Brian when she first moved to Frederickport, and he had been working on the murder investigation of the woman whose position at the library she ended up accepting. Since that time, they saw each other socially, as he was dating her neighbor, plus Brian was one of the few people who knew about the mediums—and about Olivia's experiences with astral projection.

Brian began the conversation by explaining what had gone on behind the scenes during her rescue. While Olivia understood Marie had been instrumental in her rescue, she didn't know about Allen or the extent of the mediums' participation.

When it was Olivia's turn to answer questions, she began by describing the man she had seen smoking on the porch of the cabin during her astral projection, noting he looked like one of the men she had seen on Sunday at the grocery store.

"It sounds like he never took the mask off. Which goes along with what Allen observed," Brian said.

"So we don't have any way to identify them?"

"We have their approximate heights. We also have the types of vehicles they were driving. A dark sedan and a dual-cab white pickup truck. Both with Utah plates. However, the plates on the sedan were stolen from another vehicle. The truck plates might also be stolen."

"Utah plates? You said Allen overheard one of them mentioning staying at a motel in Frederickport while the other one stayed at the cabin with me."

"Right, but he didn't say which motel."

"There aren't that many motels in Frederickport. Can't you check all of them? If anyone staying there has a dark sedan and a white truck with Utah plates, that would be them."

Brian smiled at Olivia. "Yes, we already checked that out. It seems white dual-cab trucks are rather common. We found several of them around town—including two at the Seahorse Motel—none of them with Utah plates. And we found one dark sedan, also not with Utah plates, and it wasn't at the same motel as any of the white trucks."

"So they probably left town?"

"Perhaps. But either way, we need to find out why they took you."

"They wanted me dead." Olivia then told Brian all that she remembered the kidnapper telling her, and what she had overheard. "Honestly, I can't remember everything I overheard during the astral projection. I was trying to figure out where I was and trying to focus because I didn't want to go back to my body without learning where they had me. It had been months since I had tried astral projecting. It was more difficult than I remembered. I suspect part of it was because I was so nervous and scared. Before, when I did it, I wasn't under any kind of pressure. So it was a totally different experience."

"You didn't recognize his voice?"

"No."

"Do you have any idea who would want to kill you?"

Olivia shook her head.

"Do you know anyone in Utah?"

Olivia frowned. "Utah?"

"Both cars had Utah license plates. And just because we know one plate was stolen doesn't mean your kidnappers weren't from Utah."

"I don't know anyone in Utah. I've never even been to the state."

SHANICE SHOWED UP AT THE HOSPITAL ABOUT THIRTY MINUTES AFTER Brian finished his interview and returned to the police station. The two sisters were alone in the hospital room, with Shanice sitting in a chair pulled up close to the hospital bed and the two sisters holding hands. They had just finished sharing their experiences since Sunday afternoon, after their missed FaceTime call.

"After Brian left, I kept asking myself the question he asked me. Who would want me dead? I told him I had no idea, but after he left, I started thinking about all the murder mysteries I've read. Motives are typically love, revenge, money, power, or envy. I haven't been in a romantic relationship for over a decade, so unrequited love is unlikely. Not some jilted lover or a woman who's jealous over me. I don't see anyone envying me, or how my death would give anyone power. And even though I have been a horrible sister at times, I don't see you knocking me off so you can get my house and my savings account."

Shanice squeezed her hand. "You weren't a horrible sister."

"Yes, I was. You have no idea how grateful I am you forgave me."

Shanice shrugged. "I just gave you grace, Liv. That kind of indoctrination—grooming—is powerful stuff. You were young and very naïve. Believed you were madly in love and had this purpose. Frankly, Mom and Dad were more at fault, and I forgave them. They should have protected you. And in the end, you suffered more than anyone."

Olivia squeezed her sister's hand back, and the two women sat in silence for several minutes, each lost in their own private thoughts.

"The life insurance," Shanice blurted as she abruptly stood, releasing hold of her sister's hand.

Olivia frowned up at Shanice. "What life insurance?"

Shanice stood by Olivia's bedside, her clenched fists resting on her hips as she looked down at Olivia with fierce determination. "The two-million-dollar life insurance policy."

"What two…" Olivia didn't finish the sentence. "I…I haven't thought about that in years."

"When is Aaron's birthday?" Shanice demanded.

"Um, March 31."

"How old is he going to be this year?"

Olivia stared at her sister, not answering immediately. Finally, she said, "Thirty."

"Well, we now have a motive. Two million dollars."

CHAPTER TWENTY-TWO

On Wednesday morning after breakfast, Cassandra sat at the garage apartment's kitchen table, her dark hair pulled into two pigtails as she worked on her math worksheets. Mary sat across the kitchen table from her, looking through today's newspaper.

Cassandra worked silently on the pages for about twenty minutes before looking up at her mother. Mary now had a pad of paper sitting next to her, a pen in hand, as she continued to look through the newspaper while scribbling something on the tablet.

"Mom, what are you doing?"

Mary looked up at her daughter and smiled, the pen in her right hand now still. "I'm looking for a job."

"Aren't you going to work for Mr. and Mrs. Marlow?"

"That's not full-time. And I'm not sure if I have the job, although Ms. Johnson asked me to come back tomorrow."

"Oh. So we're staying here?"

"For now."

"What about Dad?"

"For now, it's you and me. Your dad has some things to work

out." Mary looked back down at the newspaper, silently dismissing her daughter.

A few minutes later, Cassandra finished the worksheet, set her pencil down on the table, and looked up at her mother. "I'm done. Can I watch a little television, please?"

Mary looked up from the newspaper and glanced at the wall clock. After checking the time, she looked back at Cassandra. "Okay, but when I'm finished here, we're reading together from your science book."

Cassandra nodded, got up from the table, ran to the sofa, and sat down. A few minutes later she had the TV remote in hand while she moved through the channels, looking for a program her mother would approve of. She landed on an Oregon news station and was about to flip to the next channel when a familiar face filled the screen. The unseen newscaster said the woman's name—Olivia Davis, Frederickport librarian, who had been missing since Sunday. Cassandra recognized the woman in the newscast.

The newscaster hadn't finished talking about Olivia when Mary turned around in her chair to face her daughter and the television. "Cassandra, turn the channel. You don't need to be watching that."

Cassandra was about to do what her mother told her when a video replaced Olivia's picture, showing Olivia's house in Frederickport, where the police speculated she had been abducted, and as the camera panned the area, one corner of Marlow House came into view.

Cassandra pointed to the TV and said, "Mom, that's Marlow House."

"I told you, change the channel or turn the television off."

BRIAN HENDERSON HADN'T BEEN AT THE POLICE STATION FOR EVEN an hour when he got a phone call from Shanice, asking him if he would return to the hospital because she'd found a motive for murder that she wanted to discuss with him.

"I'm sorry my sister dragged you back down here," Olivia apologized when Brian walked into her hospital room twenty minutes later. "Shanice is confident she has come up with a motive for murder. But it's not a motive."

"Two million dollars is not a motive for murder?" Shanice asked incredulously.

"Two million? What are you talking about?" Brian asked.

Instead of answering, Olivia shook her head. "It's nothing."

"It might be something. Why don't we let Officer Henderson tell us if it's something or not," Shanice said.

"Go ahead." Olivia shrugged. She looked away from Brian and her sister and stared out the nearby hospital window.

Shanice faced Brian. "There is a two-million-dollar life insurance policy on my sister."

"Life insurance policy?" Brian glanced over at Olivia. "You didn't mention you have a life insurance policy."

Olivia shrugged again. "I forgot."

"I'm confused. How does one forget about a life insurance policy—especially one that size and knowing someone is trying to kill you? Who is the beneficiary?"

Olivia didn't answer the question. Instead, she continued to stare out the window. Shanice studied her sister for a moment before she let out a deep sigh, walked over to the hospital bed, and gave Olivia a gentle pat on her shoulder. She turned to Brian. "My sister endured a bitter divorce about ten years ago…"

"Twelve," Olivia corrected, still staring out the window.

"Okay, twelve." Shanice glanced briefly at her sister and looked back at Brian. "Olivia left her husband with basically the clothes on her back. They were living in Texas. Our parents sent her a plane ticket so she could go to California, where they lived. After leaving her husband, Olivia stayed with our parents. Her youngest son, Aaron, had just turned eighteen. While her husband owned a construction company, it technically belonged to his family's trust, as did the home she had been living in since she got married. So there were no marital assets to split, and she didn't have any money to hire an attorney to fight in court, anyway."

"I didn't want any of their money," Olivia whispered.

Shanice looked over to her sister. "You were entitled to something. You spent twenty years as an unpaid maid, raising Mark's children, keeping his home, following his rules, and enduring his abuse."

"He never hit me." Olivia refused to look at her sister; instead, she stared at the window.

Shanice's voice softened. "I'm sorry, Liv. You don't need to listen to all this. You've been through enough, and getting upset won't help your recovery. We'll go out in the hall."

Olivia said nothing; she simply nodded.

Brian and Shanice stepped out of the hospital room. The police officer standing guard outside the door gave them a nod. Brian glanced over to the nearby waiting room and suggested that he and Shanice talk there. They walked over to the waiting area. It was empty. They both sat down on a sofa.

"I'm afraid I get pissed off whenever I talk about it—and it's something that Olivia doesn't like talking about in the first place. Which I understand; that was a painful time for her."

"What is this about a life insurance policy? I don't understand how someone forgets they have two million in life insurance."

"Let me start with her marriage, which helps explain the life insurance. When Olivia got married, she planned to have a big family, lots of babies. That's what Mark wanted; that's what Mark's father convinced her was her duty as a wife. But she only had two children, both boys. She almost died when giving birth to her youngest, Aaron. And after that, she wasn't able to have any more children. After she almost died, Mark decided it was a good idea to get life insurance on Olivia."

"It's not uncommon to get life insurance on both parents, even one who doesn't work outside the home."

"True. But until that time, I doubt Mark ever considered getting a policy on her because he didn't think she had any value. Men like Mark say they want their wives to stay at home, raise their children, and take care of their families—but they don't respect their wives. They feel their wives owe them because they pay for their room and board. And the money Mark earned was his money. Olivia had an allowance, which he controlled how she spent."

"I don't believe all men think that way."

"I didn't say all men. I said men like Mark. My mother, for example, was a stay-at-home mom. Dad was the one who financially supported the family, and Mom didn't start working outside the home until we were in high school. And it was only part-time. But my father always respected Mom. I remember him saying her job was more important than his. And what he earned, it was always family money. In fact, Mom was the one who handled all the finances, paid the bills."

"So your ex-brother-in-law's first impulse after almost losing his wife was to take out a life insurance policy on her?"

Shanice let out a snort. "Something like that. When they first married, I doubt Mark ever considered the possibility Olivia might die early in their marriage. Young people rarely worry about things like that. But when everything went wrong during labor, and Mark faced the possibility of his wife dying, instead of being horrified at almost losing the love of his life, he wondered who would care for his sons if something happened to their mother. Who would take care of them when Mark was working? Who would clean his house, do his laundry, do the grocery shopping, make his meals, raise his children? The answer, of course, came to him: a life insurance policy on his wife would pay for domestic labor until he found a new wife to take care of him and his children. And of course, Olivia went along with it."

"Were her sons the beneficiaries?"

Shanice shook her head. "No, it all went to Mark."

"Normally, during a divorce, an ex doesn't remain a beneficiary of a life insurance policy."

"Olivia just wanted out of the marriage. She allowed him to keep the policy, providing he paid the monthly premiums, with the understanding the money was to be used to help their sons. And even though Mark was a crappy husband, I guess he really did love his sons in his own twisted way. Olivia obviously never worried about Mark coming to California and killing her; she didn't fight it. It was a term life insurance."

"Term?"

"Yes. The life insurance policy was for thirty years. They purchased it right after Aaron was born. Aaron turns thirty next month."

Brian arched his eyebrows. "So, this two-million-dollar life insurance policy that Olivia's ex took out on her—that he has been paying for each month—expires next month?"

Shanice nodded. "Exactly. If my sister dies before Aaron turns thirty, there is a big payout for his dad. But if Olivia makes it to April and then gets hit by a car and killed, not a dime to Mark. I'd say that's an excellent motive for murder."

***

LATE WEDNESDAY AFTERNOON, AFTER FINISHING HER SCHOOLWORK, Cassandra asked if she could go outside and play. It wasn't raining outside, and there was a swing in one of the nearby trees she wanted to try. Mary said yes but warned her daughter to stay in the yard.

Cassandra was swinging on the tree swing when Allen suddenly appeared. Upon seeing the ghost, Cassandra stopped swinging but remained sitting in the swing, each hand gripping the swing's ropes while the tips of her shoes pressed onto the ground below, keeping her from moving.

"Afternoon, Cassandra. I didn't mean to bother you. But I saw you on the swing. I put that swing up when my daughter, Gina, was your age. Of course, I had to change the ropes a few times over the years."

"Oh, do you want me not to use it?" she asked sincerely.

Allen smiled. "You are more than welcome to swing in it."

"Can I ask you a question?"

"Sure, what?"

"You know that lady named Olivia, the one you said needed our help? But that she is okay now?"

Allen nodded. "Yes, she's fine now. You don't need to worry about her."

"But that's what I don't understand. She's a ghost."

Allen frowned. "No, Olivia is alive, not a ghost yet, thankfully. Like I said, she is okay now."

Cassandra shook her head. "No. She's a ghost. I've seen her before."

Allen considered Cassandra's words a moment and then smiled. "Well, you are a medium; I suppose it's possible you saw her around here when she was trying to astral project."

Cassandra frowned at Allen. "I don't know what that means. But I didn't see her around here. I saw her a long time ago. At home. I saw her a couple of times, but when I tried talking to her, she disappeared, and she never came back."

"Home, where?"

"Back in Texas. She was there."

Kelly sat alone in a small booth in Pier Café, looking through the menu when Carla walked up to the table, order pad in hand.

"You waiting for someone? Joe, your brother?" Carla asked.

Kelly glanced up at the server and smiled. "I'm meeting Joe here for an early dinner. He's been putting in a lot of hours. We decided to meet here for dinner during his break. He won't be here for another fifteen minutes. Hope you don't mind if I take up the table while I wait for him."

Carla glanced around the almost empty diner and laughed. While dropping her order pad into her apron's pocket, she said, "I don't think that's going to be a problem. We're pretty dead at this time of year anyway, especially midweek." Carla took a seat in the booth across from Kelly. "If it's going to be fifteen minutes, I won't be the one taking your order."

"Your shift ending?"

"No. I'm going on break in ten minutes. I promised Earl I'd drop off some of his soup at the hospital."

"Earl? The cook here?"

Carla nodded. "Yeah. One of our regular customers is in the

hospital. Earl stopped by to see him this morning before coming to work, and the guy started complaining about the hospital food. Told Earl he would kill for some of our broccoli cheese soup. Since that was the soup Earl planned to make for today, Earl asked if I'd take some over to the hospital on my break. The guy is a good customer and a pretty good tipper, so I said sure."

"That's nice of you."

Carla grinned and said, "I imagine Joe's putting in a lot of hours lately, with Olivia being missing. Any news?"

"I haven't heard anything. But I haven't talked to Joe since this morning. I'm hoping he'll have good news when I see him for dinner."

"I hope she's okay and they find her soon. She's a nice lady. Comes in here a lot."

"Her sister is in town, arrived Monday. I guess she had some sister-sixth-sense that Olivia was in trouble."

"Olivia told me about her sister and about the Christmas cruise she gifted her. She showed me the pictures. That is one generous sister. I have one sibling, a brother, and the best thing he ever gave me for Christmas was a music CD. And it wasn't one he bought, it was one he made, and it wasn't even music I like."

Kelly laughed. "I have to say, I have a generous brother; he pretty much paid for our wedding."

"I guess some of you won the sibling lottery. But I'll admit, when Olivia showed me the pictures from the cruise, I was a little surprised her sister is Black."

Kelly smiled at Carla. "My grandma used to tell me families come in all colors."

"Isn't that the truth?"

***

After delivering the soup, Carla stayed at the hospital and visited with the patient for about twenty minutes before announcing she needed to head back to work. A few minutes later, when approaching the hospital exit on the first floor, she spied a

Black woman walking ahead of her, who was also leaving the hospital.

Carla noticed the woman's long braids. She stared at them as she stepped outside. While walking to the parking lot, the Black woman remained in front of her, walking to the same section of the parking lot where Carla had parked her car.

Carla continued to stare at the braids. She absently touched the ends of her own purple hair, pinching the tips between her fingertips. Regularly changing her hair color was something Carla enjoyed doing, yet she secretly envied the braids Black women sometimes wore. Danielle's fishtail braid was nice, but it wasn't anything Carla would consider wearing.

With a sigh, Carla released hold of her hair, which felt a little dry, and she speculated it would probably break off if she tried those intricate braids. She continued to her own car.

By the time Carla pulled out of the parking lot, the woman with the braids was already down the road in a powder-blue SUV. But as Carla continued to Pier Café, the woman's car remained some distance in front of her.

As Carla approached Marlow House, she saw the woman pull in front of Olivia's house and park.

That must be Olivia's sister, Carla thought.

AFTER PARKING IN FRONT OF HER SISTER'S HOUSE, SHANICE WALKED over to Marlow House. Earlier that day, Danielle had sent her a message, inviting her to come over for dinner. Shanice had accepted the offer.

Twenty minutes later, Shanice sat in Marlow House's living room with Walt and Danielle, enjoying a cocktail before dinner, while Jack and Addison sat on a quilt spread over the floor with an assortment of random baby toys.

Shanice had just finished telling Walt and Danielle about the insurance policy.

"So, what now?" Danielle asked Shanice.

"I haven't talked to Brian since he left the hospital. I know he was going back to the station and looking closer at Mark."

"Do you really believe your ex-brother-in-law is capable of plotting the murder of the mother of his children?" Danielle asked.

"He's the only one who benefits if she dies," Shanice reminded her.

"I understand. But it's been twelve years."

"Perhaps that's the point," Walt said. "He could have been hoping something would have happened by now. That she would have gotten cancer or had a car accident. A death where there was no reason to suspect he was involved with her death—because he wouldn't have been. But that policy is about to expire, and he might realize the only way he'll see a payoff, especially after all those years of paying a monthly premium, is to make sure she dies before that policy expires."

Danielle wrinkled her nose. "I suppose. But it's so cold."

"Isn't murder always cold?" Shanice asked.

"She's still the mother of his children." Danielle looked over at her own babies. Jack was currently tugging on one eye of a teddy bear while Addison gummed a plastic toy, drool running down her chin.

"Their divorce was bitter. Mark was angry when she left. He had no idea she was planning to leave. He was clueless, if you ask me. How do you not realize your spouse is that unhappy?"

"And if you're right, not just clueless, but also homicidal," Danielle said.

"I find it odd she let him keep the life insurance policy with him as the beneficiary. You say one reason she didn't object was that she wanted it for her sons. But they were both legal adults; why not change the policy to make the sons the beneficiaries and not the ex?" Walt asked.

"I think they had an informal agreement that he would eventually do that. Back then, I remember hearing something about the sons not being mature enough to handle that kind of money if something happened to Olivia and they ended up inheriting. They were both barely out of high school when Olivia left."

"And she never saw them again?" Walt asked.

Shanice shook her head. "When she got on the airplane that day, she didn't say goodbye to them. She didn't tell anyone she was leaving. But she left them a note in their room for them to find when they got home from school. She worried that if she told them earlier, they would tell their father before she could leave. Olivia was afraid Mark would find some way to stop her. He might have forcibly taken away the plane ticket and money my parents sent. Take away the car keys. She wanted to avoid a confrontation with Mark, especially in front of their sons."

"Olivia once mentioned that to me," Danielle said. "How they each wrote back, told her she was dead to them."

Shanice nodded. "Yes. She kept sending them letters. They never responded again. Finally, she received a letter from their father's attorney; it read like a cease and desist letter. Told her not to contact them again. When they were ready, they would contact her. They never did."

AN HOUR LATER, SHANICE SAT WITH WALT AND DANIELLE AT THE kitchen table, the twins nearby in the highchairs. They had just finished dinner and now each ate a piece of chocolate cake—all but the twins, who were instead each munching on an oatmeal cookie.

Brian had called Shanice fifteen minutes earlier, telling her he was leaving work and heading home, but would like to stop by and speak to her. She told him she was at Marlow House, which was why they weren't surprised when he walked in the kitchen door.

"Evening, Brian, want a piece of chocolate cake?" Danielle asked from the table, not bothering to get up as she took another bite of her cake.

Brian stood inside the kitchen door, Max weaving in and out between his feet in greeting, as the twins waved half-eaten cookies at him while Walt and Shanice both gave a hello.

Brian eyed the cake appreciatively and let out a sigh. "That looks really good, but I haven't had dinner, and eating sugar on an empty stomach will spike my blood sugar. So, no, thanks."

"Looks like you're putting in long hours. What are your plans for dinner after you leave here? Meeting Heather somewhere?" Danielle asked.

Brian shook his head. "No. Heather is putting in long hours too. They're working on taxes over at the foundation. I plan to grab a burger on my way home."

Danielle stood up. "Sit down. We have plenty of pot roast and mashed potatoes left over."

"It was really delicious," Shanice said. "I would take her up on the offer."

Ten minutes later, Brian sat at the kitchen table with Shanice, Walt, and Danielle, eating a dinner of pot roast, mashed potatoes, green beans, and homemade rolls while the other adults finished their dessert.

"What I found out so far, your ex-brother-in-law is having major financial problems."

Shanice arched a brow. "Really?"

"That construction company of his, it was sued. Then it filed for bankruptcy, and according to the information I found, it looks like they're losing the business." Brian scooped up some mashed potatoes with his fork and took a bite.

"That gives him even more motive," Walt said.

Brian nodded. "He's also remarried."

"I'm not surprised. I would have expected him to remarry quickly. After Olivia's sons cut her off, she never kept tabs on what Mark was doing. All her friends back there—her wonderful church friends—they pretty much cut her off too. I assume he has more kids?"

"According to what I've found online, he's only been married twice. The first, obviously to Olivia, but his current wife, they've only been married for a little over a year. I couldn't find any birth certificates showing any other children, but it's entirely possible his new wife is pregnant, but I could only do a brief online dive. Most of the information on his business I got from online court documents."

"I'm surprised Mark waited so long to remarry."

"Is there any way to tell if he is still the beneficiary on the insurance policy?" Danielle asked. "It's possible he could have made the sons beneficiaries by now."

Brian shook his head. "That's not so easy to find out. We don't know who the policy is with. Olivia couldn't remember. And if we knew who that was, it would probably require a warrant for the insurance company to release that information. But considering his recent financial problems and the fact that the policy ends next month, I'd say we have a prime suspect."

CHAPTER TWENTY-FOUR

"We're going to breakfast at Pier Café," Mary announced after Cassandra got out of bed on Thursday morning.

"What's that?"

"Pier Café is a little restaurant Ms. Johnson told me about. It's at the end of the pier, walking distance from Marlow House. We're supposed to be at Marlow House at ten this morning, so I thought we could have breakfast out before we go over. It will be a celebration breakfast."

"What are we celebrating?"

"When Ms. Johnson called me last night to confirm me going over there today, she said she spoke to the Marlows, and if I want the job, it's mine."

"You said it was walking distance. Are we walking to the restaurant?"

Mary laughed. "No, we'll be driving. It's not walking distance from here."

Before leaving for Pier Café, Mary handed Cassandra a pink backpack. "I put today's worksheets in here, along with a reading list and the books. There are also some snacks and a sandwich for lunch because I don't want Mrs. Marlow to feel obligated to feed you. It was nice of her to give you cookies the other day, but the next time she offers food, politely tell her no thank you, and tell her you brought your own food. I also filled up your water bottle, it's on the kitchen table, so make sure to grab that before we leave."

They left the apartment about twenty minutes later, each bundled up, wearing a heavy jacket, gloves, and a wool cap. Their first stop: Pier Café. After parking in the pier parking lot, both Cassandra and Mary shivered when getting out of the car. The temperature seemed colder near the pier, with the ocean breeze adding to the frigid weather. The two hurried toward the pier and then to the café.

When Mary pushed through the front door of Pier Café, Cassandra right behind her, her focus was on getting inside to warmer temperatures. Once inside, Mary glanced around for an empty booth—then she saw him.

"Joshua," she whispered under her breath. He sat in a booth with another man, the man's back to her. While she couldn't see the other man's face, she had a good guess who he was. Joshua seemed to be deep in conversation with the other man and hadn't looked her way.

Cassandra, oblivious to the diners currently in the restaurant, was preoccupied with rubbing her hands together, attempting to generate warmth without removing her gloves.

Mary snatched one of Cassandra's gloved hands and spun her around to face the door. Before Cassandra could ask what her mother was doing, Cassandra found herself being pulled back outside.

"Why are we leaving?" Cassandra asked while her mother practically dragged her down the pier, away from the diner and back toward the parking lot.

"I decided I don't want to have breakfast here. We can get something at the drive-through. It'll be quicker."

THE TWO MEN ALLEN KNEW AS BUD AND DUDE SAT ACROSS FROM each other at a booth in Pier Café. Of course, if Allen came in, he wouldn't recognize them without their masks.

They had already placed their order with an overly friendly purple-haired waitress, who for a moment Bud thought was going to linger after taking their order. Just as she was about to say something to them, someone from the kitchen started hitting the bell in the pass-through window, catching her attention. She abruptly excused herself and left their booth.

"It's been almost two days now," Bud said as he flipped through the local newspaper he had picked up before entering the diner. "According to this, there's still no sign of her." He slapped the newspaper down on the table and looked across the booth at his partner.

"Does this mean she's lying dead somewhere up there on one of the dirt roads by the cabin?" Dude asked in a whisper.

"Let's not forget Marie. Where is she? Why hasn't she contacted the authorities?"

"How ironic would it be if she's actually dead out there, and someone finds her body, just like we intended, but they don't find her until summer?"

Bud gave a shrug. "If that happens, it could work out, I guess. If they could determine her time of death, then who knows."

"Well, I'm not counting on that happening. I just wish we could hear something one way or another. Her vanishing without a trace with this Marie person is freaking me out."

"I still say we should never have left her alone. Up until that point, everything had been going exactly as we planned. Better, in fact. We didn't even have to take her out of the house like we planned. Just pulled up and pow. It was slick. Then it all fell apart."

"If one of us had been at the cabin when Marie—whoever she is—showed up, then things could have gotten a lot more complicated."

"Not necessarily. If she were someone just snooping around, she may never have gotten inside or found what we had in the basement."

"All this what-if crap is a useless waste of time. We knew when we started this, we might have to—as you yourself called it—abort the mission. There was no guarantee this was going to work out, and all I want to do is get away from this place and put this behind us."

"We will. Just wait a few more days. Our reservation is through Monday, and we don't want to check out early and attract attention."

"When I went down to get some coffee this morning, that guy who checked us in, he asked me how the crabbing was going." Dude gave a snort. "We don't need to stay. We should tell him it sucks, and that's why we're leaving early."

They stopped talking when the server walked up to the table with their order. Bud glanced up and noticed her name tag. It read Carla. He hadn't noticed the name tag when she took their order. Bud moved the newspaper to the bench seat next to him so Carla could set his breakfast plate on the table before him.

"Here you go, guys, bacon and eggs over easy." Carla set the plate in front of Bud. "And pancakes and sausage." She set the other plate in front of Dude. "Is there anything else I can get you?"

Bud glanced over his plate while picking up his silverware. He smiled up at Carla. "No, looks like I have everything I need."

"You guys just passing through, or are you staying for a few days? Maybe have family in town?"

Dude smiled up at Carla. "Maybe we live in Frederickport."

Carla laughed. "I know everyone in town."

Dude arched his brows. "Everyone?"

Carla shrugged and flashed him a smile.

"We're staying over at the Seahorse Motel for a few days. Doing a little crabbing," Bud told her.

"How are you doing? The weather hasn't been bad the last couple of days. Have you had any luck?"

"To be honest, we're not that good at it," Dude said with a laugh as he picked up a sausage link.

"Well, I'll leave you boys to your breakfast. But if you get any crab, I really like seafood. Name's Carla, by the way."

After flashing them both a flirtatious smile, Carla turned to leave when Bud suddenly called her back.

"Hey, Carla, can I ask you something?"

Carla turned back to the booth. "Sure, what?"

Bud picked up the newspaper next to him. "I read in the newspaper about some local woman going missing. Have you heard if they found her?"

"While I haven't heard any official updates, I think she's been found. It'll probably be in tomorrow's paper."

Dude, who was about to take a bite of food, froze for a moment. "Why do you say that?"

"Her sister is in town, got here the day after she went missing. I saw her leaving the hospital yesterday. It's not like she knows anyone in town—other than her sister. So I assume that's who she was visiting."

"Are you suggesting the missing woman is in the hospital?" Bud asked.

"I don't know for sure. But I'd put money on it."

After Carla left the table a few minutes later and was out of earshot, Dude asked, "Why did you ask the waitress about her? I thought we weren't supposed to give anyone a reason to connect her to us?"

"That doesn't mean we ignore the case, especially since it's been on the front page of the local paper for the last couple of days. This type of story is going to spike the interest—and even concern—of any visitor. Plus, she said she knows everyone in town. I suspect this place gets a lot of local foot traffic, and waitresses like that typically know all the dirt. And, apparently, I was right."

"Now what? Do you think she's really at the hospital?"

"We need to finish our breakfast and talk about this back in our room."

When Bud and Dude returned to the Seahorse Motel forty minutes later, Bud tossed the car keys on his bed after entering their room while Dude closed the door behind them. Bud removed his jacket and tossed it on the bed next to the keys after slipping his cell phone from his jacket pocket. He sat down on the edge of the mattress and began surfing through his phone.

"What are you doing?" Dude asked while removing his coat.

"Getting the phone number for the hospital." He reached a hand out to Dude while still looking down at his phone. "Give me the burner phone. I don't want to call from the motel room or from my cell phone."

Dude didn't ask Bud why he was calling the hospital. He just dug the burner phone out of his jacket pocket and handed it over before tossing his jacket onto a nearby chair. Dude walked over to his bed, sat on the edge of the mattress, and watched as Bud used the burner phone to make the call.

After someone from the hospital answered, Bud said, "Hi. I just heard Olivia Davis was found and admitted to the hospital. I understand you can't give me any information about her condition, but I would really like to send her some flowers; she's always been so helpful to my kids at the library. Is there any way you could at least give me her room number so I can send flowers?"

There was silence on the line for a few minutes. Finally, the operator said, "We can't give any patient information out, not even room numbers."

"Oh, I understand. But if I just send the flowers to the front desk, can someone get them to her?"

Again, there was silence on the line. Finally, the operator said, "I can't talk about patients. Perhaps you can give me your number, and I'll have someone call you."

"Oh, that's okay. I'll wait until she's back at home." Bud hung up.

"Well?" Dude asked.

"I think she's there. But I don't think they want anyone to know it."

"Why do you say that?"

"Everyone in town knows she's missing. If she wasn't there, the operator would have just come out and told me she wasn't there and ended the call."

"We need to get out of here. If she's at the hospital, that probably means she's talked to the police, and they know about us."

"So?" Bud tossed both phones onto the mattress and stood up. "Even if she or her white-knight Marie tells the cops about the cabin, they won't find anything when they check it out. It's entirely possible this Marie character is some eccentric hermit who lives in the mountains. We never saw any other cars up there. This Marie had to have been on foot. Both could be seen as unstable by the cops. So if we're lucky, she dies in the hospital, and it all works out. But if she happens to die when she gets home, perhaps when falling down the stairs, people might assume she hadn't fully recovered and she slipped."

"If you will recall, I'm the one who suggested we simply push her down the stairs. After all, from what I read, that's what happened to the last person who lived in her house. Was a lot less complicated than all this. So what's changed now?"

"I'm starting to see things differently; we've come this far; maybe aborting the mission was premature."

CHAPTER TWENTY-FIVE

Walt walked into the parlor and found Jack sleeping on a quilt spread out on the floor, a cozy fire crackling in the fireplace, and Max dozing next to the baby. Addison sat in Danielle's lap. Mother and daughter stared into each other's eyes while Addison's little fists each clutched her mother's index fingers. Addison's stocking feet wiggled happily, and drool slipped down her chin.

"Are you two having a staring contest?" Walt asked after entering the room, keeping his voice low so as not to wake Jack.

Danielle glanced up at Walt and smiled before looking back at their daughter. "I was just thinking about how we all thought their eyes were blue."

"Not everyone. I seem to recall Heather talking about how a baby's eye color can change during the first year, and the twins could end up with brown eyes like you. For some reason, you dismissed that suggestion altogether."

"But they were so blue at first. Just like yours. I was certain they'd stay that color."

Walt sat on the sofa next to Danielle. Addison immediately released her mother's fingers and reached out to her father. Walt leaned over and took Addison from Danielle, setting the baby on his lap. He absently used Addison's T-shirt to wipe up the drool from her chin. "They have my wife's beautiful brown eyes."

Danielle leaned back on the sofa, propped her feet on the coffee table, and crossed her arms over her chest while she looked over and watched her daughter gurgle at Walt. "I remember when Lily's mom said they had your eyes. I assumed those recessive blue genes from one of my grandmothers got through."

"I personally love a brown-eyed beauty," Walt said before kissing Addison's forehead. After the kiss, Addison shoved her fist into her mouth and gummed her knuckles.

Danielle's expression softened as she watched her daughter. "Poor thing, she's really teething."

The doorbell rang, waking Jack. He began to cry.

"That's probably Mary." Danielle stood from the sofa and then picked up Jack before answering the front door.

"THANK YOU AGAIN FOR LETTING ME BRING CASSANDRA," MARY told Danielle as she and her daughter stepped into the house, Cassandra wearing her pink backpack.

Carrying Jack on her hip, Danielle closed the front door behind them. The four stood in the entry hall, while Walt and Addison remained in the parlor.

"It's really no problem. We're used to having people around. Before the twins, Marlow House was a bed-and-breakfast."

Mary nodded. "Joanne was telling me about the B&B. She said you might reopen?"

"Someday, maybe. But no hurry. By the way, Joanne is not here yet. She's running a little late; car trouble." Danielle looked at Cassandra, who was just taking off her backpack. "Did you bring your schoolwork with you?"

Before Cassandra had a chance to answer, Mary said, "She did. Where would you like her to do her schoolwork? We don't want to get in your way."

Danielle briefly pointed toward the open parlor door. "I have a desk in the parlor; she's welcome to use it. Or she can work at the kitchen table if she wants. There's also a desk and computer in the library that we initially set up for our B&B guests, which she's welcome to use."

Mary shook her head. "Thank you, but I don't let Cassandra get on a computer unless she's with me. Actually, she's not allowed to use any digital devices."

"I understand." Danielle repositioned Jack in her arms. "I think this guy might need a diaper change. So, if you'll excuse me while I do that."

Mary glanced over to the staircase and back to Danielle. "You must get a lot of exercise carrying the babies up and down the stairs to change diapers. That must be exhausting."

Danielle laughed. "That's why we keep extra diapers and wipes in the living room, along with the portable cribs." Danielle looked over to Cassandra. "Max is in the parlor, if you want to say hi. Walt is also in there with Addison. But he should be coming out soon. After Joanne gets here, we're leaving to run some errands."

"Are you taking the babies?" Mary asked.

"No. It will be their naptime, and Joanne said she'd watch them for us. But don't worry, when you take over for Joanne—should you decide you want the job—babysitting isn't part of the job description."

Before Mary could respond, Walt stepped out of the parlor, carrying Addison. He said hello to Mary and Cassandra and then took a now squirming Jack from Danielle. With a baby in each arm, he excused himself to change the twins' diapers.

Cassandra asked if she could go to the parlor, to which her mother silently nodded while watching Walt walk away holding both babies. When she and Danielle were alone in the entry hall, she turned to Danielle and asked, "Does he really change diapers?"

"Yes. Walt's a hands-on-dad. Probably because he waited so long to have kids."

Mary frowned. "He doesn't look that old."

"Technically, he's not that old. But I always think of him as an old soul." Danielle grinned. "And for a long time, he never thought he was going to have children."

"Well, he seems like a wonderful father."

"He is."

Mary let out a sigh. "Cassandra's father, I don't think he ever changed a diaper. According to his father, that's a mother's job."

Danielle nodded. "Some people still think that way, I suppose."

They said a few more words, and Danielle was about to leave to join Walt when Mary asked, "Can I ask you something?"

Danielle, who had just started for the living room, stopped and turned back to face Mary. "Sure, what?"

"Joanne told me about your neighbor. That she disappeared."

Danielle nodded. "Yes."

"Has there been any news? Updates? Have they found her, or know what happened?"

Danielle stared at Mary for a moment. She thought of Cassandra and how the child knew about the missing neighbor—and about the rescue. She also knew Mary thought mediums were demonic, which meant Mary was not a safe person for Cassandra to confide in, a thought that broke Danielle's heart. Danielle felt wrong about keeping secrets from Mary regarding her daughter, and she didn't doubt Mary's love for Cassandra.

After a moment, Danielle said, "There has been nothing on the news about it. But I am staying positive and believe she'll come home, safe and sound."

WALT AND DANIELLE WERE STILL IN THE LIVING ROOM WITH THE twins when Allen suddenly appeared. The ghost started when he saw Walt and Danielle—and they in turn seemed taken aback by the ghost's unexpected appearance. The twins, now in dry diapers under their pants, played together on the floor and seemed only momentarily startled at the ghost's sudden appearance and quickly returned to their play.

"Oh, I'm sorry," Allen apologized. "It's rude of me to just barge into your home like this. I'm trying to get used to this ghost thing. And I haven't figured out how to knock on doors or ring doorbells."

Danielle smiled at Allen. "That's okay. We're rather used to ghosts dropping in."

Allen grinned at Danielle. "I wasn't expecting all this when I died. I'd read about the white light and all. But so far, no white light."

"I suspect it wasn't your time to move on. The universe has other plans for you," Danielle said.

Allen frowned. "Universe?"

"Some call it God."

"Is there a God?"

"A higher power? Yeah, I'm pretty sure there is," Danielle said.

"So, what do you mean the Universe—or God—has a plan for me?"

Danielle looked at Walt. "You want to explain?"

Walt flashed his wife a smile before looking back at Allen. "If it weren't for you, Olivia could have died. While it was your time to pass over to the other side—I understand you've been sick for some time—but something wanted you to stick around for a while. You needed to go to your cabin first. And before you did, you needed to understand there were people with whom you could communicate —which is probably one reason Cassandra was nudged, so to speak, into your path."

"You might be right. I never intended to go to the cabin. I just, well, I just thought about it, and then I was there. And then I found her."

"Walt pretty much summed up what we've both been thinking," Danielle said. "And when you're ready to move on, then I think you'll see that white light."

"I understand what you're saying—but can't this higher power…umm…move more directly?"

Walt laughed at the question. "As our dear friend Eva constantly reminds us, there are things we are not meant to understand during our lifetime—or immediately after passing over. But when you move on in your journey, it will probably make more sense."

"I also suspect this higher power is not personally handling what happens to each of the seven-plus billion people on this planet. That task might be assigned to angels or guardian angels or spirit guides who might intervene. Some of them are just better at helping people than others, and of course, there is that free-will thing," Danielle suggested with a shrug. "But that's just my theory."

"As Danielle says, it is only our theory. We don't have the answers, but from what we've experienced, we've come to certain conclusions. Now, I suspect you showed up in our living room for a reason. How can we help you?"

"I actually came looking for Marie. It's about Cassandra."

"Cassandra? She's here now. In the parlor."

"Oh…" Allen looked anxiously at the door leading to the entry hall, which led to the parlor. "I don't want Cassandra to hear this. I was going to tell Marie, but I guess I could tell you."

Allen then told Walt and Danielle how Cassandra had insisted she had seen Olivia back in Texas, where she used to live.

CHAPTER TWENTY-SIX

Chief MacDonald sat at his office desk, looking through papers. A knock from the open doorway got his attention. He looked up to see Walt and Danielle standing there. He smiled and waved them in.

"Surprised to see you two. Who's watching Addison and Jack?"

"They're with Joanne. It's their naptime, although these days naptime doesn't last as long as it used to. But she's good with them," Danielle said.

"Do you have a few minutes?" Walt asked. "We're out running some errands and decided to stop by and see if there's been any update. But we understand if you're busy."

The chief motioned to the two empty chairs facing his desk. "I always have time for you two. Plus, I need a break from this paperwork." He gathered up the papers he had been looking at and set them aside.

As Walt and Danielle each sat down, the chief asked, "So she's really retiring?"

"It looks that way. She and her new guy friend are planning a trip for this summer. I'm happy for her, but we're going to miss her.

Today she's not really housecleaning so much as supervising the housecleaning while also watching the twins," Danielle said.

Edward nodded in understanding. "She's still training her replacement?"

Danielle let out a sigh. "Yes. While Mary seems like a nice person and a hard worker, I hope we don't regret offering her the job. It's all a little complicated with Cassandra."

"Because she's a medium and you can't tell her mother?" the chief asked.

"Exactly." Danielle slumped back in the chair. "Some people are safe to discuss this with—some people aren't. I have a gut feeling Mary is not a safe person to tell. Which makes things complicated. And heartbreaking, when I consider Cassandra, knowing what she's going through."

Edward absently picked up the pen on his desk and fiddled with it as he talked. "If that's how you feel, I'm surprised you're offering her the job. Wouldn't it be easier if she didn't work for you? If she plans to keep homeschooling her daughter and bringing her to work, there will be other encounters. Frankly, I don't understand how Joanne isn't aware, considering all that's gone on over at your house while she's been there."

"I suspect Joanne knows," Walt said. "She just doesn't understand what she knows or the extent of it."

"I think she feels the house used to be haunted but believes the ghost has moved on. She's mentioned more than once that she no longer smells the cigar smoke." Danielle looked at Walt and added, "And sometimes I see her looking at you, and it's like she's trying to figure out a puzzle."

Walt smiled. "I remember how she once disliked my dear cousin."

Danielle turned back to the chief. "But enough about hauntings. We stopped by to see if there're any updates on Olivia's case, and if you've been told when she's coming home."

"The doctor says she'll probably be released this weekend. As for the case, last night I was confident Olivia's ex was behind the kidnapping. He had the motive."

Danielle frowned. "The way you say that, it sounds like you've changed your mind."

"We've since learned more about the ex. It seems he had a stroke right around the same time his company was served in the lawsuit. Since that time, he's been in a nursing home, and from what Brian learned, the ex's medical condition basically provides him with a solid alibi."

"Couldn't he still arrange a kidnapping from his hospital room?" Danielle suggested.

"Since the stroke, he's been confined to bed and is nonverbal."

"Hmm, perhaps Marie needs to take a visit to Texas. Eva could go with her," Danielle suggested.

The chief arched his brows at Danielle. "What are you thinking?"

"Not sure whom Brian spoke to, but it would be interesting for Marie and Eva to visit him at the nursing home. See if his condition is really that severe. Have a closer look at whoever else might benefit from Olivia's death if insurance was the motive behind all this. If the beneficiary is still Olivia's ex's name, what would happen to the insurance money if Olivia had died? Who could access the money if it was deposited into the ex's bank account? But it's also possible he already changed the beneficiary on the policy to his sons. After all, that was the basic understanding at the time of the divorce."

"Danielle has a good point," Walt said. "While you could have one of your own people go to Texas and interview the parties of interest, it would be quicker, less expensive, and you'd probably learn more having Marie and Eva do some eavesdropping."

"Technically, none of this is legal," the chief pointed out.

Danielle laughed. "Please show me in the statutes where it says you can't have a ghost surveil a suspect."

"You know what I mean. It's like listening in on a suspect talking to his attorney."

Danielle shrugged. "Last I heard, there is no client privilege between a suspect and what a ghost overhears."

The office phone rang. MacDonald picked up the receiver while Walt and Danielle remained silent. The chief ended the call a few minutes later, hung up the phone, and looked at Walt and Danielle. "That was Brian. Apparently, the hospital contacted him; someone was asking about Olivia."

Danielle frowned. "Asking what? No one is supposed to know she's there."

"They called the hospital, asking for her room number. Claimed they wanted to send her flowers. Acted like they already knew she was there."

"They were fishing," Walt said.

The chief nodded. "That's what I assume." He recounted the conversation between the hospital's operator and the man who had called about sending Olivia flowers.

"So she basically confirmed Olivia was at the hospital without saying it?" Danielle asked.

"Ironically, the operator hadn't been told Olivia was at the hospital. Very few people were told. The operator was aware of Olivia's disappearance, and after getting the call, she wondered if Olivia was in fact at the hospital. So, she went to her supervisor and asked if Olivia was a patient and explained the call."

"What did the supervisor tell her?"

"That she did the right thing but didn't elaborate. The supervisor called Brian and told him what had happened. It might be the kidnappers fishing, wondering if she was found and at the hospital, which is where she would obviously have been taken—or it's also possible that one of the attending doctors, nurses, or other staff members—or someone from the ambulance—told a friend in confidence. And maybe it wasn't the kidnappers who called the hospital fishing, but someone who knew Olivia from the library and heard through the rumor mill that she had been checked into the hospital."

"Now what?" Danielle asked.

"As I said, Olivia should be able to go home by this weekend. Considering the phone call, it is probably time we issued a press release informing the public that Olivia has been found. Sounds like the information might be out there anyway. And your suggestion about Marie and Eva is probably a good idea."

After leaving the chief's office, Walt and Danielle drove directly to the Glandon Foundation offices to see Heather and Chris. On the drive over, Danielle called home, checking on the twins, and Joanne told her they were both fine and to take their time getting home. Danielle's next call was to Heather, informing her that she and Walt were on the way over and needed to talk to her and Chris.

When they arrived at the foundation headquarters, Heather took Walt and Danielle to Chris's private office, where Chris was already waiting.

Not long after their arrival at the foundation headquarters, the four mediums sat in Chris's office, its doors closed. Danielle explained what they had learned at the chief's office, her idea about Marie and Eva, and what Cassandra had told Allen about seeing Olivia in Texas.

When Danielle finished telling them everything, Chris let out a long whistle and leaned back in his chair. "That's a lot to unpack."

"Have you seen Marie and Eva today?" Danielle asked.

Chris and Heather exchanged quick glances, looked back at Danielle, and both said, "No."

"I'm kind of curious about what Cassandra said. That's pretty crazy," Heather said.

"Did you ask Cassandra about it?" Chris asked.

"I feel funny bringing up anything about ghosts with Cassandra —unless it's absolutely necessary. Knowing how her mother feels about the topic." Danielle cringed. "I can't imagine what Mary might say if she overheard me talking to her daughter about seeing ghosts—or if Cassandra decided she needed to tell her mother that we saw ghosts too. Feels a little predatory."

Chris frowned at Danielle. "What do you mean?"

"If an adult tells a child to keep a secret from their parent— that's just—creepy and wrong. Makes me think of those pervs who groom children and tell them not to tell their mom—because what they have is special, and their mom won't understand."

"It's not the same thing," Chris argued.

"I get where Danielle's coming from," Heather interrupted. "From what I understand, her mother believes a ghost is really a demon—and pervs are pretty much demons."

"Are you suggesting one of the mediums try talking to Mary instead of Cassandra? Show her the truth?" Chris asked.

Heather shook her head no. "We're not equipped to handle that —you forget, Mary's outlook on ghosts stems from a place of faith —her religion. I don't know about the rest of you, but I feel it's overstepping to tell someone their religion is wrong—unless they're killing puppies as part of their rituals. Otherwise, that's kind of their own personal journey."

"Heather has a good point," Danielle said.

"Plus, there is something else about Mary and Cassandra that no one else seems to have noticed."

They all looked at Heather. "What?" Danielle asked.

"They are from Texas."

Chris frowned at Heather. "So?"

Heather groaned at Chris and gave him a dramatic eyeroll. "Olivia is from Texas. The person who is behind this kidnapping is probably from Texas—or at least that's what Brian seems to think."

"Are you suggesting Mary is behind the kidnapping?" Chris asked.

"Of course not. But I find it interesting that Cassandra claims to have seen Olivia in Texas."

"Olivia left Texas twelve years ago," Chris reminded her. "What is Cassandra, nine?"

Heather looked at Chris, her expression not of a woman who is looking at an incredibly handsome man, but an incredibly stupid one.

"Cassandra assumed it was a ghost. It sounds to me Cassandra may have seen Olivia the same way I first saw Olivia in front of my house before she actually arrived in town. So, my question is, why did Olivia astral project into Cassandra's home?"

CHAPTER TWENTY-SEVEN

Lily was in her bedroom alone, putting away her clean laundry, when her cell phone rang. She grabbed the phone from her dresser, saw the caller was Danielle, and then sat on the edge of her mattress to answer the call.

"Hey, Dani. June told me she passed you and Walt in the Packard. Out gallivanting around. Who's watching the twins?"

"Seriously, when you and Ian are out together without your kids, do people greet you with *Who's watching Connor and Emily Ann?*"

While listening to Danielle's question, Lily scooted all the way onto the bed, kicking her slippers off as she did. Once comfortable on her side of the mattress, her head propped up on her pillows, she said, "I don't know. Ian and I never get out without the kids."

Danielle laughed. "You guys went out to Pearl Cove with all of us the other day."

"True. And now that I think about it, Adam asked who was watching the kids."

"I just find it funny. That seems to be the first thing anyone asks me when they see me without the twins. I wonder if they ask Ian or Walt those questions when they are out without us and the kids."

"That's motherhood for you. Our new identity. So, is motherhood getting overwhelming? Is that why you're calling? I'm here for you, Dani."

Lily's cheerful delivery made Danielle smile. "You must admit it's kind of funny how that always seems to be the first thing someone asks me now. Like a new version of *Hi, how's it going?*"

Lily heard Walt's voice in the background yet couldn't make out what he had said. "I hear Walt. So where are you off galivanting to? And who has the twins? Stop deflecting the question. Do I need to report you to CPS?"

"They're with Joanne. And I'm calling to see if Marie's over there."

"I haven't seen her."

"Funny. Can you leave a message on the board that I need to talk to her?"

Lily glanced over to the closed bedroom door. "I'd love to, Dani. But June's here. And it looks like she'll be here for a while. So unless I walk into a room and see something flying around, and June's not within hearing distance, I don't think I can help you."

"Crud. So, why's June there?"

"There was some plumbing issue with the septic over at their rental. The landlord has a repair team working on it. She can't use the bathroom, so she's staying here. Which has been working out. She's been helpful lately. Ever since Ian told her to stop giving me unsolicited advice on how I should live my life, she's gotten a lot better."

"That's good."

Lily glanced down at the tattoo on her arm. "Although, when I wear short sleeves, she still looks at my arm like I was in an accident and it's severely deformed. Her mouth does this puckery thing, like she wants to say something but knows she can't, or her son will get on her case again."

Danielle snickered.

"So, you never told me what you and Walt are off doing, or why you need to talk to Marie."

"At the moment, we're pulling into our garage. We just got back from the Glandon Foundation."

"Why were you there?"

As Lily asked the question, Walt turned off the engine. "We had to talk to Chris and Heather." Danielle remained sitting in the car while filling Lily in on why they had gone to the foundation, all that had happened that day, and why she wanted to talk to Marie.

Walt stood in the garage, waiting for Danielle to finish talking to Lily. When the call ended and Danielle got out of the car, Walt said, "I was thinking about what Cassandra said."

"You mean about seeing Olivia's ghost?"

"Why don't we get a picture of Cassandra and show it to Olivia? See if she recognizes her? She might be able to give some context to Cassandra's claim. She won't be home until this weekend, but you could call her, explain what Cassandra said to Allen, and text the picture to her phone."

"How are we getting a picture of Cassandra without it seeming creepy? We can't take a picture of someone else's child without their permission."

"I expected you to say that. Which is why we get Max to help us."

Danielle frowned. "Max, how?"

"Imagine Cassandra sitting on the sofa in the parlor, doing her homework, and Max jumps up on the sofa and assumes a photo-worthy pose. You happen to be in the room, your phone in hand, and you respond to Max's pose by calling out Cassandra's name. She looks in your direction, you get a picture of her face, and Max doesn't move until after you take the picture. Afterwards, you show it to her mother, explaining how you happened to walk in on such an adorable sight, and offer to send her the picture. It won't be creepy in that context."

"Okay. Might work. But I'll need to keep my phone with me."

"Which is probably the easiest part of this plan—you always seem to have your phone on you. Everyone here has their phone on them."

As Danielle started toward the garage door leading to the back-yard, she gave Walt a playful pat on his backside. "Okay, gramps, you don't need to go into your monologue about how in your day telephones were wired to houses, and most houses didn't even have phones."

DANIELLE AND WALT FOUND THE TWINS IN THE LIVING ROOM, sitting on the quilt with Cassandra. Jack was attempting to assemble a stacking toy with Cassandra's assistance, while Addison lay on her back, kicking her feet while gumming what looked like a miniature pink balloon tire. The moment the twins noticed their parents had walked into the room, Jack abandoned the stacking toy and began crawling toward Mom and Dad. Addison rolled over onto her tummy, joining her brother in the crawl while dragging along her impromptu teething ring in a clutched fist.

Joanne, who had been polishing the fireplace mantel, turned and greeted Walt and Danielle while Cassandra said, "I finished my homework, and Mrs. Johnson said I could play with the twins."

Danielle, who had just scooped Addison up in her arms while Walt picked up Jack, smiled down at the girl. "I'm sure they enjoyed playing with you. Thank you for helping Joanne take care of them."

Cassandra grinned up at Danielle. "I don't think Addison wanted to play, she just kept putting everything in her mouth, but Jack likes playing with the puzzles and the stacking rings."

ABOUT THREE HOURS AFTER WALT AND DANIELLE RETURNED HOME, Joanne and Mary had finished cleaning Marlow House. By this time, the twins were upstairs taking a nap again, and Cassandra was back in the parlor, reading one of her books.

Danielle still had not taken a picture of Cassandra. Walt had communicated to Max what needed to be done, after which the cat had stayed in whatever room Cassandra had been in, waiting for Danielle to enter with her cell phone and give him his cue. Unfortunately, since arriving home, the photo opportunity had been delayed, once after Addison managed to unscrew her milk bottle and empty its contents on her brother's head, resulting in a need to bathe Jack.

Cell phone in hand, Danielle stepped out into the entry hall where Mary and Joanne were talking to Walt, chatting about how the day had gone and when they should return. Not long after Danielle joined the conversation, Mary said, "Excuse me while I get Cassandra."

Danielle realized this was her last chance to get a picture before they left. "I'll go with you; I need to get something out of my desk."

When the two women stepped into the parlor a few moments later, they found Cassandra reading her book, Max on her lap.

"Time to go, Cassandra," Mary said.

Danielle stepped closer to her sofa and looked at the little girl, now closing her book, while the cat remained on her lap. "Oh, I see Max has found a friend. He seems to really like you." Danielle coughed—the cue Walt had told Max to listen for.

Cassandra set her now-closed book on the sofa next to her and smiled up at Danielle as she stroked the cat's back. "He's really sweet."

"Well, you need to say goodbye to the kitty, because we have to go and let the Marlows have their house back."

Max let out a loud meow, stood, and leaned toward Cassandra, nuzzling his face against the child's shoulder before turning toward Danielle, posing for the camera.

Mary laughed at the unexpected sight, and Cassandra turned toward her mother and the camera. Danielle didn't need to call out Cassandra's name for her to look her way, so she snapped the picture. After she did, Max jumped down from the sofa.

Danielle looked at the picture she had taken. It was a clear shot of Cassandra's face. "Mary, I have to send this to you. It's so cute!"

Instead of being annoyed at Danielle for taking her daughter's photograph without permission, Mary happily accepted the image when Danielle sent it to her phone.

WALT AND DANIELLE SAT TOGETHER IN THE NURSERY, EACH ON A rocking chair, and the twins playing on the floor with Max. Joanne, Mary, and Cassandra had left about fifteen minutes earlier. Before Danielle had the time to show Walt the photograph she had taken, they heard the twins crying from the baby monitor.

Now sitting in the motionless rocking chair so as not to rock on the little ones, Walt held Danielle's cell phone and studied the picture she had taken and handed the phone back to Danielle. "You've got a good shot. When are you calling her?"

"I was just thinking, she may not have her cell phone with her at the hospital. Not unless Shanice took it to her."

"If she doesn't, you can either wait until she gets home this weekend or see if Brian or Shanice can show her the picture. I suspect this is more about curiosity than urgency."

"What's urgent?" Marie's apparition appeared, floating several feet above the floor on the other side of the room. The twins looked over at Marie, flashed her a smile and then went back to playing, as if a grandmotherly figure suddenly appearing in their room while hovering over the floor was the most natural thing in the world.

"Where have you been?" Danielle asked.

"Sleuthing." Marie's apparition wore her favorite flowered sundress, the straw garden hat askew atop her gray hair.

"Sleuthing where?" Walt asked.

"I just left Eva. We were sleuthing together, like Sherlock Holmes and Watson. Don't ask me which of us is Sherlock. We visited all the local motels."

"And?" Danielle asked.

Marie shrugged. "We focused on the ones where guests had white dual-cab pickup trucks and dark sedans."

"Did you find anything?" Walt asked.

"Most of the guests who were with those vehicles didn't match the description for our kidnappers. Too short, too old, and the wrong gender. Although I suppose it's possible one of the kidnappers was a very large woman."

"You said most, so did you find something?"

"At the Seahorse, there are two white pickup trucks that match

Allen's description. Although neither of them has a Utah license plate. But if they were switching plates on the sedan, they might have on the truck. The guests in both rooms were two men who matched the kidnappers' physical descriptions. One truck has fishing equipment in it; it looks like they've been crabbing."

"Did you look to see if either of them has masks, maybe check their trucks?" Danielle asked.

"Of course I looked, and no, I didn't find any masks. Eva and I spent considerable time with them—I with the fishermen and Eva with the other pair. And they said nothing suspicious; they weren't a very talkative bunch. Spent most of their time watching TV and looking through their cell phones. I searched through their rooms and their vehicles and found nothing suspicious."

"The kidnappers might have already left town," Walt said.

"Are you up for more sleuthing? Perhaps a trip to Texas?" Danielle asked Marie.

CHAPTER TWENTY-EIGHT

While Marie left to find Eva, Walt and Danielle took the twins downstairs for dinner. After they secured the pair in their highchairs and handed them each some shredded mozzarella cheese to keep them busy for a few minutes, Danielle made a call to the chief.

While she was on the phone, Walt removed the ingredients for dinner from the refrigerator. They were keeping it simple tonight—ravioli they had purchased from the grocery store, which needed three minutes in boiling water, and a salad Danielle had prepared earlier that day, along with some diced-up fruit. Before heating the water, Walt took a loaf of Heather's homemade sourdough bread from the breadbox and cut several slices.

Eva and Marie arrived to find Walt and Danielle at the kitchen table, eating their dinner, while the twins sat in the nearby highchairs, picking up pieces of ravioli with their sticky little fingers and shoving them into their mouths.

They didn't arrive with Eva's trademark glitter or seasonal

snowflakes, but her arrival caused both Danielle and Walt to pause for a moment in stunned silence while they each looked Eva up and down. Upon seeing the spirits, the twins gleefully pounded their highchair trays. Marie turned her attention to the twins, cooing at them in a grandmotherly voice while encouraging them both to resume eating their dinner.

Meanwhile, Walt and Danielle stared at Eva, whose fashion choices typically shifted from the Gay Nineties to the Edwardian era, with an occasional flapper vibe thrown in when the mood suited her. This evening she had selected a new fashion choice—at least new to Walt and Danielle. Wearing what Walt would later describe as Eva's Annie Oakley look, with her open-crown cowboy hat atop her mop of curls, a fringed-sleeved leather jacket, with matching skirt and a pair of cowboy boots. Eva grinned mischievously at Walt and Danielle, shifting her pose as if modeling her outfit.

"Okay, what is with that getup?" Walt finally asked while putting down his fork.

Placing her right hand on her right hip, Eva lifted her chin, her gaze meeting Walt's. "I would think it obvious."

Marie turned from the twins, who were again happily eating their dinner and no longer distracted by the ghosts' sudden appearance, rolled her eyes at Eva, and looked over to Walt and Danielle. "It's because we're going to Texas."

Walt suppressed a laugh. "What are you planning to do when you get there? Some sharp shooting?"

Eva's right hand moved quickly from her hip and back, grabbing a pistol from a hip holster that hadn't been there a moment earlier. "I could." Eva laughed. She shot the pistol, releasing a burst of glitter instead of a bullet, and the next moment the gun and holster disappeared while the glitter slowly dissolved. The twins excitedly pounded their highchair trays at the sight of the glitter. Marie quickly diverted their attention back to their dinner.

Walt let out a laugh. His eyes twinkling, he looked at Eva. "Are you going for a Helen Gibson look?"

Danielle looked at Walt. "Helen Gibson?"

"She was a colleague of Eva's," Walt explained.

"We never worked on a movie together. I met her in Pendleton, Oregon. Helen Gibson was her stage name. Her real name was Rose. But she was rather extraordinary. Many consider her the first stuntwoman in film. I suppose I was a bit in awe of her."

"Eva was telling me they used to film a number of silent westerns near Austin, Texas," Marie said.

"Did you ever make a movie there?" Danielle asked.

Eva shook her head. "No. My movies were typically filmed in Southern California. This will be my first trip to Texas."

Marie looked at Danielle. "Did you find out where we need to go?"

"Yes." Danielle stood from the table, walked to the kitchen counter, and picked up her cell phone. She scrolled for a moment before showing the phone's screen to Marie. The picture on the screen showed a medical facility with an address beneath the picture. "That's the nursing home Olivia's ex is in. His name is Mark Davis, and according to the chief, he's in room 240."

THE SUN WAS SETTING WHEN EVA AND MARIE ARRIVED IN TEXAS. They stood in the parking lot outside the medical facility Danielle had shown them on her cell phone. Marie glanced over at Eva, giving her a quick look up and down. "Are you really wearing that in there?"

Eva glanced down at her outfit. "I think it looks adorable. I just wish I had a mirror—at least one where I could see my reflection instead of my body from this angle."

Marie chuckled and turned from Eva to face the building. "On with our investigation. According to Danielle, he's in room 240, which I assume is on the second floor."

Marie and Eva moved from the parking lot into the building, going directly to the second floor. They found themselves standing in a hallway, next to room 230. Marie glanced behind her and pointed in the opposite direction and said, "His room should be down there."

While it was entirely possible for them to go directly from Marlow House into Mark's room from the information Danielle had given them, Marie and Eva had decided they wanted to get a feel for the hospital and its immediate surroundings before arriving in his room.

They found the corridor quiet, and the only person in sight was a nurse sitting at a desk, silently reading a medical chart. As they moved past the nurse, one of the doors down the corridor opened, and a young woman stepped out, closed the door behind her, and walked in their direction. Had Eva not moved quickly, the woman would have walked through her.

When they reached the door the woman had exited, they saw it was to room 240, Mark's room. Marie didn't bother opening the door; instead, they moved through the wall, into the room. Inside they found a man alone, lying in a hospital bed. He wore a hospital gown with a blanket thrown over his body, pulled up to his chest. They had him hooked up to various monitors and an IV. His eyes were open, and he stared ahead blankly.

"He's not sleeping," Marie said.

"What exactly are we looking for here? We already know he had a stroke and is a patient."

"For one thing, determine if he's capable of plotting Olivia's murder from his hospital bed."

Eva stood by Mark's bed and studied his face. She cocked her head slightly from side to side.

"What are you doing?" Marie stepped closer to Eva and looked at Mark.

"His eyes are open. But that doesn't really tell us anything. Even if one of the nurses comes in here right now and he is perfectly cognizant and able to communicate, he might pretend he can't.

That could very well be his alibi strategy. The only way we might disprove his incapacity is if one of his accomplices visits him."

"Or we could try this." Marie focused her energy on a box of tissues sitting on the table next to Mark's bed. The box floated off the table and moved along the side of the bed toward Mark's feet. When it reached his knees, the box floated over the bed. After the tissue box moved into Mark's line of vision, Mark didn't lurch in surprise, yet his eyes blinked rapidly, noticeably widening.

"He's obviously in there," Eva said. "But I would expect more of a reaction if he were faking his condition. Let out a scream, sit up, or maybe try grabbing the box."

Mark's eyes blinked again, but his body remained in place. Marie's energy was about to return the box of tissues to the night-stand when the hospital room door opened and the same woman they had seen leaving the room moments earlier walked in. Marie lost focus, and the box dropped to the bed, landing on Mark's hip before rolling off the hospital bed, landing on the floor, making a noticeable thud.

The woman who had entered the room witnessed the box falling and let out a gasp and ran to Mark's bedside, taking hold of his arm while looking into his face. "Mark! Mark!"

Several feet away, Marie and Eva silently watched the interaction.

"Is she the wife?" Eva asked.

"Looks more like his daughter."

"I didn't think Olivia had a daughter."

"She doesn't," Marie said dully.

"Oh, the young and pretty wife."

They watched as the woman moved around Mark, her hands caressing his arms, his face, begging him for some response. He blinked his eyes at her, but she begged him to try saying something. When she didn't get her desired response, the woman ran to the door, opened it, stepped into the hall, and frantically called for the nurse.

A few minutes later, the nurse, who had been sitting at the desk, walked into the room. "Is there a problem, Mrs. Davis?"

"It is the wife," Marie told Eva.

Mrs. Davis, who now stood at Mark's bedside, turned to face the nurse, not realizing Eva and Marie stood in front of her, blocking the nurse from her view. Well, they would have blocked her from view had she been a medium.

"My husband. He moved the box of tissues. He moved it!"

"I don't understand."

Mrs. Davis leaned down and picked up the box of tissues from the floor. She carried it to the nurse. Had Eva and Marie not quickly moved to the side, she would have walked through them.

"When I stepped out of the room to talk to you, this was sitting on his nightstand. I remember because I took a tissue from the box. When I came back, it was sitting on his bed with him. He had to have gotten it. He moved! He must be getting better!"

The nurse frowned at Mrs. Davis, took the box of tissues from her, and walked toward the patient. After setting the box back on the nightstand, the nurse checked Mark's vitals while Mrs. Davis hovered nearby, incessantly asking questions that went unanswered.

"She seems to care about her husband," Eva observed.

"I must admit, I feel somewhat guilty. It's entirely possible Olivia's ex-husband had nothing to do with Olivia's kidnapping, and now I've gotten his poor wife's hopes up."

Eva and Marie spent the next thirty minutes watching from the sidelines. A doctor was eventually called in, and after rechecking the patient, the doctor and nurse stepped into the hallway, leaving Mrs. Davis hovering anxiously over her husband.

Marie followed the doctor and nurse into the hallway while Eva remained in the room.

"He's the same," the doctor told the nurse.

"She insists the tissue box was on the nightstand when she stepped out of the room. And it was on the bed when she returned a couple of minutes later. I was at my desk; no one else entered his room while she was talking to me. How else would the tissue box move from the table to his bed if he didn't move it?"

"I know how it got there, and our patient didn't move it."

"You do?" Marie asked aloud, curious what the doctor thought he knew.

"Please tell me," the nurse said.

"It's not that complicated. Joy Davis has been spending every afternoon with her husband for the last couple of weeks. She's exhausted. Emotionally drained. It's obvious to me she moved the box herself and just doesn't remember."

The nurse considered the doctor's suggestion before saying, "Well, she said she took a tissue from the box, so I suppose she might have absently picked it up without thinking and then didn't remember."

CHAPTER TWENTY-NINE

Marie had the woman's name now: Joy Davis. Marie guessed the second Mrs. Davis was in her mid to late twenties, and from what she had heard about Olivia's sons, this made Joy younger than her two stepsons. Joy wore her silky, dark, shoulder-length hair in a pageboy hairstyle with bangs. Marie might describe her as pleasantly attractive, but not someone with stunning good looks like her granddaughter-in-law, Melony.

Joy's dress reminded Marie of something a conservative girl might have worn to church in the early 1960s, before trends and styles began changing with the hippie movement. If Joy removed the cardigan sweater she wore with her dress and exposed her arms, Marie doubted she would see any tattoos. There were no facial piercings, and even the simple pearl earrings Joy wore appeared to be clip-ons.

Marie and Eva watched as Joy stood next to her husband's bed, as if staring long enough might will him to talk.

"I know you can hear me, Mark."

Mark's eyes moved, his gaze shifting to his young wife.

Joy smiled. "They don't believe you moved that box, but I know you did. It really doesn't matter what they believe. Just keep fighting. Fight for me. Fight for us."

Joy closed her eyes, her hands now resting on Mark's right shoulder. After a moment, she opened her eyes and looked at her husband. "I have to go soon. I'd stay longer, but your father called me earlier. He's stopping by the house tonight. He says we need to talk."

Mark's eyes blinked in rapid succession. Joy reached out, stroked the side of his face, and then leaned over and gave him a gentle kiss on one cheek. "I know you can hear me. And you're probably wondering why Aaron and Joshua haven't come to see you lately." She paused for a moment, her eyes never leaving her husband's face. After absently licking her lips, she said, "They're just busy with the business. They're taking care of everything, so you don't have to worry. They don't want you to worry. They just want you to get better. We all do. We need you, Mark. We need you to get better. We need you to fight."

"Who are Aaron and Joshua?" Eva asked.

"I believe those are the names of Olivia and Mark's sons."

Eva looked at Marie. "Didn't you tell me Olivia's ex-husband was losing his business?"

"Yes, according to what Edward told Walt and Danielle, notice of the lawsuit happened before his stroke. I'm not sure how long before. And I don't know if the business filed for bankruptcy before or after the stroke. Edward wasn't clear on that. But if he wasn't aware of the severity of the situation prior to the stroke, it would explain her comments."

"I can understand a wife not wanting her husband to worry about something he can't control, especially when he needs to focus on getting better."

Marie and Eva continued to watch Joy, who dutifully attended to Mark by rearranging his blanket, stroking his face, checking his pillow, and whispering words of encouragement.

Finally, Joy looked at her watch and then looked back at her husband before stepping closer. "I must go now, love. Your father is coming to the house in about thirty minutes, and we know how he is. I can't be late." She leaned over the bed, kissed his forehead, and whispered a final, "Goodbye, I love you."

MARIE AND EVA SAT IN THE BACK SEAT OF JOY'S CAR AS THEY DROVE away from the nursing home.

"Do you really think she's taking us to her home?" Eva asked.

Marie shrugged. "Considering how she's dressed, I don't think she's planning to stop at a bar and find someone closer to her age. And she seems quite smitten with her husband."

Eva shrugged. "Or it might be an excellent performance."

Marie glanced over at Eva. "Why do you say that?"

"I was thinking about how well Anthony performed for me. Of course, he left me when I got ill, so perhaps she does love her husband."

Marie understood what Eva meant. Eva's husband, an actor named Anthony Taylor, had wooed her, then married her for her money, and left her when she became ill—after stealing from her.

"True, but she wasn't aware she had an audience."

"But she believes her husband can hear her and might get better. And as long as she believes that's possible, she'd be wise to keep up the act, if it is an act."

"Eva, I don't remember you being this much of a cynic."

"My time in the theater taught me pretty young women rarely go after much older men for love."

Marie let out a sigh. "According to Edward, there isn't much left for Mark Davis to offer her financially. And don't forget Heather, she's certainly not with Brian for his money."

Eva laughed. "Heather is not your typical pretty young woman, and she has proven time and time again that she is the antithesis of a gold digger."

They arrived at a large Tudor-style home on an acre lot in an upscale neighborhood. After pulling into the driveway, Joy used her remote to open the garage door. The car sat for a moment in the driveway, the engine running, while waiting for the garage door to open all the way. Once it was open, Joy pulled into the three-car garage, parked, turned off the engine, and pressed the remote to close the garage door.

Marie and Eva moved out of the car while Joy removed her seatbelt and gathered up her purse and jacket. While waiting for Joy, the spirits looked around the large garage. A blue truck was parked next to Joy's car. What looked like storage—cardboard boxes and file cabinets—filled the third parking space on the other side of the truck.

After Joy got out of her car, Marie and Eva followed her into the house. Eva stayed with Joy while Marie moved through the rooms on the second floor, looking for any information or clues that might lead them to the kidnappers, should Mark be involved.

Joy entered the house through the garage entrance and walked directly to a coat closet, where she hung up her jacket and purse. From there she visited the downstairs bathroom. Joy stepped out of the bathroom a few minutes later and immediately scurried around the rooms on the first floor. She gathered up the used coffee cup left on a living room table, straightened the pillows on the sofa, walked into the kitchen and quickly moved all the dishes from the sink into the dishwasher, along with the mug she had brought from the living room.

Eva watched as Joy rushed around the rooms, hastily tidying up. About fifteen minutes after arriving home, the doorbell rang. Joy froze for a moment, stood straight, and moved her palms over her hair, coaxing the waves back into a pageboy before answering the door.

JOY CALLED HIM PASTOR DAVIS. SHE DIDN'T CALL HIM DAD OR USE his first name. He looked to be about the age Marie presented—eighties—not as spry, with a full head of white hair. He walked with a cane and didn't wait for Joy to invite him in. The moment she opened the door, he walked straight into the house and to the living room, not bothering to shut the door behind him.

Joy silently shut the front door and followed her father-in-law into the living room. He took a seat on the only leather recliner in the room, reminding Eva of a king claiming his throne. He didn't recline the chair; Eva doubted he could get back up if he did. Instead, he sat hunched in the chair while his hand remained firmly on the cane's handle, the base of the cane next to his right foot.

"Can I get you anything to drink?" Joy asked, still standing.

Pastor Davis pointed to the sofa with his cane. "No. Sit down so we can talk."

Joy nodded and obediently sat down. As she did, Marie entered the room.

"I assume this is the father-in-law she mentioned?" Marie asked Eva.

"I'm pretty sure he is. She called him Pastor Davis when she greeted him."

"How is my son?" Pastor Davis asked.

"He's improved." Joy smiled.

Pastor Davis arched his brows. "He has? How so?"

Joy told him about the tissue box and how the doctor didn't seem to believe her.

"I suspect this is a sign from the Good Lord. We need to bring him home. You can take care of him here."

"He's not ready to come home. And I don't think we can afford to hire a home nurse."

"Mark does not need a home nurse; he has a wife. Joy, when you married Mark, you understood your job as a wife was to give your husband children, make a home, and be your husband's helpmate. It has been over a year, and I wonder, how are you fulfilling your duties as a wife?"

"Pastor Davis, I've been a devoted wife to Mark. And I want to give him children. But...the Lord just hasn't blessed us. And now..."

"And now, yes. Perhaps this is what the Lord intended for you."

Joy frowned. "I don't understand?"

"You are his wife, and we are bringing him home. And you will care for him. He belongs at home with his family. And if the Lord is willing, Mark will get better, and you will give him children. But for now, you need to prepare for his homecoming."

"She doesn't look excited about that suggestion," Eva said.

"I don't think it was a suggestion. Sounded like an order," Marie said.

"But—" Joy started to say something, but Pastor Davis cut her off.

"You need to remember something, Joy. This house you live in does not belong to Mark. If you aren't willing to care for your husband here, then that means he will be staying in the nursing home. If he does that, there is no reason for me to keep this house. I might as well sell it. Do you understand?"

Joy sat rigidly on the sofa and stared at Pastor Davis, her hands twisting together in her lap. After a moment, she gave a nod.

Pastor Davis smiled at his daughter-in-law and glanced at his watch before looking back at her. "When are my grandsons going to be here?"

"Um…I couldn't get ahold of them."

"I told you to tell them to meet us here this evening."

"They didn't answer their phones. I don't think they're back."

Pastor Davis frowned. "I might be old, but I am aware of cell phones. It no longer requires being at home for a person to answer their phone. And just where are they?"

Joy shook her head. "They didn't tell me. The only reason I even know they're gone is because Joshua told the nurses that they wouldn't be coming in to see Mark for a while because they would be out of town indefinitely. I assumed they told you."

"What do you mean out of town? Indefinitely? This is no time to be out of town. What about Mark's office?"

"They did what you told them to do. The office was emptied before the bank came in."

"That's impossible. I checked this morning, and they haven't put anything in the church's storage room."

"They didn't take it there. Everything is in the garage."

Pastor Davis's voice rose. "What garage?"

Joy pointed toward her garage. "There was plenty of room."

"I told them explicitly to bring everything to the church and put it in the storage room. Why did they bring it here?"

Joy shrugged. "I don't know why they brought it here. I assumed you had changed your mind."

"Have you gone through any of it?" Pastor Davis demanded.

Joy frowned. "No. Why would I? I heard you tell them to just quickly box everything up and move it and not to go through it until you were there."

"Why didn't you tell me the boys were gone when I called you this morning?"

"I…um…actually, I started to, but you hung up before I could."

Pastor Davis scowled. "First, they stop coming to church services, then they can't follow simple instructions, and now they disappear while their father is in the nursing home, telling no one where they went. This is unacceptable!" Firmly gripping the handle of his cane, he lifted it from the floor and then slammed it down, making a cracking sound on the hardwood floor.

"He's a charming man," Eva noted.

CHAPTER THIRTY

Brian and Heather arrived first at Pier Café on Friday morning and secured a booth large enough for their group. Before Walt and Danielle arrived with Addison and Jack, Heather had already gotten Carla to bring over two highchairs to their table. Carla looked a little insulted when Heather recleaned the highchair trays after Carla had just wiped them down, but she said nothing.

Chris's car pulled into the pier parking lot at the same time as Danielle's Flex. They parked next to each other. When they walked into Pier Café a few minutes later, Chris was carrying Jack, Walt had Addison, and Danielle carried the diaper bag, while the double stroller remained in the back of the Flex.

It wasn't until they were all settled at the table, and Carla had brought them coffee, taken their order, and left to put in the order, that they started talking about Olivia.

"Marie and Eva aren't back?" Heather asked.

Danielle, who had just picked up her cup of coffee, paused before taking a sip and said, "They haven't stopped by Marlow House. Chris said he hasn't seen them, and I assume you haven't either."

"I wonder if they're still there." Heather reached over to the highchair closest to her and pretended to grab a piece of fruit Danielle had set on the tray. Addison quickly snatched it from Heather, shoved it into her own mouth, and giggled. Heather grinned at the little face.

"According to the chief, he's releasing information to the press this afternoon about Olivia being found," Brian told them.

"What exactly is he planning to tell them?" Walt asked.

"Just that she's at the hospital but doing well and should go home this afternoon."

"This afternoon? I thought it wouldn't be until this weekend," Danielle said.

Brian shrugged. "They're letting her go home today. But it won't be until this afternoon."

"What else is he telling the press?" Danielle asked. "He's not going to say she was kidnapped or where she was held, is he?"

"No. He'll say it's still an active investigation, and all that he can tell them is that she has been found, and while she was suffering severe dehydration, she is doing better now."

"And you found nothing at the cabin that could help find the kidnappers?" Chris asked.

"We couldn't go to the cabin until after the doctor said Olivia was well enough to be interviewed," Brian began.

"Yeah, they couldn't really explain to Joe and the others how they knew which cabin it was, since Olivia hadn't been able to answer questions yet."

"When our people got out there, it was exactly as Marie said, cleaned out. Joe and some others were convinced Olivia was confused, and it was a different cabin, because there was no cage and they couldn't see how the kidnappers could have removed something that size between the time we found her and they got there. But they expanded the search, looking at the other cabins in the area, and found a stack of wire panels dumped off one of the side roads. They hadn't been there long; no rust. And it looks like it could be the cage Olivia described. It's all in pieces, but we're confident that's what was in that basement. It appeared to be homemade, and so far, we haven't had any luck tracing its origins."

They stopped discussing Olivia's case when Carla returned to the table with their order. After she handed out all the food, she looked at Brian and asked, "When's the police department announcing Olivia's been found? I figured it would be in this morning's newspaper."

Brian stared at Carla for a moment before answering, "What are you talking about?"

With one hand on hip and a sigh, Carla rolled her eyes at Brian. "I know she's at the hospital. Is it supposed to be some secret?"

"Why do you say that?"

Carla's confidence slipped, as did her hand from her hip. "You mean Olivia isn't at the hospital?"

Brian begrudgingly conceded, "Yes, she is. But how did you know?"

Carla's confidence returned, as did her smile. "I saw her sister at the hospital when I dropped something off for one of our regulars. Figured she had to be visiting her sister. I mean, why else would she be there? Is Olivia okay? What happened?"

"She's going to be fine, but I can't really discuss it, as it's still an open investigation."

"An open investigation? Why? What happened?"

"Carla, yesterday, did you mention anything about Olivia being at the hospital to anyone?" Walt asked before Brian could respond to Carla's question.

Carla looked over to Walt and absently chewed her lower lip a moment before answering, "I might have said something to Earl when he asked if I had taken the soup over to the hospital."

"Earl? The cook?"

"Yeah. Although he said just because I saw Olivia's sister at the hospital doesn't mean Olivia was there. The only other people I remember mentioning it to, a couple of fishermen I waited on. One of them was reading the paper and asked me if the woman had been found. I told him I thought she had been because I saw her sister at the hospital, and since she didn't live here, I figured she was there visiting Olivia."

CARLA HAD LEFT THE TABLE, AND THEY WERE IN THE MIDDLE OF eating breakfast when Marie suddenly appeared. "I saw your note," Marie announced, referring to the note Danielle had left on the kitchen table that morning, saying they would be at Pier Café having breakfast.

"Marie's here," Heather told Brian, although he had already figured that out when the twins suddenly got excited, and then a piece of scrambled egg floated up from Jack's highchair tray and into Jack's open mouth.

"Where is Eva?" Danielle asked.

"She's back at Marlow House, waiting for us. We should probably talk there," Marie said.

AFTER FINISHING BREAKFAST, THE GROUP LEFT PIER CAFÉ AND joined Eva at Marlow House. They all gathered in the living room, with Addison and Jack on the floor with Heather sitting between them. Heather quietly listened to what Eva and Marie had to say while passively allowing Addison to play with her hair, and Jack piled puzzle pieces on her lap.

Marie had just recounted all they had witnessed at the nursing home and the encounter between Joy Davis and her father-in-law.

"So you don't think the husband has anything to do with the kidnapping?" Danielle asked after recounting for Brian what Marie had said.

Marie shrugged. "I don't see how he could have. Didn't he have his stroke weeks before the kidnapping? And that man we saw, while he's still in there, it doesn't look like someone capable of masterminding anything. If we're going on the premise that the motive for the kidnapping was to kill Olivia, and the motive for the murder was to cash out on the insurance policy, Mark Davis would have to be the one behind this. I suppose it's possible he planned this before his stroke, but if someone hired you to kill someone for money—assuming he hired someone—would you go through with the murder if he couldn't pay you?"

Again, Danielle repeated, as best she could, what Marie had said for Brian, and then added, "Unless he has an accomplice who could pay the kidnappers."

"Like his wife?" Heather asked.

Danielle shrugged. "If the policy is still in Olivia's ex's name, his current wife could be his accomplice. If the lawsuit came before the stroke, then it's possible he was afraid of losing everything and then remembered the life insurance policy. Maybe he told his wife about his plan. Maybe she helped him."

"Marie went back to the nursing home and stayed with the husband after the charming pastor left. The young wife did nothing to make me think she was involved. If anything, I felt a little sorry for her. I don't imagine this is the life she signed up for. She did a lot of crying," Eva explained.

"As for the husband, he slept off and on, and when he woke up, nothing suggested he's faking his condition," Marie added.

Heather repeated for Brian what Eva and Marie had just said.

"Even if Davis had conspired with his wife and the kidnappers were successful in killing Olivia, I'm not sure his new wife could have gotten her hands on that insurance money. I'd expect his sons to fight her in court, and if I were a hitman, I wouldn't risk prison without a guarantee of payment," Chris said.

"Before Pastor Davis arrived, I searched through the house, and while I found nothing incriminating regarding the kidnapping, I learned something interesting about the young wife, which makes me wonder about their marriage," Marie said.

"What?" Heather asked.

"I found a packet of birth control pills hidden in a box of tampons in the bathroom. The prescription is hers."

"Strange place to store your birth control pills," Heather mused, "but what was interesting about it?"

Brian frowned at Heather, wondering what Marie or Eva had said about birth control pills and what they had to do with the conversation. But he remained silent, waiting for someone to explain.

"From the conversation we overheard between the young wife and her father-in-law, it sounded like she was trying to get pregnant. Which she obviously wasn't. What I found interesting, the prescription for the pills was not from a local pharmacy. Which makes me wonder, did her husband realize she was on the pill, or did he believe they were trying for a baby?"

"You never know what goes on in a marriage, but if she did marry a much older man more for his money, and then discovered his business was having problems, it's not surprising she wouldn't be eager to get pregnant," Danielle said.

"From the conversation Marie and I overheard between her and her father-in-law, it didn't sound like the young bride knew much about her husband's company. Didn't Olivia tell you her husband had been controlling? Why would he change now with his new wife? While she seemed to care for him, she might also be a little afraid. From what the nice pastor said, if she doesn't agree to become a nurse to her husband, she'll be out on the street," Eva said.

"So, we've checked off Olivia's ex and his new bride as possible suspects. The ex because the only way he could have been involved at this point was if he hired someone, who likely would not get paid now that he's practically in a coma. And the new wife would have a hard time accessing the funds, another reason hitmen would walk away. Plus, considering the controlling history of Olivia's ex, is he really the type to bring his young wife into this? That would give her too much power over him," Chris summarized.

"Don't forget the sons," Danielle reminded them. "It's possible they were added as the beneficiaries years ago, and the money wouldn't go to their father anyway."

"And according to the young bride, they are both missing," Eva said.

Brian left Marlow House that morning with more questions than answers, while Heather and Chris said their goodbyes and headed back to work at the foundation headquarters.

Right after they left, Danielle called Shanice with an offer. The offer was for Marie to stay with them after Olivia came home—until the kidnappers were caught. Shanice asked, "What happens if they are never caught?" Danielle didn't have an answer for her.

Friday afternoon, Police Chief MacDonald sent out a press release, informing the community that Olivia Davis had been found, and no details would be released at this time. When Olivia was released from the hospital, Shanice didn't pick her up; instead, Brian brought her home.

Danielle, Shanice, Marie, and Olivia sat in Olivia's living room late Friday afternoon. Brian had left twenty minutes earlier, and Olivia spent most of that time thanking Danielle and Marie for all their help. Shanice sat quietly, listening to her sister, while her gaze continually drifted to the rocking chair in the corner where Marie currently sat. She didn't know the ghost sat on the chair because Danielle had told her—it was the steady rocking that convinced her this was all real.

"I need to show you something," Danielle announced during a lull in the conversation. She stood up and walked to Olivia, her cell phone in hand. "Do you recognize this little girl? Have you ever seen her before?"

Danielle opened her photo app, found the photo of Cassandra and Max, and handed the phone to Olivia.

Curious, Olivia took the phone from Danielle and looked at it. She froze momentarily, and her eyes widened. Olivia stared at the phone, saying nothing.

"Do you know who it is?" Danielle asked again.

Olivia didn't respond immediately. Instead, she continued to stare at the picture on the screen. Finally, she nodded and said in a quiet voice, her eyes never leaving the picture, "Yes. It's my grand-daughter."

CHAPTER THIRTY-ONE

Shanice frowned at her sister. "Granddaughter? What are you talking about?"

Still clutching the cell phone, Olivia closed her eyes and absently licked her lips. When she opened her eyes again, she said, "I'm sorry, Shanice. I didn't tell you because, well, at the time I didn't really expect you to believe me when I told you about astral projecting."

"What does this have to do with astral projecting?"

Ignoring her sister's question, Olivia looked up into Danielle's eyes. "I don't understand, why do you have Cassandra's picture? Is that your cat, Max, with her?"

Danielle took the phone from Olivia and sat on the sofa next to her. "You're saying Cassandra is your granddaughter?"

Olivia took the phone back and looked again at the picture on the screen. She nodded. "She's grown up in the last year."

Shanice stood up and hurried across the room, snatching the phone from her sister's hand. She looked at the picture and then back at Olivia. "Since when do you have a granddaughter?"

"I promise I'll explain. But first, tell me, is Cassandra at Marlow House?" Olivia asked.

Shanice handed the cell phone to Danielle and returned to her seat.

"She was, but she isn't right now. But she is in Frederickport."

"With her parents?" Olivia asked.

"With her mother."

Olivia's forehead furrowed. "Not her father?"

"No. But please explain," Danielle urged.

The living room at Olivia's house went quiet for a few minutes while Olivia collected her thoughts. Finally, she said, "After I left Mark, my sons made it very clear they wanted nothing to do with me. I had lost all my friends when I left Mark, I had no one there to keep me updated on how my boys were doing, so I did what most people do these days; I followed them on social media. In my case, that was Facebook."

"But you deleted your Facebook account," Shanice said.

Olivia smiled apologetically at her sister and looked back to Danielle. "I tried calling my sons the day after arriving at my parents' house. I figured by that time they had read the letter I left and understood why I had to leave without telling them. But they had blocked me on their phones. I started looking at their Facebook accounts every day; I just wanted to see them. They had posted nothing on social media about me leaving, and I didn't try reaching them through DM. But by the end of the week, they had both blocked me on Facebook. Our church had a Facebook account, and I was blocked on that one too. All the people who I thought were my friends from church, they also blocked me. I tried calling a few, but they didn't answer their phones. It was painful; I couldn't even watch my sons through social media."

"I'm so sorry," Danielle whispered.

"Shanice told me I was just torturing myself and to delete my Facebook account. She was right. I was dead to people whom I had loved, and who I believed had loved me. And every time I logged into my account, I was reminded of that."

"I assume you created a new account?" Danielle asked.

"It was a few years later. I didn't do it right away. I created a fake persona, using a picture of a dog I'd taken as my profile picture. In my account profile, I identified as a dog mom and made it look like the profile pic was my dog, Bosco. Of course, I didn't really have a dog. I didn't tell Shanice, or anyone, about my fake account, not wanting them to worry about me. I spent time lurking. Discovered Joshua had gotten married to a pretty girl named Mary. From what I pasted together from their social media posts, she had moved to town around the same time that I left, and they started dating not long after that. And then they had a baby…Cassandra. The following year, Aaron married. He now has three children."

"You have four grandchildren, and you never told me?" Shanice asked.

"I understood how much you worried about me after the boys refused to talk to me, especially after they had the attorney send me that letter. So I said nothing."

"And you astral projected to Cassandra?" Danielle asked.

"Not right away, of course. I didn't start exploring astral projection until much later. But a few months before I moved here, I started visiting my grandchildren when they were at church. It was the one place I could see them all at the same time. But the last time I did it, I decided to go to Joshua's house, and when Cassandra saw me, she smiled at me and said, *You're the lady from church*. Her words surprised me—she could see me. It scared me, and my spirit-self returned to my body. It wasn't something I consciously did. One minute my granddaughter is asking me a question, and the next I'm in my body again. I never returned. I didn't understand why she could see me. Not until I moved here. Cassandra is a medium, isn't she?"

W HEN D ANIELLE RETURNED TO M ARLOW H OUSE, SHE DID something without telling Olivia—she called Police Chief MacDonald and told him about the connection between Cassandra and Olivia. She felt a little guilty about not telling Olivia what she intended to do, but Olivia was still recovering from her harrowing experience, and she didn't want her to worry about the police interviewing her daughter-in-law. Olivia was also confused why her daughter-in-law had moved to Frederickport with her grand-daughter and was now cleaning houses. Danielle didn't have an answer for Olivia, but she hoped the chief would find it for her.

MARY LEARNED THE NEWS HER MOTHER-IN-LAW HAD BEEN FOUND from her landlord, Allen's wife, Nancy Martin. Of course, Nancy wasn't aware her tenant had a connection to the missing librarian, and what information she had to share was minimal; at least, nothing more than—*Did you hear they found the missing librarian? She's alive and I guess okay. They haven't said where she was.*

Cassandra sat at the kitchen table, practicing her cursive handwriting. Mary, wanting more information on Olivia, joined her daughter at the table and began using her tablet to surf for news about Olivia. She had only been sitting at the table for about five minutes when a knock came at her door. Assuming it was her landlord, whom she had been talking to ten minutes earlier, she threw the door open without checking the peephole. To her surprise, she found a female police officer standing at the door.

"Ms. Walsh?" the officer asked.

"Yes?" Mary glanced briefly at the kitchen table. Cassandra had stopped writing and watched her mother and the officer from the table. Mary looked back at the police officer.

The officer handed Mary a business card. "I'm Officer Carpenter."

Mary took the card from the woman's hand and looked at it.

"Is your legal name Mary Davis?"

Still holding the card in her hand, Mary looked up at Officer Carpenter. "Umm…yes. But Walsh is my maiden name."

"I need you to come down to the police station with me."

Mary sat nervously at the table in the interrogation room, Officer Brian Henderson sitting across from her. They had assured her Cassandra would be safe with Officer Carpenter and was just down the hall with her in the break room. There were some cookies in the break room, they told her, and if it was okay with Mary, Cassandra could have some. Mary gave her permission.

"I don't understand why I'm here."

"What is your relationship with Olivia Davis?"

"Um…I don't have a relationship with Olivia Davis. I've never met her."

"So you don't know who she is? You have no familial connection with her?"

"Um…I didn't say that. I know who she is. But I've never met her."

"And the fact that your legal surname is the same as her surname is merely a coincidence?"

Mary shifted uncomfortably in her seat. "She's my daughter's paternal grandmother. But neither of us has ever met her before."

"What do you know of her disappearance?"

Mary, who had been staring down at the table, looked up at Brian. "Just what I've read in the newspaper and from what was said over at Marlow House. But I didn't realize she was missing until Mr. Marlow told me. My landlord mentioned this afternoon that she has been found. Is she okay? Where was she?"

"Why are you in Frederickport? Why are you using your maiden name?"

Mary looked back down at the table and licked her lips before answering, "I left my husband."

"Why did you come to Frederickport?"

Mary looked back up at Brian. "I wanted to meet my mother-in-law. I wanted to talk to her. But I didn't want to just show up on her doorstep. After I rented a room through Frederickport Vacation Properties, I couldn't believe my good luck, because Adam Nichols got me a job interview with the Marlows, and they live right next door to my mother-in-law. I thought it was divine intervention. But then Mr. Marlow told me she was missing."

"Why was it so important to meet the mother-in-law you had never met, especially if you had just left her son?"

Mary shrugged. "It's personal."

Brian leaned forward, resting his elbows on the table. "Mrs. Davis—or Walsh, whichever you want to call yourself—things that one might consider personal become public when murder is involved."

Mary's eyes widened. "Murder?"

"Attempted murder. Someone tried to kill your mother-in-law, and we are trying to find out who. So, once again, I am asking you, why did you want to visit Olivia Davis?"

TALL AND LANKY, CHIEF MACDONALD'S YOUNGEST SON, EVAN, looked older than his twelve years. Last week he had convinced his father he didn't need a haircut, and while his hair didn't touch his shoulders, his dark curls were thick and wild. His maturity for his age didn't surprise the adults closest to him. When a boy grows up seeing and talking to ghosts, it tends to mature them.

Instead of going straight home after school, he had gone to the police station. His older brother, Eddy Jr., was meeting him there because they planned to go out for tacos after their dad got off work.

But when he got to the station, they told him his dad was busy, something about monitoring an interview with a person of interest, so Evan waited for his father in the break room. The lady at the front desk mentioned something about cookies in there, and he was always hungry when he got home from school.

When Evan walked into the break room, he was surprised to find a little girl sitting at a table with Officer Carpenter.

"Hi, Evan. How was school?" Carpenter greeted.

"It was okay." Evan walked to the plate of cookies and picked up two. When doing so, he smiled at the girl and said, "Hello."

"Cassandra, I'd like you to meet Evan," Carpenter introduced. "And Evan, this is Cassandra. Her mother is in with Brian, and

Cassandra is waiting for her here, with me. Cassandra, Evan is the police chief's son."

Cassandra smiled up at Evan. "Hello."

Recognition dawned for Evan—his father had told him about the little nine-year-old girl named Cassandra—a medium.

"Evan, are you going to be here for a little bit?" Carpenter asked.

"Yeah. Waiting for Dad and Eddy. When Dad gets off work, we're going out for tacos."

Carpenter stood. "Would you mind staying with Cassandra a few minutes, keep her company until her mother is done? I need to…umm…visit the ladies' room; then I need to check on something."

"Sure, no problem."

Evan took a seat at the table, across from Cassandra.

"You'll be in safe hands, Cassandra. If you need anything, just ask Evan."

Cassandra nodded shyly but said nothing. She looked over at Evan—he looked back.

Once Carpenter was out of earshot, Evan said, "I'm kind of glad she left. I wanted to tell you something."

Cassandra frowned. "What?"

"I heard about you."

"Heard what?"

Evan took a bite of his cookie after saying, "That you can see ghosts."

Cassandra's eyes widened. Evan thought she might bolt.

"Don't panic, but I just wanted you to know in case you need someone to talk to—someone instead of an adult. I'm like you. I've been seeing ghosts all my life."

CHAPTER THIRTY-TWO

Cassandra didn't immediately respond to Evan's declaration. Instead, she stared at him until she finally asked, "Who told you about me?"

Evan's first impulse was to tell the truth—his father had told him. But Evan stopped himself, understanding that should Cassandra—a girl he had just met—decide to finally tell her mother she was a medium—a mother who, according to his father, believed seeing spirits meant a person was consorting with demons—and that the police chief accepted his own son could see ghosts—well, that could ultimately cause his dad major problems. If Cassandra's mother confronted his father and asked, *Police Chief MacDonald, do you believe your son can see ghosts?* Would his father feel compelled to tell the truth? And if he told the truth, it could blow up his career.

Evan cringed to think of the implications of that. So instead of answering her question directly, he said, "I know you've talked to Marie. The man who rented your mom the place you're staying at, his name is Adam Nichols. Marie is Adam's grandma. She died a few years ago. But she decided to stick around for a while. Marie helps people. She's a friend of mine. I know you saw her, talked to her. You also saw the ghost of Allen Martin. I've never met him, but I've heard about him."

Cassandra studied Evan for a moment and then asked, "Have you met Mrs. Marlow?"

"You mean Danielle? Yeah. She's a friend of mine, and she was the first person who helped me. Danielle's like you and me. She's been seeing ghosts since she was a little girl. Her parents thought she was crazy, so she stopped telling them. This isn't something you go around telling people. Even people you love. It wasn't that long ago that I finally told my older brother."

<hr>

BACK IN THE INTERROGATION ROOM, BRIAN AGAIN ASKED MARY, "Why did you want to meet with Olivia Davis?"

Mary sat up straight in the chair, staring down at her hands folded before her on the tabletop. After a moment she looked up to Brian. "Well…I wanted Cassandra to meet her grandmother."

"But why now?"

Mary glanced back down at her hands still clutched together on the table, each thumb now moving quickly around the other thumb. Without looking up, she said, "One reason, my husband never wanted his mother in his daughter's life. But he was wrong, and after we separated, I thought it might be good for Cassandra to meet her grandmother."

"It's one thing to reach out to a relative you've never met, and another to move to their town when you have no other connection to that town, without a job or a place to stay. It would make more sense to me if you had tried meeting her when you first arrived in Frederickport—or checked into a motel instead of a long-term rental. You claim you didn't realize Olivia was missing when you showed up to work at Marlow House that first day. You obviously assumed she was next door. What were you waiting for? Why didn't you go to her house? Why rent an apartment and look for a job first?"

Mary shrugged and looked up at Brian. "I didn't want to rent a motel; it was too expensive. I had to stay somewhere, so it just made sense to get something for a month; it was cheaper in the long run. And knocking on someone's front door and introducing yourself as their daughter-in-law is not all that easy. Why does any of this matter? Can I just leave?"

Brian's cell phone rang. He looked at it and stood. "I'll be right back."

Brian stepped out into the hallway at the same time as Chief MacDonald, who had been in the adjoining room, monitoring the interview.

"We have no grounds to hold Ms. Walsh," the chief began.

"You mean Mrs. Davis."

"Either one, but she just asked if she could leave, and as we both know, she can. But I would like to find out more about why she came to visit Olivia—why now? I don't believe in coincidences."

Hands on hips, Brian glanced back to the closed door of the interrogation room. "Her being in Frederickport is in some way connected to the kidnapping."

"I agree. While we have to let her leave, there is another way we can get the information from her."

"How's that?"

"Let her talk to Olivia."

WHEN BRIAN RETURNED TO THE INTERROGATION ROOM, HE FOUND Mary still sitting at the table, now clutching her purse. "Can I go?"

"It's your right to refuse to answer my questions; I can't make you stay. You're free to go. But I understand Officer Carpenter drove you here. Instead of driving you back to your apartment, I'd like you to let me take you and your daughter somewhere else."

Frowning, Mary clutched her purse tighter. "Where?"

"Olivia Davis's house."

"Why would you take me there? I—"

Brian raised his palm, silently asking Mary to let him finish. "Olivia Davis is already aware that you and your daughter are in

Frederickport. She knows who you are. Who your daughter is. That's who told me who you are. If you don't want to tell me the real reason you came to Frederickport, then you can just tell her. After all, according to you, that's why you're here, to meet her, to talk to her."

"Now?" Mary squeaked.

Brian glanced at the clock on the wall. "Not this minute; it will take at least twenty minutes to get to her house because I assume before we leave the station, you'll want to take a little time and explain to your daughter where we're going and whom she'll be meeting. I can bring Cassandra here, where you can talk to her in private."

Mary considered Brian's proposal for a moment. Finally, she asked, "Olivia knows I'm here?"

Brian nodded. "Yes."

"There's only one problem: I would rather talk to Olivia alone before introducing her to my daughter. There are things I need to tell her that I don't want to say in front of Cassandra. To be honest, it's one reason I didn't just knock on her door. I needed to find a safe place for Cassandra to stay when I first talked to her."

"Would you have a problem with Cassandra staying next door with Danielle when you talk to her?"

"Mrs. Marlow?"

Brian smiled. "Yes. Danielle is a friend of mine, and I'm aware your daughter has already spent some time with her. Danielle and Olivia are friends, not just neighbors. She is also aware Cassandra is Olivia's granddaughter."

"She is? How?"

"I suppose you can ask Olivia about that when you meet her. I understand Danielle spent the afternoon with Olivia and her sister."

"SHE'S COMING NOW?" OLIVIA ASKED. DANIELLE HAD JUST returned to Olivia's house after getting off the phone with Chief MacDonald. She stood in the living room, while Shanice and

Olivia sat on the sofa together, and Marie hovered nearby, listening.

"I'm sorry, but with everything going on and trying to find out who is behind your kidnapping, I had to tell the chief about Mary being your daughter-in-law."

Olivia nodded. "I understand. Mary is a stranger to me. And I'll admit, the fact she showed up in Frederickport now, it's troubling."

"Mary told Brian she came to Frederickport because she wanted to meet you. Why she came now, she wouldn't explain to him, although she said she and your son were separated."

Olivia arched her brows. "Separated?"

Danielle nodded. "Brian asked her to explain why she chose now to come, and she wouldn't say much aside from wanting her daughter to meet her grandmother. And while the chief doesn't feel she's part of the kidnapping, he wonders if something about her reason for coming might in some way be linked to the kidnapping attempt. He wants you to talk to her alone." Danielle paused for a moment and looked over at Marie and back to Olivia. "But you won't be alone. It would probably be best if Marie stayed with you."

AFTER DROPPING CASSANDRA OFF AT MARLOW HOUSE, BRIAN TOOK Mary next door to Olivia's. After formally introducing Mary to Olivia and Shanice, Brian and Shanice retreated to the kitchen while Olivia and Mary remained in the living room, with Olivia sitting on the sofa and Mary sitting on the chair next to the sofa.

They sat in uncomfortable silence for a few minutes before Mary asked, "How did you find out I was your daughter-in-law?"

"Facebook." Olivia smiled softly. "I suppose I've been stalking you since you married Joshua. But it was Cassandra I recognized."

Mary frowned. "I don't understand."

"After I got home this afternoon, Danielle came over from next door to welcome me home. We were chatting, and Danielle was trying to get my mind off my recent ordeal, and she started telling me about something funny Max—her cat—did. She showed me that picture she'd taken of him. I recognized Cassandra."

It wasn't entirely a lie. But Danielle had explained why she had taken that picture, and Olivia didn't want Mary to learn Danielle had had an alternative motive when photographing Cassandra.

"Oh my, what a strange coincidence," Mary murmured. She looked down at her folded hands.

"There are no coincidences," Marie muttered. Of course, neither Mary nor Olivia heard her.

"So why have you come? Why now? From what you told the police, you've left my son. Why? Why did you leave him?"

Mary looked up from her hands. "I left him for the same reason you left Joshua's father. But I took Cassandra with me because I couldn't leave her behind and let them fill my daughter's head with lies, like they did your sons."

CHAPTER THIRTY-THREE

Olivia sat quietly on her sofa, her eyes on Mary, waiting for her to explain what she had just said.

"I was raised by my grandmother. We moved from Austin during my senior year. Grandma and I started going to Pastor Davis's church; that's where I met Joshua. He was a year ahead of me. He'd already graduated, but we hit it off. I suppose one reason, he needed someone to talk to. He was so angry."

"This was right after I left his father," Olivia said softly.

Mary nodded, her hands still clasped together in her lap. "When he first met me, he asked about my parents. It was the second time I had gone to church with my grandmother. It was after the service, and we were in the fellowship hall. He knew I'd come to church with my grandmother and asked if my parents would ever come to church with us. I told him my father had died a long time ago, and my mother didn't want me. She'd taken off with a boyfriend, and my grandma took me in. I'm not sure why I blurted it out like that. But something made me say it."

"You said Joshua was so angry back then."

"Joshua once told me he never met anyone whose mother didn't want them, like his mother didn't want him—until me. I suppose that shared experience was the start of our relationship."

"I'm sorry about your mother. But I always wanted Joshua. I didn't leave him—I left his father."

Mary smiled sadly. "Yes, I understand that now. But you see, Joshua didn't back then; neither did I. Anyway, we kept seeing each other, we fell in love, and I got married right after high school graduation. Joshua was already working for his father's construction company. My grandma wasn't thrilled about me getting married so young, but she liked Joshua back then, and he had a good job."

"Back then? Did she come to not like him?"

Mary shrugged. "I understood marrying Joshua meant we would have a traditional marriage, a biblical marriage. I wanted that. He would be the head of the household. He promised to take care of me, and I vowed to love, cherish, and obey him until death do us part. And I meant it. We were happy for the first few years. I loved being a mother. Joshua made good money working for his father and was a good provider. I enjoyed fixing up our home, cooking, and taking care of my family. We wanted more children, but after Cassandra's birth, it wasn't happening. I suggested we talk to a doctor, but Pastor Davis told Joshua we just needed to pray on it."

"When did you stop being happy in your marriage?"

"When the controlling became suffocating. You asked if my grandma came to dislike Joshua. Not that she disliked him, but she felt he was too controlling. When Cassandra was about ready to start school, I realized I would have more free time. I told Joshua I wanted to get a job while she was in school or maybe take some classes at the junior college. He said no. He forbad me from getting a job, and he said if he didn't go to college, he wasn't going to spend money to send his wife to college, plus Pastor Davis did not approve of women going to college."

"Sounds like his father."

"Whenever I brought up college or getting a job, he'd get angry, tell me I was acting like his mother. He would say things like, are you going to run off and leave Cassandra like my mother left me… like your mother left you?"

"Sounds like that boy needs therapy," Marie muttered.

"Joshua also brought up homeschooling during these—*discussions*. We'd once talked about homeschooling when I was pregnant. Back then, we had agreed on sending our children to public school. But when I mentioned wanting to get a part-time job or going to school myself, he suddenly wanted me to homeschool Cassandra. After a while, I didn't want to argue anymore, so I agreed. Later, at church, Pastor Davis approached me, told me his grandson had told him I wanted to get a job, and if that was still true, he had one for me, and Joshua had already agreed I could accept it. The job, which I accepted, was working in the church nursery every Sunday. I didn't get paid. I never had my own money, not until about two years before my grandmother's death."

Olivia frowned. "What happened at that time?"

"One day my grandmother came to the house to see me. Joshua was at work, and Cassandra was playing in her room. Grandma sat me down and handed me a fat envelope. It had ten thousand dollars in cash in it. She told me she had been slowly emptying her savings account; she didn't want the tellers to start asking questions if she took out large amounts. It was most of her savings. Grandma didn't have any other real assets; she lived in a rented apartment and lived on her social security. She left about a thousand dollars in her account but gave me everything else."

"Why?"

"Grandma told me she had been planning this for some time. She assumed that if she lived long enough, she would eventually need to go into a nursing home, which happened the next year. She also understood her savings would cover maybe two months in a nursing home. So, she figured, since she would have to go on Medicaid anyway, it was wasteful to leave her money in her savings account, when it would be gobbled up before she went on Medicaid. So, every month for a couple of years, she would take money out of her savings and hide it in her freezer."

"Gives a new meaning to cold cash," Marie murmured.

"And she wanted you to have it?"

"Yes. She said if she died before going to a nursing home and left me the money in a will, she felt Joshua would demand I give it to him to manage. Even though he didn't have the right to take it, she knew I would give it to him to avoid conflict. She also knew, if she died before giving me the money, I would find it in her freezer because I would be the one to clean out her house, and when I lived with her, that's where she would keep our emergency fund. Growing up, she had always told me if something happened to her to take the money out of the freezer, keep it, and tell no one."

"She wanted you to have your own safety net?"

"Yes. She told me to hide it and not tell Joshua. Said this way, if I stayed with Joshua, it was because I wanted to stay, not because I had to."

"What made you decide to finally leave?"

"When I learned it had all been a lie. When Joshua learned it had all been a lie."

Olivia frowned. "What had been a lie?"

"About you leaving. How you didn't leave Joshua like he had been told."

"I still don't understand."

"Not sure how much you know, but your ex-husband's construction company was sued a while back. I don't have all the details—Joshua doesn't share those kinds of things with me. I just know they had to declare bankruptcy. But then Mark had a stroke, and he went from the hospital into a nursing home. Then one day, Pastor Davis calls up Joshua and tells him to get Aaron to help him remove everything from Mark's office because he heard through one of his parishioners that something had happened to the status of the bankruptcy and the bank would probably be coming in and locking down everything."

"I'm trying to follow this. Officer Henderson told me about the business and about Mark's stroke. But what does this have to do with me?"

"When moving the boxes, they came across something they weren't supposed to find."

"What?"

"A box filled with papers about your divorce. When Joshua realized what was inside the box, he brought it home instead of keeping it with the rest of the things he moved from his father's office. Frankly, I'm surprised Mark kept it all. I would have expected him to burn it all, not keep it for his sons to find someday."

"What kind of papers?"

"Legal papers, notes about the divorce, and letters you had written to Aaron and Joshua. Letters he never showed them. He told his sons that you only stuck around as long as you did because you were legally obligated to stay until they were eighteen. There was a draft of a letter you had supposedly left Aaron and Joshua when you took off. It was short. So short, I memorized it. It said, *I'm sorry, but I never wanted to be a mother. I have fulfilled my obligation. Have a good life with your father. Don't try contacting me.*"

"I never wrote that."

"We figured that out. Also in the box were the actual letters you left for them. Letters they never received."

"Mark lied to them," Olivia whispered.

"When you first left and Mark gave them that fake note from you, Joshua initially assumed you had some sort of mental breakdown. He tried contacting your parents. He didn't have their phone number, only their address. Mark obviously intercepted the letter Joshua sent, because they found it in the box, along with a rough draft of a letter from your parents' attorney telling Aaron and Joshua not to try contacting you again or they would get a restraining order."

"My parents never hired an attorney."

"I understand that now. But it was a rough draft of a letter that Aaron and Joshua actually received after Joshua tried contacting your parents. Obviously, Mark wrote that letter. After that, Mark suggested they block you on social media. He told them they needed to accept your decision and move on."

"I thought I was married to a putz," Marie muttered. "Olivia's ex makes my husband seem like a sweetheart."

"So why did this make you leave Joshua?"

"Because I realized for all these years, Mark had been lying to Joshua and Aaron about you. And for most of my marriage, I had accepted everything Joshua demanded of me, because if I didn't, that meant I was like you. Like my mother. But everything was a lie. And from what we learned by reading those papers, Pastor Davis didn't just know about what was in that box; he was part of it. There are notes from him to Mark, telling him things to do, to cut you out of their lives. He didn't want his grandsons to ever have contact with you again."

"Pastor Davis was part of it?"

"Yes. I told Joshua I would no longer attend his grandfather's church. I told him I was not walking away from God or from Jesus, but I was walking away from a false teacher. What we read in that box was not something a true man of God, a follower of Jesus, would condone."

"What did he say?"

"I suppose he was still trying to process everything. He kept telling me there had to be something we were missing. I told him I refused to find justification for what his father and grandfather had clearly done, and I was done being the obedient wife, when the source of his rules came from a tainted well. I told him I was leaving him and taking Cassandra with me while he figured things out, and that I would contact him later."

"And he let you leave?"

"He tried forbidding it, but I told him I would tell everyone about his father's lies—about his grandfather's lies. This was probably bad of me, but I had already taken pictures of what we'd found in that box. So, by the time I told him I was leaving, he understood I had ammunition against his father and grandfather, ammunition I would use. He didn't argue with me after that, but he also didn't think I would leave. After all, he assumed the only money I had was the small allowance he gave me, and he never let me have a credit card."

"You never told him about the money your grandmother gave you?"

"No, not until after I left. With the business basically shut down, Joshua and Aaron, who had both worked for their father, started doing side jobs to pay the bills. One day, while Joshua was on a side job, I packed up and left with Cassandra. I left Joshua a note, telling him I would contact him. I also told him not to worry, I had some money my grandmother had given me."

"It's still not clear; why did you want to meet me?"

Mary's gaze met Olivia's. "As a mother, I felt you deserved to learn the truth. And it was the only way I could see to stop this cycle of abuse."

CHAPTER THIRTY-FOUR

While Mary explained to Olivia why she had initially come to Frederickport, Danielle and Cassandra sat in the kitchen of Marlow House, each eating a cinnamon roll. Meanwhile, Walt was upstairs, giving the twins a bath.

"These are really good." Cassandra tore another piece from her roll.

"We probably shouldn't be eating them so close to dinner." Danielle licked frosting off her fingers.

Cassandra looked up at Danielle. "Mom told me your next-door neighbor is my grandma."

"That's true." Danielle took a bite of her roll.

"You already knew that, didn't you?"

"I didn't until I showed Olivia the picture I took of you and Max."

"I don't understand." Cassandra set the last piece of cinnamon roll on her napkin and looked up at Danielle.

"Maybe I can help you. What exactly don't you understand?"

"I understand my grandmother is the Olivia who Marie helped. But I also saw her at church a few times. Then she showed up at our house. And when I talked to her, she disappeared. I thought she was a ghost. But they say she's not a ghost. I don't understand."

Danielle smiled sadly. "It's confusing. And I don't think it's important to understand everything all at once. But you have a gift—sometimes it seems like a curse. You can see spirits. Marie is an earthbound spirit, and we typically call those ghosts. But when a spirit moves on—like going to a place some call heaven—they are just spirits then, no longer a ghost. And sometimes a person's spirit can leave their body without them being dead. Some people believe that when we dream, our spirit can leave our bodies, and when our body wakes up, the spirit is pulled back into the body."

"Is that what happened to my grandmother? Was she dreaming, and her spirit left her body, and I saw it?"

"Something like that. Not exactly, but that's close. It's one of those things that's best not to tell people who don't believe in mediums."

"I met the police chief's son. He told me he's a medium like me."

Danielle smiled. "Ah, Evan."

"He told me I should be careful before I tell someone I can see ghosts. Even someone close to me."

"I need to tell you something before your mom comes to get you to meet your grandmother."

"What?"

"I think it would be best if you didn't say anything to anyone about seeing Olivia's spirit. And when you go over to meet Olivia, Marie will be there, so you'll want to pretend not to see her."

"You mean I shouldn't say anything to Mom?"

Danielle cringed. "Cassandra, I am not sure how to say this. No adult should tell you to keep a secret from your mother. You should be able to tell your mother anything, and if someone insists you keep a secret from your parents, then you should tell your mom immediately."

"So I should tell Mom I can see ghosts?"

Danielle let out a sigh. "I won't tell you what to tell your mom. That's not my place. But I will tell you my own experiences as a medium, and what I learned when I was a child. I will tell you what I decided was the right thing for me. You must decide what is best for you."

"How do I do that?"

"First, unless you are a professional medium, someone who makes money talking to spirits, it's best not to go around telling everyone you can see ghosts."

"Because they will think I am crazy."

"Exactly. As for those people we choose to tell—people close to us—we have to decide when it is the right time to tell them. When they are ready to accept the information. They may never be ready. And that's okay. I have people in my life whom I'm close to who would never understand. So that is a part of me I choose not to share with them even though I care deeply about them. It's better for both of us."

***

"WOULD YOU LIKE TO MEET YOUR GRANDDAUGHTER?" MARY ASKED Olivia.

Olivia grinned. "I would love that."

Before leaving to get Cassandra, Mary went to the kitchen and told Shanice and Brian she was running next door to get her daughter. Brian and Shanice walked into the living room just as Mary stepped outside, closing the door behind her.

"Well? Did you learn anything?" Shanice asked.

Olivia did a quick recap of what Mary had told her, mindful that Mary and Cassandra would be returning shortly, and she didn't want them to walk in while she was rehashing the private conversation to her sister and a police officer.

After Olivia finished the telling, Brian quietly processed the information. When Mary returned with her daughter, she found the officer and Shanice sitting in the living room with her mother-in-law. Who she didn't see was Marie, who had been there since she arrived at Olivia's house.

Cassandra stood shyly at her mother's side, holding her hand, while Mary introduced Cassandra to everyone—everyone but Marie.

"You've already met Officer Henderson," Mary said before turning to Shanice. "This is your grandmother's sister." Mary hesitated a moment, trying to remember the sister's surname.

Before Mary could remember, Shanice smiled at Cassandra and said, "I hope you call me Auntie Shanice. I'm your great-aunt."

Cassandra studied Shanice as if trying to figure out a puzzle.

"Dear, tell her hello, nice to meet you," Marie nudged.

Cassandra glanced at Marie and then smiled at Shanice and said, "Hello. Nice to meet you."

Shanice grinned back. "Nice to meet you, too."

Mary turned Cassandra to Olivia. "And this is your grandmother, Olivia Davis. Olivia is your father and Uncle Aaron's mother."

Olivia smiled at her granddaughter. "Hello, Cassandra. I'm so happy to finally meet you."

"What should I call you? I used to call Mom's grandmother GG."

"That's because she was your great-grandmother," Mary explained.

"I would love for you to call me grandma. I've never been called grandma before."

"Grandma. I like that. I've never had a grandma before."

Neither Olivia nor Cassandra moved to hug each other. Instead, they started chatting, trying to get to know each other. Olivia asked her if she liked to read. Cassandra said yes. Olivia told her granddaughter she was a librarian, and Cassandra told her she loved visiting their library back home. They began talking about books they liked, with Shanice chiming in with some of her favorites from her childhood.

After a bit, Cassandra looked from her grandmother to Shanice and then back to her grandmother. "Grandma," Cassandra said, using the moniker *grandma* for the first time, "I didn't think you and Auntie Shanice looked like sisters, but I see it now. You have the same hair."

The seriousness in Cassandra's tone over the absurd observation caught the adults off guard. "Cassandra, dear, what do you mean?" Olivia asked, choking back a laugh.

"Your hair. You both have pretty hair, but…different."

Shanice's gaze met Olivia's. The sisters smiled, understanding what Cassandra was saying. Their hair's uniqueness—from the child's perspective—was a physical attribute the two sisters had in common.

"Thank you, Cassandra. I'll take that as a compliment," Olivia said.

IT WAS GETTING CLOSE TO DINNERTIME, AND MARY SUGGESTED THEY let Officer Henderson take her and Cassandra home. After all, he probably wanted to go home himself, and perhaps they could all meet tomorrow. Shanice asked Cassandra and Mary to stay for dinner and offered to take them home so Brian wouldn't have to take them back to their apartment.

While they discussed their plans, the doorbell rang.

"I'll get it," Brian offered. No one objected. The women continued talking amongst themselves.

Brian walked to the front door and opened it. He found two young white men, who looked to be in their late twenties or early thirties, standing on the front porch. They startled when they saw Brian standing at the door in his police uniform.

"Can I help you?" Brian asked.

The shorter of the two men frowned at Brian and said, "We're here to see Olivia Davis. Is everything alright? Why is a police officer answering her door?"

Before Brian could respond, a child's voice called out, "Daddy!" The next moment Cassandra ran past Brian to the man who had just asked to see Olivia.

"Cassandra?" the man said in surprise, scooping the girl up in his arms. "What are you doing here?"

"We're seeing Grandma." Cassandra then shouted, "Mom, Dad's here!"

Voices from the living room called out, "Joshua?" First from Mary, and then a hesitant one from Olivia. The men walked into the house without being invited in, walking past Brian, while Cassandra's father carried her into the living room.

Brian didn't attempt to stop them. Instead, he closed the front door, but when doing so, he glanced outside and noticed the white dual-cab pickup truck parked in front of Shanice's vehicle. Brian had parked the police car in the back alley. But he was pretty sure, when he first arrived, Shanice's vehicle had been the only one parked in front of the house.

Closing the door, Brian stepped back into the living room and was met with a chorus of voices—questions and awkward greetings. Brian remained standing on the perimeter of the living room while witnessing a chaos of conversation, going from an awkward reunion between mother and sons to spousal interrogations, with each party asking what the other person was doing in Frederickport.

Shanice, like Brian, observed, and while Brian couldn't see Marie, he understood she was there, also observing, and in this moment, he was especially grateful for her presence.

Finally, Brian cleared his throat before saying in a loud voice, "Excuse me, may I have your attention, please?" The room went quiet, and they all turned to Brian, whose hand now rested near his holster.

Olivia stood. "Oh Brian, these are my sons, Aaron and Joshua. Joshua is Cassandra's father."

"Yes, I figured that out. But I am going to have to ask Aaron and Joshua to come down to the station with me for some questions."

CHAPTER THIRTY-FIVE

Chief MacDonald stood in the office next to the interrogation room, talking with Brian Henderson while they looked through the one-way mirror at Joshua Davis, who sat quietly at the table in the interrogation room, waiting for Brian. Meanwhile, Joe had taken Aaron into another room to wait his turn with Brian.

"You didn't need to come back to the office for this," Brian said.

"True, but when you called and said Olivia's sons were in town, and you were bringing them in for questioning, I wasn't about to stay home. Do you honestly think they were involved in the murder attempt?"

"Considering Mary told Olivia her husband recently found a box of papers about the divorce, the timeline fits."

"Yes, but from what you told me, it sounds like what they found contradicted everything their father told them about their mother and showed her in a favorable light. If anything, I'd think that would make them want to reconnect, not murder her."

"But what if one thing they found in that box was the life insurance policy on their mother—one that was running out next month?"

The chief turned to Brian. "Did Mrs. Davis mention finding the life insurance policy?"

"No. But Olivia didn't ask her about the policy."

"WHEN DID YOU ARRIVE IN FREDERICKPORT?" BRIAN ASKED JOSHUA. The two sat in the interrogation room across the table from each other.

"Sunday."

"Where have you been staying since you've been here?"

"The Seahorse Motel."

"Why did you come to Frederickport?"

"To see my mother."

"Did you try to contact her on Sunday?"

"I drove by her house when I first got to town, but it looked like she had company. So I didn't stop."

"What time was this?"

After Joshua described the time and the people he observed, Brian realized it was after Olivia had been taken.

"You didn't call your mother ahead of time, tell her you were coming. According to your mother, she hasn't seen you in over ten years. Why now?"

Joshua shifted in his seat. "What is this about?"

"You are aware that your mother was kidnapped?"

Joshua stopped moving around in his chair. He stared at Brian for a moment. "No, I wasn't. I read she was missing, but I didn't think someone had taken her. Have they been arrested? I didn't read about any of that in the newspaper."

Instead of answering Joshua's question, Brian asked, "When did you learn your mother was missing?"

"I read an article in the local newspaper at breakfast on Tuesday."

Brian leaned back in the chair and studied Joshua for a moment. "So, you decided to come all the way from Texas to visit your mother, whom you haven't talked to in over a decade. You don't bother telling her you're coming, and you're here for a few days and don't try seeing her."

"I told you I drove by her house on Sunday. And I drove by again the next day, but I thought she had company."

"But then you read in the newspaper that your mother is missing, and you don't bother coming to the police station for additional information on her disappearance?"

Joshua stared at Brian but said nothing.

"When did your brother arrive in Frederickport?"

"Monday morning."

"So, what have you two been doing all week, just hanging out at the Seahorse Motel, wondering where your mom disappeared to, but not curious enough to come to the police station and ask questions or find out if there was some way you could help?"

"We didn't read about her being missing until Tuesday. And from how that article read, sounded like she just didn't show up for work, and people fail to show up for work all the time, and it doesn't mean something nefarious happened. We figured she had just gone somewhere for a few days and didn't bother telling anyone, and something got messed up at her work and they thought she was supposed to come in. Yesterday, someone said she was at the hospital, so I figured that's probably where she had been all along. Got sick, missed work, and some small-town reporter turned it all into a missing person case. That's why we were at her house tonight; we heard she had just been released from the hospital."

"How did you find out on Thursday that she was in the hospital? That information wasn't released until today."

"We heard it at the diner when having breakfast."

"What diner? Who did you hear it from?"

Joshua shrugged. "The one on the pier. One of the guys sitting at the table next to us asked the waitress about the missing woman. She mentioned she must have been found because she was at the hospital. So, what is this about a kidnapping?"

"What can you tell me about your mother's life insurance policy?"

Joshua frowned. "What life insurance policy?"

"You don't know about her two-million-dollar life insurance policy?"

"No. And why would my mother pay for something like that? She lives alone; she isn't even married. People get life insurance when they have kids at home, not when their kids are grown adults. Something like that would cost a fortune for someone my mother's age."

"Not if she took out the policy thirty years ago."

Joshua shook his head. "I don't know anything about a life insurance policy. Why am I here?"

"I understand you and your brother worked for your father's construction company until it recently closed down."

"Yes. What does that have to do with anything?"

"I understand you recently came across a box with papers about your parents' divorce."

Joshua stared at Brian and said nothing.

"Is that true?"

Joshua shrugged. "So?"

"I was wondering if you might have found something in that box about a life insurance policy. Maybe one on your mother, for two million, that would expire next month. And if something happened to your mother before next month, your father, or possibly you and your brother, might be the beneficiaries. I imagine that money could help your family about now."

Joshua stared dumbly at Brian. "Are you suggesting I kidnapped my mother for her life insurance policy? How would that work exactly? And what was my plan? If it were a life insurance policy, wouldn't it only pay off if I killed her? What? I kidnapped her and let her go? Anyway, I don't know about any life insurance policy."

BRIAN SAT WITH THE CHIEF IN THE CHIEF'S OFFICE. JOE HAD JUST left for home, and the Davis brothers had been released. When Brian had questioned Aaron after Jason, Aaron said nothing that contradicted what his brother had said. In truth, Brian and

MacDonald hadn't been that concerned about the interviews; they were waiting to find out what the brothers would say when they returned to the Seahorse Motel.

"Sometimes this feels unethical," the chief told Brian.

"What, having Marie follow the Davis boys back to their motel room and listen to what they say about the kidnapping when not in an interrogation room?"

The chief shrugged, to which Brian let out a laugh.

THE MEN ALLEN HAD REFERRED TO AS DUDE AND BUD SAT IN THEIR room at the Seahorse Motel.

"I say we do it tonight," Bud announced. "We should do it while her sister is still here."

"Why would we want to do it when someone is with her?"

"Because that way, we can make it look like murder. It doesn't have to look like an accident."

Dude frowned at Bud. "I'm not following you."

"You know how I felt about staging it to look like an accident?"

Dude did know. When they had first planned Olivia's demise, Dude wanted to keep it simple and break into her house and push her down the stairs. People would assume she had fallen. But Bud argued that falls didn't always kill a person. Giving her an additional whack over the head would tell the police she had been murdered, and it wasn't an accident. Or the fall might be fatal, yet she could linger for a while before actually dying. This meant they would have to stick around to make sure she died and risk some neighbor stopping by.

"Yes, but I'm still not following you."

"Now we can stage it as a murder—one where we give them a suspect: her adopted sister. Being murdered doesn't mean the life insurance won't pay out—that only happens if the beneficiary on the policy murdered her. But the adopted sister has plenty of motive to murder her without an insurance policy. She probably figures she'll inherit her sister's Frederickport house and whatever money she has. Even if that's not true, she only needs to believe she's in the will for a motive. You can't tell me the adopted sister didn't harbor some resentment over how she was treated after her sister got married. She'll be a perfect suspect."

"And also, a witness."

Bud laughed. "Who said we're leaving a witness behind? We can scruff them both up a little bit, then stage the scene before rigor sets in. I have a few ideas. You know how I like to be creative."

Yes, Dude knew how Bud liked to get creative. He was the one who came up with the elaborate kidnap and weaponless murder plot, which Dude had ironically called overkill—which ended up not killing anyone. But Dude wasn't going to bother arguing with Bud. He had been going along with him since they were kids, and it was too late to stand up to him now.

Plus, he appreciated Bud's attention to detail—it was almost a compulsion. Like how they had not only stolen license plates when driving from Texas to Oregon, but the sedan they used when taking Olivia, instead of keeping the car, they ditched it and never drove in it without wearing the masks. Dude believed Bud's attention to those types of details would get them through this without landing them in prison.

CHAPTER THIRTY-SIX

Danielle had just gotten the twins down for the night and walked into her bedroom when her cell phone rang. Grabbing the phone off her bedroom dresser, thinking it might be Walt, she looked at it and saw Lily was calling.

"Hey, Lily," Danielle answered the phone as she flopped down on the small sofa in her bedroom; flames flickered in the nearby fireplace.

"Can you talk?"

"Yeah. Twins are sleeping; Walt's over at Olivia's. And I was debating about taking a shower now or waiting until Walt gets back, in case they wake up."

"That's why I was calling."

"What, you coming over so I can shower?"

Lily laughed. "Yeah, right. No, I was wondering how everything worked out with Olivia." Danielle had called Lily after Mary picked up Cassandra to go meet her grandmother.

"It got kind of crazy. If I weren't alone with the twins, I would have called you sooner. But guess who showed up when Cassandra was meeting her grandma?"

"Who?"

"Olivia's two sons."

Max jumped up on the sofa with Danielle.

"No! The same sons she hasn't seen since she left her husband?"

Danielle reached out and stroked Max as he curled up next to her. "As far as I know, they're her only sons."

"So many questions! Like, what did Mary tell Olivia about why she came, and what did the sons have to say?" Lily asked excitedly.

Danielle, her bare feet now up on the sofa as she leaned against one sofa arm, continued to stroke Max. "I don't think they had time to say much at the house, Brian was there, and he asked them to come down to the station and answer some questions."

"They don't think they had something to do with the kidnapping?"

"I'm not sure what they think. But after the sons showed up, Brian asked them to come to the station with him, and before he left, he called Walt. He asked Walt to come over and stay with Olivia and Shanice, and for him to ask Marie if she would stay with Olivia's sons while they drove to the station and follow them back to their motel and stay with them for a few hours."

"Sneaky. He wants to hear what they say to each other after the police question them."

"Exactly. Anyway, tonight, after the chief got home, he called me." Danielle recapped what Mary had told Olivia—which Olivia had then told Brian—who had then told the chief. "They didn't want to leave Shanice and Olivia alone quite yet, so Brian thought of Walt."

"Were Mary and Cassandra still there?"

"Yes. They stayed after Brian left with Olivia's sons and ate dinner with Olivia and Shanice, and then Shanice took them back to their apartment. Now it's just Olivia and Shanice over there with Walt."

"The sons didn't come back to talk to Olivia?" Lily asked.

"No. According to Walt when he called me, they agreed to come back over in the morning to talk. It's been a long day for Olivia, and they had no idea how long they would be at the police station."

"You want us to walk over to her house? It's dark outside, and it's probably going to start raining," Dude said.

"It's not that far. And rain won't kill you. Hell, people don't even use umbrellas in Oregon."

"I'm not a fan of getting wet," Dude grumbled.

"I want the truck left in front of our motel room. We're keeping the room lights on and leaving the blinds open a little bit; that way, if someone walks by our window, they'll see our television on, but they won't be able to see the beds. They'll think we're still in our room. I was thinking about arranging pillows on one of the chairs, so if someone walks by, they'll also see a shadow that looks like someone sitting in a chair watching TV."

"I get it. We're walking so people think we didn't leave our motel room." Dude stated the obvious, suppressing his irritation over Bud's penchant for obsessing on what Dude saw as unnecessary details.

"Exactly. We need to change into our black jeans and black turtlenecks. I want us dressed in black because I want to fade into the night."

Dude internally rolled his eyes at the *fade into the night* comment but said nothing.

Bud continued, "When we get to Beach Drive, we put on the ski masks. But until then, we can wear our dark hoodies with the hoods up."

"Okay. I guess you have this all figured out."

"I'll take the gun, but only to get them to do what I want. I've no intention of shooting anyone and screwing up my plan to make this look like they killed each other."

"I hope this works."

"You go change your clothes. I'm giving her a call, let her know what the plans are now. Oh, and don't forget to get whatever you need to open the lock once we get to her house. We can't break a window to get in."

"Okay." Dude turned and walked away to change his clothes, silently questioning if it really was okay.

Bud sat on the side of the bed, the phone to his ear, waiting for his party to answer.

"Hey. You still coming back on Monday?" came the familiar voice.

"Yes. But there has been a change of plan. We revoked the abort mission."

"What do you mean?"

"We decided to pay her a little visit tonight. She's home alone with her sister. And I figured, if anyone has a reason to want her dead, it's her sister. After all, didn't you tell us she treated her like trash for years. Maybe she resents their parents dividing the inheritance."

"That's just the impression I got. I'm assuming you plan to kill them both?"

"Did I say that? No, I'm sure they're going to have an argument tonight, things get out of control, and they end up killing each other." Bud laughed.

"That sounds tricky. Are you sure?"

"Hey, we're the ones taking all the risks, so what do you care?"

"Please don't get caught."

"I don't plan to. By the way, have you figured out how long it's going to take for the insurance to pay out?"

"No. I'm not asking those questions until after she's dead. Don't you think that would look a little suspicious if I started asking now?"

"I'm not suggesting calling and saying, *hey, when Olivia Davis dies, how long before you send the check?* I meant reading what it says on the policy. But don't go to their website. We don't need someone checking out your search history and finding you were looking before she was declared dead."

Dude and Bud dressed in black, from their black shoes to their jeans, turtlenecks, and oversized hooded jackets. Each had a black ski mask shoved into a jacket pocket to be put on when they got to Beach Drive. Bud wore his gun in a vest holster, but he intended to only use it for its intimidation purposes. Shooting either with his gun would only ruin the scenario he planned to set up.

Bud's chosen weapons were two heavy wrenches he had picked up at the thrift store when they stopped in Utah and picked up the purple bedspread. He'd bought the wrenches to take home with him and hoped he could find something at Olivia's house to use instead of the wrenches, because he understood he needed to leave the weapon behind when staging the murder. But if they couldn't find a suitable weapon, they'd use what they brought.

Dude kept looking out the window through the blinds, not wanting anyone to see them leave their motel room. "I think it's clear," he finally said.

As they headed toward Beach Drive, it began to drizzle. As they walked, they kept to the shadows, stepping into bushes when necessary to avoid the headlights of passing cars.

Bud carried his wrench up one sleeve of his jacket, while Dude shoved his into a pocket in his jacket's lining. He kept shoving one gloved hand under the jacket to reposition the wrench because half the tool stuck out of the pocket and kept sticking him in the ribs.

When Dude and Bud arrived at Beach Drive, they stopped a moment, removed their ski masks from their pockets, and pulled them over their heads. The masks covered their faces, with two small openings for their eyes.

They made it to Olivia's house without incident. When they reached her property, they moved around the perimeter of the house and tried peeking in the windows yet kept finding the blinds closed. But when they came to the living room window, they found the blind partially open, and Bud peeked inside. When he did and saw who was in the living room, he reached out and clutched Dude's wrist, squeezing it tightly.

Bud moved away from the window, allowing Dude to look inside. Dude saw three—not two—people sitting in the living room.

The sisters were sitting next to each other on the sofa, but across from them was a man sitting in one chair. The three seemed to be talking.

"What now?" Dude whispered.

Bud shoved Dude to one side so he could look in the window again. He silently watched for several minutes, trying to recalibrate what they should do now, but then the man stood up. One woman then stood, and it looked as if they were walking to the door.

"I think he's leaving," Bud whispered.

Bud and Dude moved away from the window and hid in the bushes, watching. A few minutes later, the side door opened, and the man walked outside.

"Thanks for staying, Walt," the adopted sister said, standing visible in the doorway.

The man she called Walt now stood right outside the door, the overhang keeping the rain off him. "No problem, happy to help. Now that my replacement is here, I'm sure you'll be safe. But get Olivia to bed. She looks exhausted."

The woman standing in the doorway glanced back briefly at Olivia and back to Walt. "She's had an emotional day; I'm not sure how she's processing all this."

"We're next door if you need us. Give us a call, or you can send Marie over."

She laughed. "I'm finding it awkward talking to someone I can't see."

Walt laughed. "Yeah, that's what our friend Lily tells us. But she's getting better at it. She often leaves messages for Marie on a dry-erase board, and Marie responds in writing."

"That must be interesting."

"The only problem, Lily has to be careful someone doesn't see what she wrote—or worse—a note Marie wrote."

The woman laughed again.

Dude and Bud remained in the bushes, listening to Walt's footsteps disappear into the night. When they finally heard the faint sound of a door closing over at Marlow House, they emerged from their hiding place.

"They were talking about a Marie," Bud whispered from the shadows, his gaze looking over at Marlow House.

"You don't think they were talking about the same Marie who wrote that note?"

Bud shook his head. "I don't know what to think."

"What now?"

Bud turned his attention from Marlow House to Olivia's house. "I think we get this done."

They needed to get into the house without making it look like a break-in. Fortunately, one of Dude's skills included picking locks. He decided on the kitchen door, as it was far enough from the living room so the sisters wouldn't hear anyone messing with the door. Bud stood guard at the window, watching the women sitting on the sofa, talking with each other. Should one of them get up and head for the kitchen, Bud would signal to Dude.

But the women didn't move, and by the time Dude unlocked the kitchen door, the women were still sitting on the sofa, oblivious to the intruders about to enter the house. By the time Bud moved from the window to the kitchen door, he already had his gun out of its holster, and the wrench he had shoved up one sleeve, he now held in his left hand.

Bud entered the house first, with Dude following him inside. They paused a moment while Dude gently shut the kitchen door and removed the annoying wrench from beneath his coat—which had been flopping around against his chest since leaving the motel —and clutched it in his right hand.

Bud gave Dude a nod, and the two moved toward the living room, thankful for the real estate photos they'd found online when researching Olivia. The photos gave a clear picture of the house's layout.

The two men burst into the living room, Bud aiming the gun at the women while his other hand held the wrench. Dude stood next to him, his posture almost defensive, considering the way he held his wrench, as if ready to smack someone.

The women looked up in surprise; each audibly gasped. But neither one stood. They stared at the two men for a moment before Olivia said, "Marie?"

CHAPTER THIRTY-SEVEN

Clutching the grip of his gun, Bud stepped toward the sofa. Dude stood behind him, still holding up his wrench, waiting for Bud's orders. Neither woman had moved since their initial surprise at the men's arrival. They continued to stare at the gun's barrel, yet instead of their faces wearing fear, Bud thought they wore an expression more of curiosity and anticipation. They were supposed to look terrified, Bud thought, not like they were watching a magic show and waiting for him to pull a rabbit out of his hat.

Bud stopped walking and stood in the middle of the living room, Dude a few feet behind him. "Who in the hell is Marie?"

Before they had a chance to answer his question, the gun flew out of his hand, sailing up toward the ceiling, and then veered to the right and floated over the staircase and up to the second-floor landing, dropping to the floor there.

Bud and Dude watched the gun's flight in stunned silence before looking back to the women, who remained sitting on the sofa, watching them as if they were watching a magic act.

Olivia looked Bud in the eyes, his only facial feature visible to her. "That was Marie." The next moment the face masks ripped off

Bud's and Dude's heads, exposing their faces. It was as if the hand of a ghost had reached down and snatched a mask from each man's head.

Unable to process what had just happened, Bud let out a guttural-sounding battle cry, raised the wrench he still held, and charged toward the sofa. Dude, not sure what he was supposed to do, followed Bud's example, but before they reached the coffee table, an invisible force ripped the wrenches from their hands, bringing the two men to an abrupt stop. They watched with a mixture of bewilderment and terror as the wrenches floated across the room and up the staircase before joining the gun on the second floor.

Now standing in front of the coffee table, the men looked down into the smiling faces of the two sisters. Bud opened his mouth to say something, but the words caught in his throat when something pushed him against Dude, and before he could utter a word, their feet lifted off the floor.

Shanice watched in fascination as the two men floated up to the ceiling, their feet kicking, hands waving, as they yelled obscenities, curses, and even a prayer. When they reached the ceiling, their backs touching it, they looked down at the living room beneath them, their eyes wide with horror. Their screaming stopped.

"I think we should call someone," Shanice finally said, still looking up at the men.

Olivia studied the intruders for a moment before saying, "Those are the men who kidnapped me. The one on the right, when he was yelling a second ago, I recognized his voice. But I don't recognize their faces. I've never seen them before."

"Olivia, like I said, we need to call someone. I'm not sure if ghosts get tired, but I'd hate for them to come crashing down in your living room. They might break something. Something of yours, I mean; frankly, I don't care if they break their necks."

"We should probably call Walt first," Olivia suggested.

WALT ARRIVED CARRYING ENOUGH ROPE TO TIE UP BOTH MEN. AFTER entering Olivia's house, he stood in the middle of the living room and looked up at the ceiling. The two men looked down at him, but neither one moved nor said a word.

"How long have they been up there?" Walt asked, his eyes not leaving the men.

"Maybe ten, fifteen minutes," Shanice said. "Everything seemed to happen so fast; it could have been longer or less."

Walt looked over to Marie, who stood by the fireplace, her attention focused on the men. "Too bad you can't bring them down one at a time."

Marie shrugged. "I imagine if I tried, they would both come down, but one much faster."

Walt chuckled. "Okay, bring them both down."

The intruders let out a gasp when they started their slow and steady descent from the ceiling. From Walt's perspective, it looked as if both men were holding their breath, afraid to move. When the soles of their shoes touched the living room floor, they started to bolt, but the next moment their feet were pulled out from under them, and they each landed on their bellies.

Later Olivia would tell Walt it looked as if he were hog-tying a calf the way he secured the two men, leaving them in the middle of the living room floor, their hands and feet bound. When they had finished securing the intruders, Walt looked at Marie. "We work well together, Marie."

One man yelled, "Who's Marie?"

Walt glanced over at the man who had just shouted the question. "Olivia's guardian angel." Turning from the prisoners, he walked to a chair, sat down, and pulled out his cell phone.

"Who are you calling?" Olivia asked.

"Brian. When walking over here, I saw his car at Heather's. We can't call 911 yet, not until we come up with a believable story on how you managed to capture the men who kidnapped you. And considering everything, it would be reasonable for me to call Brian first, since he's right next door and the lead on your case."

BY THE TIME BRIAN ARRIVED AT OLIVIA'S HOUSE, WALT HAD already retrieved the wrenches and gun from upstairs and set them on the kitchen table. Brian stood in the kitchen with Walt, discussing what had happened, while Marie remained in the living room with Olivia, Shanice, and the prisoners.

"So, what do you think we should tell Joe and the others?" Brian asked after looking over the weapons the men had brought.

"I think we'll keep it simple. Shanice having a gun works to our advantage. We say she heard someone messing with the kitchen door. When they broke in, she already had her gun drawn. She made them sit down at the kitchen table while Olivia called me. I came over, tied them up, and we called you."

"Why didn't you call 911?" Brian asked. "Why didn't they?"

"They called me because I had just left their house—which is true—and they were afraid they wouldn't be able to hold them until the police arrived, and they asked me to bring rope. After coming over and tying them up, I called you first because you were next door."

Brian smiled and gave a shrug. "I guess it could work."

"What now?"

"You said you didn't go through their pockets?"

"No. Marie brought them down from the ceiling, and she helped me tie them up. I did pat them down to make sure they didn't have another gun, which they didn't. While I could tell they each had a wallet and some keys, I figured it would be best if you dealt with that."

"Understood." Brian patted the two handcuffs hanging from his belt. "Let's go in and get these guys properly cuffed before I call this in."

Brian and Walt walked back into the living room and stopped when they got to the men tied up on the floor. Hands on hips, Brian looked down at the men and asked, "Why don't we start with you guys giving me your names?"

Instead of answering, they glared up at Brian. Brian asked again, and when they refused to answer the second time, he walked to the man closest to him, leaned down, and dragged him several feet away from his partner. Before trading the ropes for handcuffs, Brian checked the pockets of the man's jacket and pants and pulled out a wallet, several small tools, a cell phone, and a room key for the Seahorse Motel.

Brian dumped the contents of the man's pockets onto the coffee table and then picked up the wallet and opened it, pulling out a driver's license. Brian looked closely at the picture on the license and then at the man from whom he had taken it. They looked like the same person.

Still holding the license, Brian walked back over to the man and looked down at him. "Says here you're Gerald Flemming from Oklahoma. Is that right?" When the man did not answer, Brian removed a set of handcuffs from his belt, knelt, and removed the rope from around Gerald's wrists before securing the wrists in handcuffs behind Gerald's back.

After Gerald was handcuffed, Brian untied his ankles and then pulled him to his feet while giving him his Miranda rights. Once the prisoner was standing, Brian moved him to stand in the corner with Walt, preparing to give Gerald's partner the same treatment.

From the partner's pockets, he removed a wallet, cell phone, and instead of a motel key, he had a vehicle key fob. Like he had done with Gerald, Brian opened the wallet and pulled out a driver's license. Once again, the photo on the ID matched the prisoner.

"Says here your name is Harold Flemming. Does this mean you guys are brothers?" Brian asked.

Still on the floor, his wrists and ankles tied, Harold glared up at Brian without responding.

Brian smiled down at the glaring man. "Harold and Gerald Flemming? Brothers? Hmm...your parents enjoyed rhyming names? Harold and Gerald."

Harold's face reddened. Clearly not amused by Brian's mocking rhyme, the prisoner tried kicking Brian with his bound ankles, but instead of hitting Brian with the side of his shoe, he hit a solid wall of energy. Harold yelled out in pain while drawing his knees up against his body, trying to get away from whatever he had kicked.

"Let's not try that again," Brian said calmly as he walked over to the coffee table to set down the license before properly cuffing Harold. When he dropped the license on the table, he noticed a folded piece of paper sticking out of the end of the wallet. Curious, he reached down, removed the paper from the wallet, and unfolded it.

On the paper someone had written: *You aren't alone. It's Marie. I've come to help you escape.* Brian looked up from the paper and looked at Olivia. Showing her the letter, he said, "Is this the letter you told me about?"

Olivia looked at the letter and smiled. "Yes. Now we know what happened to Marie's letter."

Letter in hand, Brian walked over to Harold and showed it to him. "I found this in your wallet. Where did you get it?"

Once again, the prisoner remained silent. Brian refolded the letter and took it to the table with the rest of the items. He then returned to Harold and proceeded to properly cuff him, remove the ropes around his ankles, and mirandize him while pulling him to his feet. When that was done, he called the station.

After Brian got off the phone, he looked at Walt and said, "This is proving to be a long day."

CHAPTER THIRTY-EIGHT

Heather offered to go over and stay with Evan and Eddy while the chief went down to the police station so he could listen to Brian's interview with the two intruders. Technically speaking, Eddy was old enough to stay alone with his brother; after all, plenty of kids his age babysat. But it was late, and the boys were already asleep in bed.

At the station, Brian was with Harold in the interrogation room while Gerald was being detained in lockup. After Brian finished questioning Harold, it would be Gerald's turn. The chief watched the interview from the next office. Joe wasn't on duty, and they didn't call him in.

Brian sat down across from Harold and set a folder on the table. "According to your fingerprints, it looks like you are Harold Flemming, just like it says on your driver's license."

Harold leaned back in his chair. "I want to see my lawyer."

"That's your right," Brian said, not bothering to stand up.

Still leaning back in his chair, Harold eyed Brian and smiled. "But one thing, when you read me the Miranda, you got it wrong."

Brian arched his brows. "How so?"

"You told me I was being arrested for kidnapping and breaking and entering. What kidnapping?"

"Weren't you paying attention? I said the kidnapping of Olivia Davis."

"I have no clue what you're talking about. I don't even know Olivia Davis."

"You broke into her house."

"Not saying I did, but if I did, it doesn't mean I intended to kidnap her. In fact, I heard she was in the hospital. Me and my brother read in the paper something about her being in the hospital. According to the article, she lived alone. So maybe we figured her house was empty and we might go have a look at her house. The kitchen door might have been left unlocked; we walked in. I imagine that happens a lot in these tourist towns; people just want to see inside some of the beach houses. We weren't expecting to walk into the kitchen and find a woman pointing a gun at us. Then she calls her neighbor, and they hold us at gunpoint and tie us up."

Brian had to give Harold Flemming credit; the guy hadn't fallen apart. Which would have been a reasonable reaction, considering he'd been stuck up on Olivia's ceiling for at least ten minutes before Marie brought them down and Walt tied them up. Not only that, but Harold had also grabbed onto the story Brian had told the responders to explain their capture, which could mean lesser chargers if a jury believed Harold and Gerald were attempting a break-in of an empty house as opposed to an armed home invasion.

Gerald, on the other hand, was not doing as well. Brian suspected the guy had initially been in shock after Marie's intervention, considering his passivity while being cuffed, compared to his brother, who tried kicking him. By the time they reached the station, the reality of what had happened seemed to break through Gerald's shock, and he began ranting about Olivia's house being possessed. He was still ranting when they put him in lockup, and the other officers on duty thought it was all an act to use an insanity defense, but Brian knew the truth.

Brian took a deep breath, exhaled, and leaned back in his chair.

"I didn't say you were being arrested for attempted kidnapping. You already kidnapped Olivia Davis, but she managed to escape."

"I don't know what you're talking about."

"On Sunday, two men kidnapped Olivia Davis from her driveway. Took her up into the mountains and held her captive in a cabin that they broke into. They locked her in a cage they assembled in the cabin's basement and kept her there for several days without giving her any food or water. But then she managed to escape."

"I'm sorry that happened to her. But we had nothing to do with it."

"The kidnappers were driving a truck matching the description of your truck."

"Who said that?"

"A witness."

Harold frowned. "There are lots of trucks like ours. In fact, I saw another truck just like ours in the motel parking lot. Did the kidnappers' truck have an Oklahoma license plate?"

Brian smiled at Harold and thought, *No, it had a Utah license plate, and the only witness we have is a ghost. But that plate was probably stolen at the same time you took one for the sedan. The sedan that has since disappeared.*

Instead of answering the question, Brian opened the folder he had placed on the table when he first sat down. From the folder, he removed a piece of paper. It was a copy of the letter he had removed from Harold's wallet. He slid the letter across the table.

Harold looked down at the piece of paper and frowned. "What's that?"

Brian leaned forward, placing his elbows on the tabletop. "It's a copy of the letter I found in your wallet."

Harold leaned forward and reached out and grabbed the letter before sliding it in front of himself. After staring at it a moment, he shrugged and looked up at Brian. "What is this supposed to prove?"

"It proves you were in the cabin where Olivia was held."

Harold shook his head. "How is that?"

"When I first interviewed Olivia at the hospital after her escape, she told me she fell asleep in the cage you locked her in. When she woke up, she found that letter on the bottom of the cage and the cage door open." It was a lie, but ever since learning about the mediums and ever-present spirits, Brian had learned how to twist the truth when needing to conceal paranormal events.

Harold pulled the copy of the letter closer to him, staring down at it, his frown deepening.

Brian leaned closer. "When Olivia escaped, she left that letter in the bottom of the cage. But when we got to the cabin, we found the cage gone, and someone had taken it apart and dumped it down the road from the cabin. But that handwritten letter—it disappeared. So, tell me, how did it get from that cage to your wallet?"

Harold looked up from the letter to Brian. Their eyes met. Finally, Harold shoved the copy of the letter aside and said, "I want to talk to a lawyer."

"I'll get you a phone so you can make your one call." Brian gathered up the letter, slipped it back into the folder, and stood. "But before you do, let me tell you something. The letter I found on you proves that you were at the cabin. Olivia recognized your brother's voice as one of the kidnappers. We already have a motive—the insurance policy on Olivia that is due to expire next month."

Harold's eyes widened at the mention of the insurance policy.

"We don't think you and your brother are working alone. You're obviously working with someone who would benefit if that policy paid out. I imagine we'll find what we need on your cell phones to help us link you to the person behind this. And since there are not that many possibilities, it shouldn't be that hard."

Brian started to walk away, stopped, and then looked back. "Olivia was found with a purple bedspread. We'll be having it checked for DNA. Wonder what might show up. And just remember, one of you will probably make a plea deal and serve less time than the others. I wonder who it will be."

Joy Davis lay in her bed, staring up at the ceiling, the only light coming from the hallway. She rolled over and picked up her cell phone from the nightstand, checking the time.

Why haven't they called? she wondered. After placing the cell phone back on the nightstand, she sat up, threw off the covers, and got out of bed. Grabbing her robe off the nearby chair, she slipped it on, then grabbed her cell phone off the nightstand and slipped it into her robe's pocket.

Leaving the bedroom she had once shared with Mark, she walked down the hall and then down the stairs, heading for the garage. If she couldn't sleep, she would try to get something accomplished. Joy turned on the lights one after another as she moved through the house, from the second floor to the first floor.

In the garage, she turned on the overhead light, illuminating the large space with harsh brightness. She walked over to her car and opened the driver's door. Reaching into her vehicle, she opened the center console and pulled out the envelope she had placed there weeks ago. It was the insurance policy of Mark's ex-wife, Olivia Davis.

After removing the envelope from the middle console, Joy closed the car door. She spied Mark's office chair sitting on the other side of the garage, along with the other things Joshua and Aaron had brought from his office. Joy walked to the office chair, sat down, and then opened the envelope, removing the policy.

Joy remembered when she first found the policy. She had been looking for a pen in Mark's home office when she found it in one of the desk drawers. Mark had walked in and found her reading it. He had been angry at her for looking through his desk, but she'd asked him what the papers meant.

Annoyed, he had grabbed them from her hand, shoved the policy into its envelope, and placed it back into the drawer while saying, "It was a policy on Olivia we took out right after Aaron was born. After the divorce, she let me keep the policy, understanding the money would go to our sons if she died."

When she asked why he was listed as the beneficiary, he'd explained he'd never bothered changing it because he would still give Aaron and Joshua the money. He then went on to say it didn't matter anyway because the policy expired in March.

Weeks later Mark's business was sued, they entered bankruptcy, and then Mark had the stroke. It was after the stroke that Joy started thinking about the insurance policy and how if Mark suddenly inherited a fortune from his ex-wife's life insurance policy, that money would go into his account—an account that she, as his wife, could legally access.

Sitting in Mark's office chair, Joy read through the policy and could find nothing specific about how quickly the policy might pay off. When first removing it from the desk in Mark's home office after the stroke, Joy had gone through the desk and files in that room, looking for any other information on the policy, but found nothing.

While remembering all this, she glanced over to the boxes piled in the garage, all from Mark's business office. Perhaps—she wondered—he had some files on the policy that he had kept at his business office.

Joy refolded the policy, slipped it back into the envelope, stood up, and then set the envelope on the desk chair. She walked over to the boxes and began lifting off lids, peeking inside. With most of the boxes, she returned the lid, pushed them aside, and then went on to another one. Some boxes, she looked through each file or envelope.

Joy had gone through about ten boxes when she came to one filled with what looked like unopened mail. She quickly glanced through the sealed envelopes. Most seemed to be junk mail that should have been tossed rather than brought here. But as she thumbed through the unopened mail, she noticed the return address on several envelopes was from an insurance company—the same insurance company that had issued Olivia's policy.

Leaning over the box, Joy gathered up all the unopened envelopes from the insurance company, then walked to the chair and picked up the envelope with Olivia's policy and walked to the door leading to the kitchen.

Once in the kitchen, Joy dumped the envelopes onto the counter and began opening them. The first one she opened was dated the same week Mark's business was served. It was a past-due notice on Olivia's policy.

Joy frowned. She opened another envelope. Instead of a past-due notice, this one said the life insurance had lapsed for nonpayment. Joy's eyes widened, and she shook her head in denial. *No, that's not right.*

In a panic, she tore open all the envelopes. When finished, she stared down at the mail spread across her kitchen counter. According to these letters, Olivia's policy had lapsed before they had even decided to murder her.

Joy picked up the envelope with the policy. Removing the document, she absently dropped the now empty envelope onto the counter and began reading the policy, looking for wording that might say it would still pay out a portion of the payout; after all, Mark had been making payments for almost thirty years; it had to still be worth something.

The doorbell rang. Joy glanced toward the door and then up at the kitchen clock. It was late. Who could be here this late? Was it about Mark? Had Aaron and Joshua finally come home?

Still clutching the policy in her hand, Joy walked to the front door and looked outside through the glass panes in the door. There were two police officers standing on her front porch.

Confused, she opened the door and stared dumbly at the police officers, her right hand still clutching Olivia's life insurance policy.

"Joy Davis?" one officer asked.

"Yes?"

"You need to come with us," the other officer said.

CHAPTER THIRTY-NINE

Danielle called Olivia on Saturday morning to see how she and Shanice were doing after their traumatic evening. She didn't want to call too early, thinking they might sleep in late, but after she looked out the upstairs bedroom window and noticed Shanice's car driving away, she assumed Olivia was awake.

"Neither of us slept that well," Olivia told Danielle when she called. "But Aaron and Joshua are supposed to come over in about an hour. We didn't have time to talk last night when they showed up. We had barely said hello when Brian asked them to go to the station with him. They agreed to come over for breakfast this morning. Shanice just left to pick up some cinnamon rolls at Old Salts, and I'm starting some bacon in a minute. Have you heard from Brian? I haven't heard anything since they took those men away last night."

"No. I haven't talked to anyone yet."

OLIVIA FRETTED—TRYING TO DECIDE IF SHE WANTED TO SET THE kitchen table for the four of them, or her dining room table. She decided on the kitchen table, feeling the dining room would be too formal, and considering she and her sons were virtual strangers, the cozy, casual kitchen ambiance might foster a more comfortable environment to reunite with her sons and rekindle the closeness they once shared.

After Aaron and Joshua arrived, Olivia nervously greeted them, and they, in turn, seemed to share her nervousness. As the mood had been during their brief meeting the night before, the reunion did not start with hugs and open warmth, but with reserve and hesitation.

Olivia began by introducing her sons to their aunt. She couldn't remember if she had done it the night before. After the introductions, she quickly ushered them into the kitchen. She had already set the table, and the food would get cold if they chatted in the living room. Even though they were eating in the kitchen, she used the good china and cloth napkins, with the knives, forks, and spoons carefully placed according to the diagram she once saw in a cookbook she had received as a wedding gift those many years ago.

The cinnamon rolls Shanice had picked up sat on a plate in the center of the table. There was also a platter of crisp bacon, a small bowl of cut-up fruit, and a covered bowl with scrambled eggs that Olivia worried might cool off too quickly.

Shanice surprised Olivia when she announced she was fixing herself a plate and eating in the other room. "I think you three need some privacy. There are obviously things you need to discuss, and you don't need an audience."

THEY SAT AROUND THE KITCHEN TABLE—OLIVIA, JOSHUA, AND Aaron. Olivia had just handed her sons each a cup of coffee before she joined them at the table. She urged them to fill their plates before the food got cold.

Instead of reaching for the food, Joshua looked at his mother and said, "The police told us someone kidnapped you. When we got to town and read you were missing, we…we didn't think you were missing because of some nefarious reason, but that your boss reported you missing because you didn't come into work. We thought it was some misunderstanding."

"What happened? Are you okay? Did they hurt you?" Aaron asked.

Olivia glanced from Aaron to Joshua and then set her cup on the table. "I am okay, and they didn't hurt me. No one physically attacked me. But before we talk about that, I need you to tell me, why are you here? Why now?"

Aaron and Joshua exchanged glances. Joshua started to say something, but Olivia interrupted him and pointed to the food. "But fill your plates first. You can tell me while we're eating."

"We found out Dad had been lying to us for years," Joshua said. He looked down at his plate now filled with scrambled eggs, bacon, a little fruit, and a cinnamon roll. Hesitantly, he took a bite of the egg.

"Lying about what?" Olivia asked, though she already knew. Joshua's wife had already told her, but she wanted to hear what he had to say.

"Dad had a stroke a few months back, and he's in a nursing home. He can't speak or write. The doctor says he understands what we say, but he's lost his verbal skills and his mobility. He also lost his business." Joshua recounted what they had found when cleaning out his office, repeating what Mary had already told her, and then said, "I've done a lot of thinking since finding that box."

"So have I," Aaron said.

"I hadn't yet processed what we found when Mary left me and took Cassandra with her. Aaron and I have talked about it a lot, especially this last week after coming to Frederickport. My marriage has blown up, and Aaron has had similar issues in his marriage."

"What conclusion have you come to after all this reflecting?" Olivia asked gently.

The brothers exchanged glances again before Joshua continued, "Aaron and I remember being close to you when we were little. Dad was always working, but you were always home. In retrospect, we were pretty spoiled at home. You always did everything for us. We didn't have chores. I would come home from school and my bed was made; any of the toys I'd left out the night before were put away. After I took a bath, the dirty clothes I left on the bathroom floor magically appeared back in my closet, clean and ready to wear. I just assumed that is how things were supposed to be. Like the home-made cookies you always had ready for us when we came home from school each day. I never remember saying thank you. It never crossed my mind that it was necessary."

"I remember once when I was little, I started helping you clear the table after dinner," Aaron said. "Dad reprimanded me. Told me that was a woman's job, and then he mocked me, called me his daughter he never asked for."

"I remember that. I should have said something," Olivia whispered.

"No, Mom, you couldn't have. I remember how Dad treated you back then, too," Aaron said.

"But I was the adult," Olivia barely whispered.

"I remember you reading to us every night before tucking us in. Dad never did. But when I was about twelve, Dad started taking me to work with him. It made me feel grown-up. Plus, Dad was finally spending time with me."

"Both of us had a similar experience when Dad started bringing us into his world," Aaron said. "At least, that's how we've come to describe it: *bringing us into his world*. He was subtly—or not so subtly—teaching us that the men's role was more important, and you, our mother, were a supporting character in our family, but not the main character, and not even as important as your children. As our grandfather always said, a wife is a helpmate, and her duty is to submit to the men in her family."

"For our first twelve years, you were the most important person in our lives. But then, over the next six years, we were gradually pulled away from you by our father until, finally, we no longer respected you. Which we now understand was wrong. Although, in truth, we always knew it was wrong. I suppose a part of us always felt guilty about how we treated you during our teen years—how Dad encouraged us to treat you. But then you left, and Dad showed us that fake letter and told us you wanted nothing to do with us. It enforced all he had been gradually teaching us since we became teenagers."

"We're sorry, Mom. We want to have a relationship with you again, if possible. My wife and I have already started family counseling—and not through the church. In fact, we've left Grandfather Davis's church," Aaron explained.

"Aaron seemed to be quicker on the uptake than his older brother," Joshua said with a harsh laugh. "Until last night, I didn't know where Mary had gone. Now that I know where she is, I'm hoping she'll talk to me. I want us to try counseling, too. I'm also stepping away from Grandfather's church. This doesn't mean I'm walking away from God, but after finding out how Dad and my grandfather lied, I realize now I've been treating my wife like Dad taught me to treat you. And it's wrong. I love Mary and Cassandra, and I don't want to lose them like I lost you."

THEY CONTINUED TO TALK WHILE EATING BREAKFAST, AND WHEN they were about done, Aaron asked, "Can you tell us about the kidnapping now?"

Olivia told him everything—omitting any references to the paranormal and using the fabricated version people like Joe had been given regarding her escape. In the new version, she escaped the cage and walked to the highway, where a motorist spied her and called the police.

When she got to the part where the kidnappers showed up last night, both Aaron and Joshua were horrified at what could have happened just hours earlier. However, it was when Olivia told her sons the men's names that Joshua and Aaron both froze and stared at their mother in disbelief.

Noting their expressions, Olivia frowned. "What?"

"You said their names are Gerald and Harold Flemming?"

Olivia shrugged. "I assume that's their names. It's what was on their driver's licenses. Of course, the IDs could be fake."

"We know Gerald and Harold Flemming," Joshua said, setting down his fork. "Assuming it is the same Gerald and Harold Flemming, yet I can't imagine it could be someone else."

Olivia frowned. "You know them?"

"Well, not personally. We've never met them. But those are the names of Joy's brothers. Joy is Dad's new wife we told you about."

POLICE CHIEF MACDONALD AND OFFICER BRIAN HENDERSON SAT IN the living room of Olivia Davis. Also in the room were Olivia, Shanice, Joshua, Aaron, and Marie. Although no one realized Marie was in the room with them, not even the chief or Brian.

Marie had been at Olivia's house since Shanice returned with the cinnamon rolls, eavesdropping on the private conversation between Olivia and her sons, and she planned to eavesdrop on this conversation too. How else could she keep the mediums fully apprised of the situation?

Brian had just handed Aaron a photograph of Gerald and Harold Flemming.

"Hey, those guys are staying at the same motel as us," Aaron said. "I noticed them because they were driving a truck like ours."

"Are those your father's brothers-in-law?" Brian asked.

Joshua took the photo from his brother, looked at it, and then handed it back to Brian. "We've never met them in person. But Aaron is right; those are the guys at the motel."

"You didn't meet them when their sister married your father?"

Aaron shook his head. "No. They live in Oklahoma, but that's not why they didn't come to the wedding. Dad's wife, Joy, is originally from Oklahoma. She met Dad right after she moved to town, about two years ago. From what I understand, she comes from a poor family. Dad went to Oklahoma with her and met her family before they got engaged. That's when he met the brothers. He told Joy he didn't want them coming around or being part of their lives. Said once they started their own family, he didn't want their bad influence."

Shanice and Olivia exchanged glances but said nothing.

CHAPTER FORTY

After learning the kidnappers had used their family's cabin to hold Olivia Davis prisoner, Nancy Martin agreed with her daughter to hold her husband's funeral service at their church in Frederickport and take the ashes up to the cabin in the summer, when the weather was better and the unpleasant memory of how Martin's Hideaway had been used would not be as fresh.

On the day of the funeral, they received an enormous flower arrangement from an anonymous person. The note read: *To Allen Martin's family: you do not know me, nor have I ever met Allen Martin. But he once did a kind act that saved my life. I wanted you to know. I am sorry for your loss. From what I have heard, Allen was a fine man, and he loved his family dearly. You will be in my prayers.*

Olivia wanted to attend Allen's funeral, but she realized it would confuse Allen's wife and daughter and stir unpleasant memories of what someone had done at their family's cabin, now that it was public knowledge that the Flemming brothers had broken into the cabin and used it to hold her prisoner. Instead, she sent the flower arrangement.

While Olivia did not attend the funeral, Adam and Melony went; after all, Adam had been handling the Martins' garage apartment rental for years; and Nancy had recently asked him to handle the cabin, as she thought they might want to rent it out.

Adam would also need to find a new tenant for the garage apartment because Mary had given notice that she probably would not be staying and not renewing for another month. Mary had decided to try working on her marriage and would probably move back to Texas. This also meant Danielle and Walt would need to keep looking for a new housekeeper.

Adam and Melony stood at the end of the receiving line, a few feet away from the people in front of them, waiting to give their condolences to the grieving family. That morning, Danielle had told Adam his grandmother would be coming to the funeral with Allen and Eva.

Adam felt a gentle tug on his left earlobe. He briefly glanced behind him and then leaned over to Melony and whispered, "Grandma's here. It's a little weird thinking Allen is standing behind us with Grandma and Eva, at his own funeral."

Melony practically snorted. It was extremely unladylike, but totally appropriate for the absurdity of the situation.

DURING ALLEN'S FUNERAL, THE MEDIUMS AND THEIR ALLIES gathered at Marlow House for Mexican takeout—Lily called it a late lunch while Heather called it an early dinner. There would be no hurt feelings from Ian's sister, Kelly, who was excluded from these gatherings because she hadn't been let in on the secret—although she suspected there was some secret Ian and the others had been keeping from her. Tonight she and Joe were having dinner at Joe's parents' house, and Kelly's parents had also been invited.

Those at Marlow House included Walt, Danielle, Ian, Lily, Brian, Heather, Chris, Olivia, Shanice, Chief MacDonald, Eddy Jr., Evan, Addison, Jack, Connor, and Emily Ann, along with Sadie, Hunny, and Max.

Joanne had mopped the floor in the spacious entry hall that morning, so Walt had dragged a collection of children's toys out for

Connor and the twins to play with there. That way people wouldn't be stepping over the little ones while walking from the dining room to get food from the buffet and then taking the food into the living room.

"HOW LONG ARE YOU STAYING?" BRIAN ASKED SHANICE AS THE TWO stood at the buffet in the dining room, each filling their plates.

"I'm not in a rush to get back home. Olivia wants me to stay for a couple of weeks. It's one perk of retirement. But I'll admit, I'd rather visit Olivia during the summer."

Brian laughed. "Understood."

Lily and Olivia sat at the end of the dining room table, choosing not to take their food into the living room and eat on their laps. Plus, Lily had a clear view into the entry and could keep an eye on Connor, who played with the twins.

"Dani said your oldest son is still here?" Lily said before taking a bite of a tortilla chip.

"Yes, Joshua is staying with Mary and Cassandra. Mary checked with Adam to make sure it was okay. She must be out of the apartment by March 3, and then they plan to go back to Texas and work on their marriage. In the meantime, while they're here, I'll get an opportunity to get to know my granddaughter, daughter-in-law, and hopefully start rebuilding a relationship with my son."

Lily reached across the table and briefly patted Olivia's right hand. "I'm happy for you. Dani mentioned your other son left already?"

Olivia nodded. "Yes, he had to go back home. But he's returning next week, bringing his wife and my grandchildren for me to meet. They're staying at my house."

"How long are they staying?"

"Probably a week. He has to get back to work."

"I thought he worked for his father's company that closed?"

"He did. Both boys did. But now he's doing side jobs, and fortunately, that's been keeping them busy. From what they said, I have a feeling Joshua and Aaron are going to start their own business together, something their father and grandfather don't control."

In the kitchen at Marlow House, Chief MacDonald leaned back against the counter, talking to Chris, while Evan and Eddy Junior sat at the kitchen table, eating their food, and Eddy surfed on his cell phone.

"So, the new wife was the mastermind behind the kidnapping?" Chris asked.

"It depends on whose story you listen to. Joy Davis claims she only mentioned the policy to her brothers, and they—on their own—plotted to kill Olivia, thinking they could get her to split the money with them, or they would blackmail her to force her to share."

Chris arched his brow. "Could that be true?"

"Unlikely. For one thing, when the police showed up at her house to bring her in for questioning, she just happened to be holding a copy of Olivia's life insurance policy in her hand. And when they checked her house, they found mail spread out on the kitchen table that, according to the house's security cameras, she had just opened. One was a notice that Olivia's policy had lapsed, and by her reaction captured on the video, she did not take the news well."

Chris laughed. "So all that trouble, and if they had killed Olivia, there would be no payout?"

Edward nodded. "Exactly. And as for those security cameras, I guess the second Mrs. Davis wasn't aware her house had security cameras. Apparently, her father-in-law had them installed one day when she was visiting her husband at the nursing home."

Chris frowned. "That doesn't sound too legal."

Edward shrugged. "Apparently her father-in-law is the one who owns the house she was living in with his son. He did it to make sure his young daughter-in-law wasn't doing anything immoral while his son was in the nursing home."

"I suppose plotting murder falls into the immoral category."

"Even if the insurance policy had not lapsed, and they had been successful in killing Olivia, it is unlikely the second Mrs. Davis would have gotten any of the money," the chief added.

"Why do you say that?"

"It turns out Mark Davis's father has power of attorney for his son, something she apparently didn't know."

"How did she not know?"

MacDonald shrugged. "The more I'm hearing about her and her brothers, they aren't the brightest criminals."

"Such as?"

"When Brian was interviewing Harold Flemming, Harold said he wanted an attorney, and at that point, he should have stopped talking. But then he started asking Brian questions, which resulted in Harold throwing his siblings under the bus."

WHEN ADAM AND MELONY ARRIVED AT MARLOW HOUSE, THEY were not alone. They walked into the living room with Marie, Eva, and Allen.

"How was your funeral?" Heather asked cheerfully.

Allen smiled wistfully. "I know Gina and Nancy have been doing a lot of crying since we left the hospital together. But they held it together today; I was proud of them. It was a lovely service, and people said some really nice things about me."

Heather repeated for the non-mediums what Allen had just said.

"Allen wanted to come with us so he could say goodbye to all of you," Marie said.

Again, Heather played ghost interpreter.

"Thank you, Allen," Olivia said. "You saved my life."

"No, Marie did that," Allen argued, but Olivia couldn't hear the words, and Heather didn't bother repeating them because the non-mediums chimed in with parting words for Allen. Adam thanked him for his business and friendship, Shanice thanked him for saving her sister, and Eddy said something about how he planned to attend his own funeral someday because that sounded so lit.

After a few more comments, and Allen thanking everyone for being so kind, Eva looked at him and asked, "Well, are you ready?"

"I understand you and Marie aren't ready to move on. I might be tempted to stick around if Marie taught me how to do what she does." Allen let out a sigh. "But staying doesn't feel right to me. It's like this chapter is closed, and I need to move on. But…"

Allen was about to say, *But where is this light I read about?*

He didn't finish the sentence because in the next moment what felt like a spotlight from above turned on, illuminating the space around his body. While the non-mediums didn't see the light, everyone else in the room could, which was why all the mediums now stared at the ceiling. It seemed to have opened up, filled with bright gold-rimmed white clouds, spilling light onto Allen.

Allen's smile widened as he looked up into the light, his arms outstretched. "This feels…amazing." Eva, Marie, and the mediums watched in silence as the image of Allen drifted upward, a smile on his face, until at last, he, the light, and the clouds disappeared, and the room returned to what it had been minutes earlier.

"He's moved on," Danielle said.

It was Valentine's Day, Walt and Danielle's fourth wedding anniversary—or more accurately, the fourth anniversary of their second wedding. They had eloped the day after Memorial Day, keeping it a secret from everyone, even Lily and Marie. Their second wedding ceremony took place eight months later, on Valentine's Day, at Marlow House, in front of all their friends. Many of those friends now knew Walt and Danielle had initially eloped; some did not.

Walt and Danielle sat together in a quiet booth at Pearl Cove, each drinking a toast to—what Danielle called—our fourth fake wedding anniversary.

Back at Marlow House, Marie and Chris babysat the twins. Marie was doing most of the childcare while Chris had showed up so someone couldn't accuse Walt and Danielle of leaving their children alone.

Chris had offered to help Marie watch the twins because he understood Lily and Heather wanted to spend time with their significant others on Valentine's Day, and he had no intention of taking a woman out on Valentine's Day—with all its implied meaning. He secretly wished there were someone he would like to ask out, but the last woman he wanted to ask out on Valentine's Day, he was now babysitting her children.

AFTER THEIR TOAST, WALT TOOK A SIP OF HIS COCKTAIL AND THEN said, "It may have been a fake wedding, but it was beautiful."

Danielle grinned. "It was. And I certainly wouldn't describe our real wedding as beautiful, but it was memorable."

Walt laughed. "I can still remember how that hippie pastor kept asking me if I wanted to take a toke."

"Well, he did say it was good pot." They both laughed.

A few minutes later, the server brought them both a bowl of clam chowder. Their conversation shifted from their weddings to recent events.

"I'm glad the library gave Olivia the rest of the month off. Not only does she need the time off after all she's gone through, but this also gives her time to spend with her sons while they're in town," Danielle said.

"I don't think I mentioned it, but according to Ian, his sister has become rather obsessed with Marie's letter."

Danielle cringed. She knew exactly what Walt meant. It was the letter the kidnapper had found on the bottom of the cage, which Marie had intended to get rid of before the police arrived. "Well, on the bright side, Brian claims that letter helped get the one brother to confess."

"That may be true, but Kelly's on a tear to solve the mystery. According to Ian, she wants to do a podcast series on it. I imagine Edward wishes Joe hadn't shared that information with Kelly."

"I'm sure Joe's curious himself and wondering why the chief doesn't want to find out where the letter came from."

"Just another normal day in Frederickport," Walt said before taking a sip.

"I'm just glad Olivia is safe and that she's rebuilding a relationship with her sons. And before we know it, it will be March. I wish Madeline hadn't had to cancel her visit."

Walt knew what Danielle meant. Madeline was her ex mother-in-law, and she had planned to visit the first week in March but had to postpone the trip.

"While I would have liked to have seen Madeline and Finn again, we should probably focus on finding a new housekeeper before we have any guests. And I will admit, I am looking forward to a quiet, uneventful March."

Walt would soon learn March 2020 would not be uneventful.

THE GHOST AND DÉJÀ VU

Danielle and the mediums of Beach Drive look forward to a quiet and uneventful spring in Frederickport. Unfortunately, the Universe has other plans, and March 2020 threatens to change the world forever.

Walt promises his friends they will get through this together. It's not manufactured bravado. Walt's been on this rodeo before, and he's determined to ride it out and survive, like he did in 1918.

NON-FICTION BY
BOBBI ANN JOHNSON HOLMES

Write On, An Author's Journey
Havasu Palms, A Hostile Takeover
Where the Road Ends, Recipes & Remembrances
Motherhood, a book of poetry
The Story of the Christmas Village